OTHER WORKS BY HEATHER NOVAK

EDIE'S AUTOMOTIVE GUIDE SERIES:
Headlights, Dipsticks, & My Ex's Brother
Fire Trucks, Garter Belts, & My Perfect Ex

THE LYNCH BROTHER SERIES:
Hunting Witch Hazel
Threat of Raine
Dead Like Romi (Coming Soon)

I hope you fall in love with Grenadine!

FIRE TRUCKS, GARTER BELTS, & MY PERFECT EX

EDIE'S AUTOMOTIVE GUIDE: VOLUME 2

HEATHER NOVAK

Heather

Copyright © 2019 Heather Novak

All rights reserved under International and Pan-American Copyright Conventions

This is a work of fiction. Names, characters, places, and incidents are either the products of the author's imagination or are used fictitiously, and any resemblance to actual persons, living or dead, business establishments, events, or locales is purely coincidental.

By payment of required fees, you have been granted the *non*-exclusive, *non*-transferable right to access and read the text of this book. No part of this text may be reproduced, transmitted, downloaded, decompiled, reverse engineered, or stored in or introduced into any information storage and retrieval system, in any form or by any means, whether electronic or mechanical, now known or hereinafter invented without the express written permission of copyright owner.

Please Note

The reverse engineering, uploading, and/or distributing of this book via the internet or via any other means without the permission of the copyright owner is illegal and punishable by law. Please purchase only authorized electronic editions, and do not participate in or encourage electronic piracy of copyrighted materials. Your support of the author's rights is appreciated.

No part of this book may be reproduced or transmitted in any form or by any electronic or mechanical means, including photocopying, recording or by any information storage and retrieval system, without the written permission of the publisher, except where permitted by law.

To my family, especially my grandparents: Thank you for not leaving me on the side of the road, even though I know you were tempted many, many times. (Also, please skip the spicy scenes so it's not super awkward at holidays.)

To Mr. Heather, who's my IRL hero.

As always, for my mom. You would've loved this book! I miss you.

And to everyone who is searching for someplace to belong: this one's for you.

"Remember, you are not measured by who you love, but who loves you in return."
– Mom (quoting Frank Morgan)

Letter to Heather, 7/22/1990

CHAPTER ONE

MOM'S BUCKET LIST #1: TAKE ONE PHOTOGRAPH EVERY DAY FOR A YEAR

I STARED at the red and white sign I'd thought I'd never see again in this lifetime. *Welcome to Grenadine.* It sported a cartoon-like font, with a smiling cartoon cherry as the dot over the "i." A plethora of rainbow flowers huddled around it, butterflies and hummingbirds swooping in and out of view. If I held my breath and stood really still, I could practically hear happy music chiming, as if I were walking into a fairy tale. It was the kind of sign that should inspire the same feeling as, say, the Walt Disney World sign.

It was terrifying.

I was pretty sure this was how the plot of at least seventeen horror movies started. Reaching for my phone, I opened my group chat with my best friends, Payton and Jasmine. I snapped a picture of the sign and sent it with the caption, **This is how I die, isn't it? A small town in Michigan turns out to be more lethal than LA.**

Jas: Prob. Good thing u went red, blondes die first

Jas: Just don't shower @ night or b slutty

Payton: Too late...

I rolled my eyes. **Haha.**

I attached my phone to my selfie-stick and took a series of pictures with me in front of the Grenadine sign. I almost got stung by a bee while I heard the shutter click, so there was bound to be some great pics for this year's Payton's Playhouse holiday card. When you were co-founder of the largest female-run porn company in the United States, you got to be silly with your holiday cards.

I opened my car door, which went up instead of out, and tucked my selfie-stick away in my one suitcase. Yes, singular. I loved my 2019 Ford GT Carbon Series, even if it was the most ridiculous car I could take on a road trip. You'd think the $500,000 price tag would mean room for two suitcases, maybe even a cupholder or two, but no. This baby was built for speed.

It was fast and sexy. Like me.

In addition to the one suitcase, I had wedged in a collapsible cooler and a large tote bag that held my purse, a paper road map, and my mom's journal. After climbing into the driver's seat, I pulled out the journal. I crossed off 32. *Dye my hair to match the Grenadine sign.* from my mom's bucket list. I was lucky that the bright red went well with the yellowish undertone of my light skin.

Then I took a deep breath.

And a second.

And a third.

What was I doing here?

Did I really take a sabbatical from work for this?

I sucked in my cheeks and used my right hand to grab my seatbelt. Carefully, I stretched it over my chest. It was probably a little too soon after surgery to be road tripping, but whatever. I couldn't just sit around wasting my life.

While the stitches were gone, the swelling and bruising from a breast biopsy and subsequent removal of the massive fibroadenoma were still painful. We were being extra cautious. They had said Mom's mass was a non-cancerous fibroid as well.

It hadn't been.

Despite my doctor's reassurance that it wasn't necessary, I had asked that she remove the entire mass. Thankfully, it hadn't really affected the size of my perfect C-cup breasts. Now, two weeks after my surgery, I was back in the one place I'd vowed never to return to eleven years ago. Because that's where Mom's bucket list started.

I was too young when she died to appreciate the list. Hell, I hadn't thought about it in years. Now, the list was with me, and she was gone. She passed away two months before my high school graduation, fate refusing to grant her one last wish of seeing me walk across the stage and get my diploma. Two months and one day later, the Grenadine sign—and the first eighteen years of my life—were in my rearview mirror. But ever since waking up in my hospital bed, I'd had the unstoppable urge to complete everything my mom never got to finish.

This week I had already crossed off resizing great-grandma's wedding band so I could wear it, as well as going to a karaoke bar and singing Mom's favorite Britney tune. It had been an incredibly painful rendition for anyone within earshot. I was pretty sure it was only a matter of time before a video of that hit the internet.

I breathed deep as I pulled into town, everything somehow looking different, yet exactly the same. After checking into the local bed and breakfast—number eight on Mom's list was eating breakfast at Grenadine Manor B&B—I headed to a fundraiser down the street that was raising money for the local auto shop. I was bolstered by the fact that no one seemed to recognize me, which probably had something to do with the bright red hair, huge sunglasses, and carefully planned outfit. I had gotten a few sidelong glances and at least one double take, but no one had acknowledged me yet, and I certainly didn't acknowledge them. An "I won't tell if you don't" silent agreement.

To be fair, I was a long way from the girl with dirty brown, unmanageable curls, thrift-store clothes, and inch-thick glasses. Thank God for Lasik. And legal name changing. Gone was Vera Tompson. I was now Vera Eastman, having taken my mom's mother's maiden name. I was more likely to be recognized as Roni Vegas, porn star, but with my cherry leg tattoo covered and my naturally curly hair now straight, long, and bright red instead of the traditional blonde, it hadn't happened yet…at least not out loud.

The last hour had been a blast, but I'd made a rookie mistake entering the oil change competition. While it was gratifying to kick everyone's ass—except Edie's, the owner of the shop—it had brought both a lot of pain and a lot of attention. Neither were on my to-do list.

I stuck my arm under my boob, making a shelf for it to rest on. It was time to get out of here and rest for tomorrow. I had a water tower to climb and an estranged father to avoid.

The best-laid plans, however, were derailed when a bunch of incredibly attractive firefighters were led across a makeshift stage for a Date-A-Firefighter auction. I snapped a picture for the group text and sent it with a drooling emoji.

Me: It's like a sexy firefighter calendar up in here.

Payton: uh…

Payton: buying my plane tix, BRB

Jas: Mama's got a fire u can put out

Me: Thanks for making it weird, Jas

Jas: Ur welcome *kiss emoji*

"Grenadine, get those credit cards ready! The firefighter auction is about to start. You give us the money; you get a date with our town's sexiest men and women!"

FIRE TRUCKS, GARTER BELTS, & MY PERFECT EX

I blinked at the stage where the emcee, a beautiful woman with dark brown skin and short, natural hair, blew a kiss to the group of firefighters in tight white T-shirts and well-fitting jeans. Her name was Tamicka if memory served. "Give it up for our first firefighter, Cassie!" Cassie stepped forward and waved as the crowd cheered. She looked a few years younger than me, with a warm khaki complexion and a long, dark ponytail that shivered when she laughed.

Wowza. How was everyone in this town so attractive? It had to be something in the water.

A few things had changed in Grenadine since I'd left over a decade ago. She was probably the first female the station had employed who wasn't a cleaning lady. A low whistle from a group of older men next to me made my shoulders tighten. I gave them a sideways glance, ready to run back to the B&B, rather than be approached.

But this trio wasn't looking at me. They were looking at the stage. "She could make me dinner and then be dessert," I heard one of them say as he scratched the straw-like hair under the sweat-soaked brim of his baseball hat.

His friend, who looked like he hadn't showered in several weeks, snickered. "Everyone put in twenty and we could make it a group date." They dug crumpled bills out of their pockets and shoved them into dirty-man's outstretched hand. They elbowed each other as if their ingenious plan would mean all their sexual fantasies were about to come true.

I dipped into my pocket and fingered my credit card. I could easily beat a sixty-dollar bet and save her from a night of unwelcome advances. Sisterhood was sacred, whether or not we'd ever met before.

My palms started sweating. Bidding meant speaking. Loudly. Which meant even more attention, which meant small talk, which meant discovery.

I shivered, despite the humid August evening. Keeping a low

profile was imperative to not causing drama. I straightened my shoulders and scanned the crowd again. It wasn't that I was looking for someone in particular, it was more like avoiding them. But I hadn't seen either my dad or my ex. This was good. This was okay. Not seeing my ex was probably for the best, and I'd prefer to talk to my dad in private.

"Can I get forty dollars?" Tamicka asked.

I scoffed, offended by the low starting bid. Forty dollars wasn't going to save this shop. A hand brushed my upper arm and I tensed, instantly shrugging away.

"I'm sorry. I didn't mean to startle you," the bombshell blonde, Edie, rushed out. She had some sunburn on the ivory skin of her nose and forehead, but it didn't diminish her smile.

I shrugged with a half-smile. "I have an aversion to being touched unexpectedly." I didn't add it was because most people who randomly touched me were creepy ass men thinking a porn star was "free game."

She nodded. "Got it." She raised her hand up in apology. "You seem...annoyed."

I bit my lip, heat flooding my face. "It's just..." I cleared my throat. "Forty dollars isn't going to save the shop."

She smiled sadly as the bid only climbed by five dollars each hand raise. "Small town. Unless you're one of the guys who got work in the auto industry or real estate, it's largely blue collar. Forty dollars is a week's worth of groceries to some of these guys." She leaned closer. "She's also the newest member of the force. The bids will go up as we get to the veterans."

"Sixty dollars going twice..." the announcer said.

I looked down at my feet, willing myself to figure out what to do. My mom's voice echoed in my ears, practically shouting the answer: *24. Do something reckless to help someone else.*

Sixty dollars, my ass. Pursing my lips, I took a deep breath and threw my hand in the air. "Two hundred dollars," I shouted. My heart was pounding so hard, I could barely hear the crowd gasp around me. I couldn't believe I had just done that.

Edie squealed and wrapped herself around a dark-haired man who was smiling down at her in a way that made my stomach squeeze. She looked over her shoulder and mouthed "thank you" before burying her face in his neck. I turned away, trying not to think about how that was one of my favorite parts on a man.

The rest of the crowd applauded and stirred, looking back at the outsider who'd just showed up and outbid them. The trio next to me immediately stopped their celebrating and stared at me slack-jawed. I pushed my sunglasses higher up onto my nose, despite the fact that it was twilight and I was starting to have trouble seeing. If I had sunglasses on, they couldn't see me, right? That's how physics worked?

To my right, a group of women I had known in high school were whispering just loud enough to hear.

"Have you ever seen her before?"

"She looks so familiar..."

"Do you think she's one of those...like Ellen?"

"Hold on. I swear I know her from school. I'm checking our graduation class on Facebook. Maybe there's a pic." Their leader—Jessica? Jordan? Jennifer?—whipped a phone out of her leggings and started presumably looking through photos.

A drop of sweat ran down my spine. This was not my best move. Now that I had committed to paying, there was no way I could leave if things got dicey. Maybe I should've worn a Scream mask, like that one guy did when he'd collected his lottery winnings. I'm sure that wouldn't have raised any concerns.

To my left, a group of teens were hard at work posing for their selfies. I scooted closer to them; they wouldn't recognize me. They were trying to get the stage in the background of their kissy-face pictures. Their tank tops were conveniently tugged down to show a shadow of cleavage, their skirts rolled up, and they wore high-heeled sandals on gravel.

I wanted to impart on them the wisdom of wedges for rough terrain, but it was a lesson we all had to learn the hard way. Besides, I did *not* want to talk to teenagers. They scared me more than spiders, and I was really terrified of spiders.

Kitty-corner from them was a group of working women, some still wearing their aprons and uniforms. I recognized a few of them but couldn't remember their names. They laughed and shot their gnarled, cracked hands up with glee, elbowing their friends and generally having a good time as another two firefighters were bid on. They made even my jaded heart happy.

With the exception of Edie, the rest of the shop girls—all in the shop's coveralls—were standing in the front row and screaming, trying to get the audience to up their bids. They seemed generally happy to be there and willing to make fools of themselves for a good cause. When they got one woman to double her bid on an older man with a bald head and a baby face, even I clapped.

There was one glaring difference between everyone here and me: I was the only person here alone. I pulled out my phone again.

Me: Sooo…I maybe bid on someone…

Jas: YAS GURL!

Payton: That seems counterintuitive to keeping a low profile

Me: I didn't say it was a good idea

Jas: Take him around the block a few times & then cut loose

Me: Her

Jas: Oh! Even better.

Me: It's not like that. Was trying to save her from creepy bros

Payton: Bid on a man next. Send pics.

Me: Low profile

Jas: Too late. Live UR life!!!!!!!!!!!!!!!!!!!!!!!!!!!!

I rolled my eyes at the number of exclamation marks Jas had sent. I was tempted to count them, but they all began blurring together after the fifth one.

"Welcome to the stage the first quarterback to lead the Grenadine Tigers to a state victory, his graduating class's homecoming king and valedictorian, and winner of the highest bid for the last three auctions..."

My entire body stilled at Tamicka's words. *Jack.*

"...Jack Reeves!"

At the sound of my ex's name, years of laughter, memories of making out under the bleachers, and the feeling of his skin against mine all slammed into me at once, forcing me back a step. I mumbled an apology to whoever I'd walked into, but I didn't move. I couldn't move.

My Jack.

I dropped my phone, my hand unable to figure out how to hold it anymore. What were hands, even? All of my brain power went to staring at the amazingly sexy man who slid forward and into a dance move I had taught him when we were kids, his hips rotating as he spun around.

Eleven years had been very, very kind to this man. He had been the cutest boy I had ever seen when he was seventeen. Now he was off the charts. My mouth went dry. My eyes nearly fell out of my head.

The reddish-brown hair I had loved to rake my hands through was still short on the sides, but now a little longer on top. His once clean-shaven face now sported a close-cropped beard that I bet would feel amazing against my thighs. I had kissed every single freckle that dotted his fair skin over and over again.

He was still...

And his smile...

The way his collarbone...

Those forearms...

All the women around me, and some of the men, started murmuring and reaching into their purses and wallets.

I'd known it was a probability I'd see him while I was here, but I hadn't expected to suddenly feel like I was *home*. I twisted the gold band on my right ring finger over and over again, concentrating on yoga breathing so I didn't pass out or do something stupid.

I raised my hand, not even sure what Tamicka was saying or if bidding had begun. All I knew was that I needed to be near him again. "Three thousand dollars!" I yelled.

Well, so much for not doing something stupid.

CHAPTER TWO

GRENADINE ORDINANCE NO. 50-20-1895: NO PUBLIC FLIRTING IS ALLOWED BETWEEN A MAN AND WOMAN AFTER SUNSET.

TO BE HONEST, I didn't remember the rest of the auction. I don't even know who handed me my phone, but somehow it was back in my hand. My shaking thumbs typed out a desperate message.

Me: SOS! SOS!

Me: I did something really stupid

Me: I need a handler

Me: Get on a plane. Come help me.

Jas: K, who'd u kill? I can call my uncle

Payton: Do NOT admit to murder over a text, have I taught you nothing?

Me: No one's dead. Yet. I may die.

Jas: Sooo…no duct tape & shovels?

Payton: It can't be that bad

Me: I just bid $3k on my ex

Payton: …

Payton: *facepalm emoji*

Jas: THIS IS THE BEST THING I'VE EVER HEARD!!!!!!!!!!!!!!!!

I turned off my phone. I needed space to think about how to handle this. There was no way I could just casually go out with Jack, no matter how much I wanted to.

Game plan: pay and run.

I skirted the edge of the crowd at a brisk pace, keeping my head down. People were getting bolder with their glances and gossip. I heard my dad's name at least twice. *Focus, Vera. Pay Tamicka. Run.* Years of jogging several miles a day would officially pay off.

I whipped out my credit card as I reached her. She raised an eyebrow but took the card, her Christmas-themed nails almost making me smile. "Nice nails," I told her.

"I always need a little Christmas, girl. Doesn't matter what time of year." She gave me another once over and then hooked up a card reader to her phone.

I hopped up and down on the balls of my feet and glanced over the top of my sunglasses to Jack, who was surrounded by his adoring fans. For a moment, I swear the ground fell out from under my feet. But Tamicka cleared her throat and brought me back down to Earth.

Tamicka held up her device. "Sign with your finger." I quickly made a scribble and nodded, snatching the card from her and shoving it in my pocket. "Red suits you. Much better than brown…or blonde."

My entire face and neck went hot. She winked at me, and I mumbled a thank you, walking away so fast it could be called a light jog. And by light jog, I mean I was outright running.

"You really are good at leaving," Jack called out.

I froze and closed my eyes. *God dammit.* I took two deep breaths before lifting my sunglasses to the top of my head and turning around to face him. My first love. My first heartbreak. My first *everything.*

The moment our eyes met, everything else fell away. The space that had separated us for so long vanished. The constant humming inside of me—this unquenchable need to keep going and doing and seeing and conquering—quieted, like the last raindrop of a thunderstorm.

Jack.

His eyes widened as if I had said his name out loud, as if he knew what he did to me.

Someone pushed me gently from behind, breaking me out of the trance. I blinked hard, realizing the crowd had parted, leaving a clear path between Jack and me. All the stillness inside of me vanished, turning into a tornado of unspoken words and long-suppressed feelings. I squared my shoulders. *Do not freak out right now, Vera. He is just another man.*

Jack jumped off the stage then reached back to help Cassie down. I pretended not to notice the way his well-tailored biceps flexed with the movement. Everyone was looking between the three of us and whispering. I saw money exchange hands. Oh yeah, that's why I was freaking out. I had just walked into a reality show starring me and my impromptu decisions.

"Princess," Jack murmured, the old nickname now sharp-edged.

I ground my teeth together against the way it sliced. The memory of our last fight clawing its way to the surface. I shoved it right back down. I was now a business woman with a spine of steel. I could handle this. "Jack." My voice was cheerful and empty, void of all the emotions that were rioting inside me.

By the way his lip twitched, I knew he could see straight through me, even now. He hadn't let go of Cassie's hand yet and my chest felt empty, like I had run five miles. *Don't freak out. Channel Jasmine.* No, that was a terrible idea. She'd take them both back to her room for the night. *Channel Payton.* I stood a little straighter and put on my flirty eyes.

Jack gestured between Cassie and me. "Cassie, this is my ex, Vera Tompson."

"Eastman, now," I corrected.

He raised an eyebrow. "Vera *Eastman*, this is my friend and co-worker, Cassie Ramirez."

Cassie released his hand, then reached out to shake mine. Her grip was strong and confident, despite the weary look in her eyes. "It was a shock to get such a high bid from someone...visiting," she commented carefully.

I smiled in a reassuring way. "There were some guys who were being fucking creepy, so I jumped in. Didn't want to put you in the situation when I could do something to stop it."

Her gazed lingered on me for a long moment and then she nodded. "Thanks. You weren't putting me in any situation, but I appreciate your bid."

"It's for a good cause," I agreed.

Jack's stare was practically burning into the side of my face. Turning to face him, I plastered on a fake smile. I swallowed so hard I strained something in my neck. "Well, since you're friends and co-workers, you two can go on a date with each other. I'm not staying in town long enough to set up anything." I deserved a freaking award for how steady and nonchalant my voice sounded. Porn had taught me how to be a decent actress in nearly every scenario.

Channeling the goddess who'd bagged me six Adult Video News —AVN—awards and several million dollars, I shoved my hand in my hair, shaking it out a bit while looking bored. "Anyway, Jack, it was good to see you. Tell your family I said hi. Cassie, nice to meet you."

I turned and started walking. I was almost home free.

"You staying with family?" he asked casually. An icicle pierced my forcefield and lanced straight through my heart. "Does your dad know you're in town?"

I smiled flatly and turned back to face him. "No." I shrugged. "You'll know when he does." I leaned forward and play-whispered, "Just watch for the crowd of pitchforks and holy water."

Jack struggled not to smile, and it melted the corner of the ice shard piercing me. "He better lead the charge tonight. The use of pitchforks on Main Street is prohibited on Sundays."

I smirked. "Shovels are probably just as effective, and they're allowed on Sundays."

Jack raised a finger. "Unless it's a waning gibbous."

No. Stop flirting. I blinked, dislodging myself from the Jack Spell™ I was under. He was too damn charming, and I was too easily disarmed. I cleared my throat and nodded at him and Cassie. "Take care." I turned and walked away, head held high. I made it almost the entire way back to the B&B before I threw up in some bushes. Stupid nerves.

CHAPTER THREE

GRENADINE ORDINANCE NO. A2.98: A MAN IS NOT ALLOWED TO SCOWL AT HIS WIFE ON SUNDAYS

IN THE AGE OF INSTA-NEWS, I really should've expected an immediate reaction. When I walked through the ornate front door of Grenadine Manor, it was no more than eight minutes later. Mrs. Simons, who was probably in her sixties but didn't look a day over a well-groomed forty, walked around the front desk and directly into my path.

"Miss Eastman, I'm afraid there's been a change in room availability. I'll need you to pack your things right away."

I blinked, frowning. "Uh." I shook my head. "Pardon me?"

She folded her hands in front of her and straightened her shoulders. "You need to leave the property."

I looked back over my shoulder as if there was someone behind me who could give me some answers. "Okay..." I drew the word out, trying to tamp down my anger. This was definitely not the first time this had happened, but it was definitely the most inconvenient. "Is there a reason why you're kicking me out?" I swore all the ambient noise in the room disappeared. I was going to make this woman admit her prejudices to my face.

Mrs. Simons leaned forward and spoke as if she were interrupting a study session in a library. "We have guests who are staying with us who have young children."

I pursed my lips and lifted my eyebrows. "I assure you, children do not bother me. Girl Scout cookies are my favorite cheat food."

She laughed uncomfortably. "I don't think you understand me. The other guests feel it's not safe for you to be here."

"Because...they're sick? I've had all my vaccinations. I'm sure it'll be fine." I shrugged, reveling in her discomfort.

Frustrated, she shook her head and gestured to me. "It's because of your...*profession*." She made a face as if she smelled something bad. "They're...nervous."

"I don't perform with any actors under twenty-one by personal choice. There is no reason for anyone to be nervous."

She crossed her arms and shrugged. "I'm sorry."

She was not getting rid of me that easily. I took a step forward and nearly rolled my eyes when she took a step back. I put my hands up, placating her. "You knew my mother, Leigh Tompson?"

Mrs. Simons nodded. "She was so young. But—"

I pulled out my pleading look. "I'm trying to finish her bucket list. She always wanted to stay here and try the breakfast, but she never had the chance. Let me stay the night, you can just leave breakfast by the door, and I won't call my lawyer." I clasped my hands and looked up at her through my eyelashes. I wasn't actually going to bother my lawyer for this, but it sounded good.

For a few seconds, I thought I had convinced her. But her monotone apology made me feel cold all the way to the bone. "Please don't make me call the authorities," she added as a final twist of the knife.

I nodded, closing my eyes for a brief moment. Dammit. This was super inconvenient. Sweat stung my neck and underarms at the realization that I wouldn't complete this bucket list item. I needed space to regroup. Without wasting any more of my breath, I went to my room and grabbed my suitcase. Thankfully I hadn't bothered unpacking yet.

I left my fancy brass keys on the counter and walked out without a word. Anger burned in my stomach, and I concentrated on the feeling instead of crying. I very rarely cried, reserving it for funerals and extreme joy—like when my goddaughter was born. A deep breath steadied me.

My stomach growled as I pushed my way out of the front door, and I shushed it. I shoved my stuff into the car and locked the doors. Ray's Diner was just down the block, and it was probably the only place in this godforsaken town that was open after nine. This was probably a terrible idea, but I had eaten fast food for days and I wanted something that wasn't a dry veggie burger or wilted lettuce.

Ray's deep, "Hello, hello, hello!" made me feel like I was a teenager again, coming in for sundaes with Jack after a football game. Ray had to be in his late sixties now and the years had deepened his laugh lines. He reached out both of his hands to grab mine and squeezed tight. "You look just like your mother!" he exclaimed, and my cheeks hurt from how hard I smiled.

"Ray, I'm so happy to see you," I said, and actually meant it.

He waved over a young woman wearing a poodle skirt and a Peter Pan-collared blouse. She had his same golden complexion, dark hair, and huge smile. He said something in Kutchi to her before releasing my hands. "Vera, this is my granddaughter, Celine. She'll take your order."

Celine smiled and handed me a menu. "Nice to finally meet the infamous Vera."

I shook my head. "Be careful you don't get too friendly with me. They'll come after you with pitchforks, too."

Shrugging, she pointed to her feet. "I'm wearing sneakers. I can outrun them."

I took a look at the menu and laughed. "It's still exactly the same."

"Yeah, except we've started to add symbols to vegetarian and gluten-free options now."

"She's a vegetarian!" Ray added. "Give her the veggie lasagna and a salad." He gave me a once-over. "And a brownie. She's too skinny."

I looked over at him with a smirk. "How the hell did you remember? And I'm not too skinny, I'm fit." I worked hard to keep my body toned.

"I got old, not senile. And your grandmother would say you're too skinny." He put the cigar back in his mouth.

A pang in my chest had me clearing my throat. I missed Grandma so much. I handed Celine the menu. "What Ray said sounds perfect."

Celine nodded and made a note on her pad. "I'll get that to go for you."

Surprised, I pointed at the row of empty stools at the counter. "Oh, I'll just eat it here."

Ray shook his head. "No, you won't. Your dad comes in with his neighborhood watch group in ten minutes. Unless you want that reunion tonight..."

"Just kidding, to go is perfect!" I basically shouted. "Thanks," I said at a more reasonable volume.

I had paid Celine and was grabbing my containers when she swore under her breath. "Looks like they're early tonight."

I spun around to find my dad walking in with a group of people who used to come to my birthday parties. Neighbors, old friends' parents, and a few of my middle school teachers. But my eyes were on the man who had told me to leave and never come back.

His age was evident by the gray hair at his temples and the dulling of his once-sharp jawline. His shirt was looser in the shoulders and tighter around his midsection. But he still looked exactly like the man who'd taught me to drive and ride a bike. The man who'd never looked at me the same after he found out I was stripping two towns over.

His smile fell the moment his matching blue eyes met mine. He looked away, concentrating on something over my shoulder. All the noise in the diner stopped. Even the guy washing dishes had ceased his constant spraying and was leaning out of the pick-up window.

I took a step forward and saw his shoulders tense. I hadn't realized how much I had missed him until I saw him again. "Dad." My voice cracked and I pressed my lips together, angry at their betrayal.

He didn't say a word. He just looked down at his feet. I took a deep breath. "I'm just back for a few days. Checking some things off Mom's bucket list."

He was still for a long moment before he turned toward the door. "Excuse me," he said to the people who came with him.

Desperate not to lose this chance, I reached out and grabbed his arm. "Dad, listen to me—" He twisted out of my grip, the boxes in my hand tumbling to the floor. Lasagna splattered on my pants and shoes. I just stood there, watching him walk away. Just like I had done.

I heard Payton's voice in my head. *You have five seconds to pull yourself together, Vera.* It was the same thing she said to me every time I started to freak out.

Five.

Four.

Three.

Two.

One.

I took a deep breath and pushed my way through the crowd, shoving out of the diner and straight into a woman in an Edie's Auto jumpsuit. "I'm sorry!" I exclaimed, looking up to see a beautiful Asian woman.

She steadied me before stepping back. "Are you okay?"

"I'm great!" I didn't need a dad who didn't love me. I didn't need a B&B that didn't want my money. I didn't even need all the calories from lasagna. What I needed was to get the cheese out from between my toes.

I hurried to my car, digging out wet wipes from my purse and trying to mitigate the damage. With a heavy sigh, I tossed my shoes into a garbage can. There was no way I would get the sauce off my suede wedges.

I climbed into the safety of the driver's seat, closed and locked my door, and turned up my favorite playlist. After one peppy song, I had calmed enough to look up hotels on my phone. There was one just outside of town that boasted clean rooms and a breakfast buffet. That was good enough for me. Ignoring the thirty-seven texts—most of them were probably from Jas—I turned my phone back off, not wanting to deal with them.

As I fussed with buckling my seat belt, a knock at my door made me scream. My elbow slammed against the door handle and I swore. Stupid small-ass car. I looked up to find the Edie's Auto woman holding a bag from Ray's. I rolled down the window.

"I noticed you dropped your food. Figured you could use a redo."

I stared at her for a long moment, confused. Why would someone I hadn't met before bring me dinner? "Thanks?"

She smiled. "You really helped Edie today," she explained. "We take care of our own here." She handed me the bag. "Ray had them remake it, no charge."

"Thanks. Losing that brownie was the worst part of my day," I admitted, laughing. I reached my hand out. "I'm Vera, by the way. I don't think we've met officially."

She shook my hand in a strong grip. "Chieka. I work at the shop." She used her thumb to gesture behind her. "Come on by one of these days and we'll show you around." She gave my gunmetal gray car with red accents a longing look. "And please, *please* bring by this beautiful woman. Can I touch her?"

Her invitation surprised me, and warmth spread across my chest. "Uh, sure!"

She caressed the car from the door to the hood. "She is a beauty. I'd love to see her again. And you, of course." She chuckled.

I smiled. "Thanks, but I'm leaving in the morning."

"Ah, damn." She tugged on her long, onyx braid. "Well, I'll let you get on with your night."

I nodded. "It was nice to meet you, Chieka."

"You too." I'd started to roll up my window when she called my name. "Where'd you learn to change oil like that?"

I laughed. "The DJ at a strip club taught me. He was the shit."

She flashed me a dazzling smile. "That's awesome." She gave my car one last longing glance. "Take care of yourself, Vera."

I waved before pulling out of the parking lot and heading toward my new lodgings. But first, I wanted to make one more stop.

CHAPTER FOUR

GRENADINE ORDINANCE NO. 34-15-89: NO ADULT TOYS OR VIDEOS SHALL BE SOLD PUBLICLY WITHIN GRENADINE TOWN BORDERS.

I PULLED into the parking lot of Happy Endings, the adult novelty store my mom's mom used to own. I was officially in Crescent Hills, the city next door to Grenadine. I couldn't believe this store was still here after all these years, even though Grandma was gone.

My mom had found her passion for interior design and restoration furniture but still worked part-time with my grandma. I'd joined Grandma's staff the moment I turned eighteen, a few months before she and Dad sent me packing. My dad hated that being married to my mom meant being related to a store that sold "shameful" things.

But my grandma had stayed unapologetically herself until the day she died, and I wanted to be just like her. Pulling into the parking lot, I glanced at the clock. It was almost ten, but if the hours were still the same, it would still be open for another twenty minutes. I laughed quietly. A sex toy store closing before midnight—or closing at all—was a sign I was definitely in small-town Midwest.

I pulled some flip-flops from my bag and shoved them on my feet and then walked toward the door. I paused, my hand on the door, my head throbbing, reminding me that I hadn't had water or food in a really long time. My plan to wait until the hotel to eat was admittedly not a great one. Cautiously, I opened the door and stepped inside.

The faint smell of gardenias curled under my nose and I stopped dead, endless memories of Grandma wrapping around me. I nearly choked, struggling to get oxygen that wasn't polluted with the past. I breathed in through my mouth and steadied myself. I knew scent memories were strong, but that had been intense.

I laughed at myself. A young woman with a cleaning rag and spray can greeted me, probably thinking I was drunk. I waved her off as she continued polishing a well-lit glass case that I knew housed the high-end toys. Turning in a circle, I took in the navy-blue carpet, bright white trim, and solid wood shelves. It was set up like a library in someone's home, instead of a toy store.

Nothing had changed in eleven years.

I examined a shelf of the low-to-mid-range quality dildos and vibrators. I loved the crazy colored ones that were more fun than function. I was inspecting a sample shelf, particularly a bright purple one with flashing lights that was super amusing, when a door along the back wall opened and the smell of gardenias assaulted me again.

"Kim?" an older woman called from across the store. The young woman looked up. "I need you to call tomorrow about a missing shipment."

I stilled.

Whoever was talking sounded just like my grandma. My vision went a little fuzzy around the edges and my heart started doing a triathlon. *Holy shit.* The pain at my temples was spidering out and piercing my right eye. I needed to eat and take some medication immediately. I didn't usually have hallucinations with my migraines, but maybe this was my body telling me it needed more iron or chocolate or something.

I shoved the dildo back on the shelf, but it tipped over. In slow motion, the next dildo fell over, then the next one, then the next. It was dildo dominos. I held out my arms, trying to catch them, but they tumbled around me. The fall caused some of the vibrators to turn on, making them light up and move. One of them started to twirl. Crouching down, I gathered them, using my shirt as a carrier, and shoved them back onto the shelf, still whirling.

"Are you okay?" the clerk called.

I laughed awkwardly, embarrassed for the first time in a long time. "I'm sorry, just having a clumsy..." My words died as I saw a puff of white hair over the top of the shelves, pinned in a high bun. Just like my grandma used to wear. I pinched the bridge of my nose and took a deep breath. This town was making me insane.

I reached up and turned off the vibrators as a mixture of desperate longing to see my grandmother and exhaustion from the last several weeks washed over me. I had always envisioned coming home would be easier. My dad and I would reconnect, I'd see some of the old stomping grounds, and maybe even run into Jack, who was supposed to have gotten less attractive with age. It was supposed to be a fun way to honor my mother.

It was time to go find my bed and lock myself behind a door away from people. "Have a good night!" I called, taking two steps backward.

I stumbled into a DVD tower, sending a few cases flying. I swore, bending over to pick them up. Glancing down at them to see if I knew the actors, I froze at the face staring back at me. It was...me. I looked over the rack and found row after row of movies that I had filmed. Only my movies.

"Let me help you," the elderly woman said as she walked around the corner. She reached down and touched my arm, her skin soft and cool against mine. "Vera?" she whispered.

I looked up and saw the ghost of my grandma standing there. Standing so fast I wavered on my feet, I dropped the DVD cases and pressed my palms against my throbbing head. I took several steps backward. *This is just a migraine. You're just having some weird visual symptoms. You're not going crazy.*

"Vera?" the woman asked again.

Adrenaline burned up my spine and I considered calling for an ambulance. Could this be an aneurysm? What had the doctor said about blood clots? I had stopped every hour to walk around like she told me to do.

The ghost took another step toward me. "No, you're dead. This is just a migraine," I whispered, reassuring myself. My eyes stung as I turned around and ran out the door, stumbling over my flip-flops and nearly falling onto the sidewalk.

I dove into my car, started the engine, and threw it into reverse without bothering to look behind me. I was gasping, trying to get enough air. My head throbbed so hard I could see the veins in my eyes. "You'll be fine in five seconds. Five. Four. Three—" A hiccup sob interrupted my counting.

I needed reinforcements.

Pressing the phone button on my steering wheel, I told my system to call Payton. "No phone available." I hit the steering wheel in frustration. I had turned the damn thing off. I stuck my hand in my purse, my fingertips grazing the mirror smooth surface of the phone when my car bottomed out in a pothole. The tire warning light, indicating I had a flat tire, went on just as two brake lights in front of me went red. "Oh shit!" I yelled, slamming on my brakes.

The brakes tried their best, whining their protest, but with a flat tire, I couldn't stop fast enough. I rear-ended the Audi TT Roadster in front of me and sent it into the intersection. My airbags exploded and I choked on the dust filling the car. My poor car, my baby, was a crumpled mess.

Perfect. What a great day this turned out to be.

CHAPTER FIVE

@GRENADINEUNOFFICIAL: @THEGRENADINEPOTHOLE ON FREEMONT AND PORTER STRIKES AGAIN! WITNESSES SAY INTERSECTION IS CLOSED. #SAYNOTOPOTHOLES

I RAN my hands over my face to make sure I was in one piece. There was a spot above my eyebrow that stung and was bleeding slightly, but my nose was still intact. The headache had surprisingly subsided to a dull throb, probably as a result of all the adrenaline coursing through me.

An older man with wrinkled tan skin and thinning gray hair carefully opened my door and leaned in. "Oh my! Are you okay?" he asked, looking over the inside of the car.

I unbuckled my seatbelt and it hung slack, locked in place from the accident. I moved my neck back and forth, not feeling any sharp pain. "I think so," I answered before twisting to get out of the car. Pain radiated from my neck, down my shoulder, and across my left breast. I hissed a profanity.

The man held up his hand. "Sit there, Ms. Vegas. We'll get you checked out."

My eyes widened and I searched his face. The streetlights highlighted the slight blush high on his cheekbones. "My wife and I are longtime fans," he admitted. "I'm Gio. I heard you were in town and wanted to meet you…" He shook his head. "Preferably under better circumstances."

I smiled sadly. "You caught me not at my best, it seems."

He pulled a handkerchief out of his pocket and gestured to my forehead. "Here, this may help. It's clean; I promise. My wife, Dolores, always makes sure I have an extra clean one."

"Thanks." I pressed the fabric against my head with a slight hiss. "I really should check on the other driver."

Another person had opened the door of the Audi and the woman inside was yelling. I couldn't hear what she was saying, but I knew by her tone it was not pretty. I groaned.

Gio grimaced. "I think you should probably stay here until the cops arrive. It'll be safer."

"Safer for who?"

"You."

A police car with flashing lights whipped around the corner followed closely by a black Mercedes CLS 450 Coupe. "Looks like my homecoming parade has arrived."

Gio chuckled. "I always figured you'd be a hellion in real life, too."

That made me smile, although it made my lip sting. I must have a cut there, too. "If I was in better shape, I'd ask to take a picture with you. I love meeting fans."

He shook his head. "Once you're healed, we'll get a picture. Dolores would want to be in it, too."

The police car pulled across the intersection, effectively shutting it down. An older white man climbed out of the passenger seat and made his way to the Audi. The guy in the Mercedes ran in front of him, gently pushing the good Samaritan out of the way and crouching on the ground, inspecting the woman inside.

A young black man pushed out of the driver's side of the police car and made his way over to me. Even in the low lighting of the street lamps, I could tell he was incredibly handsome. Like, Karamo Brown levels of handsome. What did they feed these men in Grenadine?! He was definitely new in town—I would've remembered him.

"Officer Caden LeBlanc," he said by way of introduction. "Ms. Eastman, I presume?"

"Yes, officer." I squinted. "Am I that infamous already?"

The corner of his mouth twitched. "You're the only person in town with a Ford GT."

I nodded. "Word gets around." I shifted in my seat and inhaled sharply at the throb on my left side.

"Are you okay?"

I wrinkled my nose. "Probably?"

Gio cleared his throat. "She has some shoulder pain on her left side. I told her to stay in her car."

Caden nodded. "Gio, good to see you. Thanks for stopping to help."

He smiled. "I'm always happy to help. Especially a pretty lady like her."

Caden turned back to me. "Can you grab me your license, proof of insurance, and registration?"

A loud, "SHE SHOULD GO TO JAIL FOR THIS!" rang out and I jumped.

"Is she okay?" I whispered, starting to freak out that I had seriously hurt her.

Caden ground his jaw. "She's prone to...melodramatics."

Gio cleared his throat. "In my day, we called that looney tunes."

Caden fought a laugh. "Gio, why don't you head home to Dolores? I'll give you a call tomorrow morning if I need your witness statement."

Gio nodded and touched the brim of an invisible hat. "Sounds good." He turned his attention to me. I pulled the handkerchief away from my head, but he waved me off with both hands. "Keep it. It's an honor to give it to you, Ms. Vegas."

"Thank you, Gio."

Caden smirked but immediately went serious. I turned my body to reach for my purse, unable to stop the small squeak of pain that fell out of my mouth. I handed Caden my information and leaned my head back against the seat. "Are you really okay?" he asked.

I fumbled with the blood-stained cloth in my right hand. "I had surgery two weeks ago on my left…side. It's just really sore."

He nodded. "We'll have the paramedics check you out, just in case." He looked over my license and insurance. "Can you tell me what happened here?"

A woman's wail pierced the night just as an ambulance siren rang out. "I had to hit the town's crazy woman, didn't I?" I muttered. "I was going too fast. It was my fault completely. I hit a giant pothole, popped my tire, and just couldn't stop in time."

He nodded and motioned back to my car. "I'm going to call this in. Just…stay away from the dragon."

I narrowed my eyes. "The dragon?"

He pointed over his shoulder. "Cynthia. She will eat you alive."

The ambulance pulled up and the young man who had run to Cynthia's side waved them down. A white pickup truck pulled up behind me and I closed my eyes, not wanting to deal with another person. I needed to call my doctor in LA to make sure I hadn't done any serious damage.

"Vera!" a man yelled, and I swung around so I was leaning out of the car. My heart did a tap dance as Jack ran toward me, fear slicing across his beautiful face. "Are you okay?" His voice shook in a way I'd never heard. He put his hands on my knees, looking me over.

His touch was doing things to my brain. I couldn't figure out how to make words come out of my mouth. My eyes cataloged every detail of this new Jack. He now had laugh lines at his eyes, a small scar on his chin, and it seemed like his shoulders had doubled in size. But he still smelled exactly the same—like sunshine and mint.

"Vera, are you okay?" he repeated.

I nodded then winced at the soreness. "Yeah, mostly. I think I've stopped bleeding."

He shoved a hand in his hair, leaning against my legs. "I got a text from my buddy who saw a Ford GT hit Cynthia, and I panicked."

"How'd you know it was me?"

"Even if you weren't likely the only person in this state to own this car, you have California plates."

"Ah." My headache was edging back in, making my head foggy.

A woman in an EMT uniform approached us. "Ms. Eastman? Caden sent me over to check you out." Jack stood up immediately, allowing her to approach. "My name's Sharon. Can you tell me what's going on?"

"Vera, please." My eyes went to Jack's and back to Sharon's. She silently waved him back and blocked his view. "I'm fighting a migraine and I had surgery two weeks ago," I admitted quietly, explaining about the dissolving stitches and bruising.

Using herself as a shield, she lowered my shirt to examine the incision and the surrounding area. "You look okay. I would call your doctor tonight and see if they want you to go to the hospital." She continued with her instructions and things to watch out for while putting a butterfly bandage on my forehead and checking me for a concussion.

Caden came by when she was finished and gave me back my information. "I, unfortunately, need to give you a ticket."

"Understood."

He handed me the paper. "We'll have a tow truck come by. Earl will take your car to Edie's shop. She's closed tomorrow but will give you a call on Monday." He turned to Jack. "You can take her now. I'll keep an eye on things here."

Jack helped me out of the car, and I bit the insides of my cheeks to keep from crying out. I was going to be very sore tomorrow. "Let's get you in the truck and I'll grab your things."

The sound of heels smashing into pavement had me tensing up, which just made me ache even more. "She should be arrested!"

Caden stepped in front of her. "Cynthia, she's already gotten a ticket. The best thing for everyone—"

"Is to arrest her for driving drunk! Why else would she have hit me? I was clearly stopped at the traffic light."

Cynthia's champion, who was in a tie despite it being after ten thirty, approached wearing his attitude on his sleeve. "Women like her—"

"Excuse me?" I started. *Oh, hell no*, I was not listening to another lecture about how my job made me a bad citizen.

"That. Is. Enough," Jack said in a tone so low and cold, even Cynthia stilled. "This was an accident. Vera's insurance will pay for the damages. For now, I'm taking her somewhere to rest."

Cynthia stepped forward, but whatever she saw in Jack's look gave her pause. Caden cleared his throat. "Please leave Ms. Eastman alone, or I'll be forced to take you down to the station for harassment."

Without another word, Jack steered me away and helped me to his four-door pickup truck. Once he opened the door, he put his hands on my hips and lifted me onto the seat. I nearly drooled all over. It would've been a mess.

He went back to my car and grabbed my bags, then loaded them into the backseat. He and Caden shook hands before he climbed in and turned to me. I swear the truck shrank two sizes. "Where are you staying?"

I closed my eyes and pushed my fingers against my forehead, rubbing in slow circles. "Uh...the hotel near 75."

He started the truck and pulled away. The space between us was heavy with too many years of unspoken thoughts. I leaned back in the seat and stared out the window, catching slices of familiar countryside in the moonlight. "Thanks for...everything," I said softly. I looked over at him, the headlights of a passing car highlighting the stern set of his jaw.

He nodded and I looked away, not liking the way my body wanted to lean closer to his. *Not happening, body.* Jack's gaze cut to my face then back to the road. I pressed my palms against my eyes, ignoring the sting of the cut. I shook my head and sighed. "I'm starting to think coming back was a bad idea."

"Why did you come back then?"

"I wanted to finish Mom's bucket list by my thirtieth birthday."

Jack made a noise of understanding. He was the one who had held my hand throughout her illness and funeral. "And you needed to come back to Grenadine to do that?"

I stared out the window determined not to look at his face right now. "Several of her items have to happen in Grenadine. Eat breakfast at Grenadine Manor, be nominated Cherry Queen at the annual Founder's Festival, slow dance with Lance..."

Jack let out a low whistle. "That last one..."

"I think I might just call that one done. I did have what could equate to a dance-off with him at Ray's tonight."

Jack nodded, clearly having already heard about the confrontation. "You always knew how to wring the most drama from every situation."

I flinched. He wasn't wrong. "I'm sorry for just showing up. I wasn't sure what I was expecting, but this" —I made an all-encompassing gesture with my hand— "wasn't it."

Jack laughed. "Vera, you grew up here. You're a famous porn star; you drive a custom-built, rare sports car; and I don't actually think you know how to keep a low profile. What did you think was going to happen?"

I shoved my hands into my hair, massaging my scalp. "Clearly, I wasn't thinking long-term."

"Another one of your talents."

"Jack..."

"I'm sorry. That was out of line. But how could you hurt Grandma Bea?"

I swallowed hard. "That's one of my biggest regrets."

"Not that it's any of my business, but why aren't you staying with her?"

My mouth fell open and I stared at him for a long moment.

"That's not funny. You're a lot of things, Jack Reeves, but I didn't take you to be such an asshole."

Jack did a double take before refocusing on the road. His hands tightened on the steering wheel, making it squeak. "Why am I an asshole?"

I stared at him. Why did every conversation today feel like it was happening in some kind of alternate reality? "It's been eleven years. Surely the news has gotten around that Grandma Bea died."

Jack slowed down and pulled over to the side of the road. "Vera, are you okay? Is your head hurting more? Should I take you to the hospital?" His eyes roamed over me as if looking for something out of place.

I reached for my phone and searched for the email from my dad from over a decade ago, reading it out loud. "Your grandma passed away from a broken heart. Come home for the funeral this Friday." I handed him the phone. "Actually, I swear I saw her today. It's why I was driving like an asshole and not paying attention, honestly."

He released a strangled puff of air, blinked hard, and shook his head. "Your dad sent you this?"

"Yep."

He ran a hand down his face. "I don't know how to tell you this…"

I chewed on my thumbnail, an old habit I had broken when I'd gotten into porn. I hated fake nails, but weekly manicures were mandatory, so I strived to keep my natural nails in perfect condition. Jack put my phone on his dash, then reached for the hand I was chewing on. He flattened out the curled fingers and laced his hand through mine. I looked down at our joined hands and then back up at him, my stomach twisting.

He cleared his throat. "Vera, Grandma Bea is still alive."

CHAPTER SIX

"WHEN THINGS ARE BAD AND GETTING WORSE, KEEP A COOKIE IN YOUR PURSE." - GRANDMA BEA

ALIVE. The word clanged around my head. I opened my mouth to speak, but nothing came out. My entire body was strung tight, like a guitar string about to break. I wanted to tell him he was wrong, there was some mistake. I was too afraid to hope, but I also knew Jack would never lie. Not about something like this.

It felt like my chest was trying to cave in as I struggled to take a full breath. Jack put the truck in drive and drove back toward town. "Vera..." he started, but it seemed he couldn't find the words, either. He just held on to my hand.

I had missed eleven years of birthdays, holidays, long talks on the phone, and Grandma's cooking. We used to talk every day until I left. Once I got a new cell phone, it was too late. She was gone.

Except that she hadn't been.

She wasn't dead.

He rubbed the back of my hand in a circle with his thumb, like he used to do when I was upset when we were kids. His touch was like a balm to my soul, loosening the knot in my chest. "I lost eleven years with her," I finally said, the words like sandpaper against my raw throat.

He squeezed my hand. "It'll be okay. You'll figure it out."

"How do you know?"

He navigated a turn then shot me a soft smile. "She's probably the person who loves you the most in the world. She's so proud of you, do you know that? I never needed to look you up online because she always knew what was going on with you. Each time she heard you won an award she had a party at her house with her friends. She even made formal, handwritten invitations."

I laughed, although it sounded almost like a sob. I covered my mouth with my shaking hand, trying to find the strength to calm the burning that tightened my chest.

We were silent until Jack turned on Grandma's street. I must have made a sound, because Jack shook my arm gently. "It's going to be okay," he promised. "You are the most important person in her life, whether or not you knew." He pulled the truck into Grandma's driveway. He gave me one more squeeze before releasing it and getting out of the truck.

I just sat there, unable to move. Dread weighted down my limbs as I studied the house, which still looked exactly the same. A 1950s-style brick ranch with the large front window and a small garage. Grandma had added her own touches, like a pair of rocking chairs on the front porch, a small but colorful garden along the entryway, and two lanterns on either side of her driveway.

I could see her through the front window, wearing an apron, like she always did when she was baking. Jack's headlights must have warned her that there was someone in her driveway. She walked toward the front door, and every muscle in my body went tense.

Jack opened my door and unbuckled my seatbelt. I didn't move my eyes from the picture window as he helped me out of the car and onto the driveway. He gripped my right hand and I felt the strength of his arm pressed against mine.

Somehow, I put one foot in front of the other, walking through what seemed like a fever dream. When we reached the bottom of the porch steps, the front door opened. I stopped, trying to convince my leg muscles to keep working. All that stood between me and the woman I had left behind eleven years ago was a flimsy screen door.

Jack released my hand and put his arm around my lower back, softly encouraging me to walk up the stairs, but I couldn't move. Grandma turned on the porch light, opened the screen door, and stepped outside. Her hand flew to her chest. There was no more than six feet between us, but it felt like the Grand Canyon.

How did I even begin to apologize for not at least checking that she was actually dead? Why hadn't I called Jack, or any other person in town? Why had I trusted the word of a man who disowned me? I was such an idiot.

Jack cleared his throat. "Grandma Bea? I brought someone to see you."

She took a shuddering breath and held out her arms. "My grandbaby!"

Her words filled my chest with emotion. I cried out, letting go of Jack's hand and launching myself up the stairs and into her arms. She pulled me to her, holding me tight.

She was shorter than I remembered, barely up to my shoulder, but she had the grip of a bear. I don't know how long we stood there crying and hugging—it could've been a minute, it could've been two days—but it was only the start of the tears and hugs we needed to make up for.

"I thought you were a ghost," I admitted, my breath catching.

"Not yet." Her voice wasn't steady either. "I've prayed for this day for eleven years."

"Dad emailed me that you had died of a broken heart," I whispered. "I would've come home if..." A hiccup sob burst out of me and she patted my back. I hated crying, especially with a headache, but I couldn't control it now.

"It's okay. We're together now." She shushed me and pulled back, putting her hands on both sides of my face. She frowned and tutted at the cut above my eyebrow that wasn't there earlier.

"Vera's okay, but she was in an accident tonight," Jack explained.

"We should get her inside." He helped us into the house, guiding us to the kitchen. Grandma and I sat next to each other, my right side leaning against her left.

This house was still my favorite place to be. The smell of Grandma's perfume and baking was everywhere, and I inhaled deeply, drowning in the memories. Her living room still had teal carpet and floral curtains, but the kitchen had been redone. The counters were white granite, but the cabinets were still oak. Her stove and refrigerator were still white, but her dishwasher and microwave were now stainless steel. She still had a flower curtain valance on the window above the new stainless-steel sink.

My eyes followed Jack as he filled a kettle with water, then pulled out three mugs and tea bags. He followed that by going to the freezer, procuring a bag of frozen peas, and plopping them onto my left shoulder. Grandma kept touching my face and petting my hands as if making sure I was real. "Forgive me for saying this, but I'm going to kill your father," Grandma said succinctly. "I know how to use a knitting needle as a weapon."

I put my head against her shoulder, ignoring my screaming neck muscles. "And no one would suspect a nice, little old lady who makes scarves for the entire police staff." My late grandpa had been on the force, and Grandma had knitted scarves for every staff member for the holidays.

"Switched to hats this year," she explained. "They need more scarves like a hole in the head." She kissed the top of my head. "Now, tell me everything that's been going on in your life."

We were practically talking over each other in excitement, trying to cram eleven years of life into the first ten minutes of our reunion. There was so much to say, but the hard stuff could come later. The tea kettle whistled, and Jack shuffled around the kitchen, putting a spoonful of honey in Grandma's tea and a dollop of milk into mine. He set them down in front of us before taking the seat next to me. It was like he knew I needed him to be there, to witness the moment I had only dreamed about.

Grandma looked at Jack and nodded toward her counter. "Grab those cookies. We need them."

Jack nodded and stood, grabbing the large strawberry cookie jar off the counter and setting it on the table. I reached with my left hand, desperate to taste one of her cookies again, but the pain made me gasp out loud. I pulled my arm back against my body, waiting for the throbbing to subside.

"Maybe we should get you checked out again," Grandma said, starting to fuss.

Jack reached over and put his hand on top of our clasped ones. "Grandma Bea, she's okay. The paramedics checked her out."

She nodded then reached into the cookie jar and pulled out three chocolate chip cookies and set them down in front of me. "Here, these will help."

As we talked, I tried to commit her face to memory. She looked almost the same, but sadder. The years without her daughter and granddaughter showed, in her sunken eyes and thinning hair. I cleared my throat and shoved an entire cookie in my mouth. It melted on my tongue and I moaned. "The cookies really do help," I admitted around a mouthful.

Jack laughed and Grandma took a bite of a cookie, herself. "My dear girl, when will you learn that there's magic in cookies?" She finished the cookie and grabbed a napkin from the holder at the center of the table to wipe her hands. "Now then. What is this rumor I'm hearing that you spent three-thousand dollars on a date with Jack? Is he at least putting out on the date?"

I laughed so hard, I almost choked. That would be just like me—reunite with my grandma and the love of my life, then die because of a cookie.

CHAPTER SEVEN

"GOING TO CHURCH DOESN'T AUTOMATICALLY MAKE YOU A GOOD PERSON, JUST LIKE BUYING STORE-BOUGHT COOKIES DOESN'T MAKE YOU A BAKER. YOU GOTTA PUT A LITTLE EFFORT IN TO NOT SUCK." –GRANDMA BEA

I HAD KEPT Grandma up past her bedtime. She fought valiantly, but by midnight she had dozed off three times at the table. She threatened that I had better be staying in the guest room or else, and I happily accepted.

I took in the room, which still had the same floral bedspread on the queen-sized bed, but the cream-colored carpeting and flat screen television were new. The dresser had been one of my mom's refurbished pieces, and a family picture of us from a day at a lake up north adorned the top. I rubbed my forehead, my head spinning.

Jack walked into the room with my suitcase and bag and set them down. I nodded toward the bedroom door and he closed it softly. "She asleep?" he asked quietly.

I nodded. "I don't know how to thank you," I admitted, my voice as quiet as his. "This whole day feels like a dream."

The corners of his eyes crinkled. "I can only imagine." He searched my face. "You okay?"

I smirked. "I just had like four cookies and got a dozen Grandma hugs."

He laughed, more air than sound. "You're okay."

The craziness of the day, the emotions of being back, of seeing him, of seeing Grandma, and exhaustion hit me like a thousand-pound weight and my legs nearly gave out. I sat on the edge of my bed, rubbing my hands over my face. "So... what's new with you?"

He smiled and shook his head, putting his hands in his pockets and rocking back on his heels. "Listen, it's been a long day. Let's catch up another time."

I sighed and nodded, knowing he was right. "You were always the logical one." I stood and walked over to him and without thinking about it, I wrapped him in a hug. "Thanks for everything today."

He tensed for a moment before his arms came around me, his chin resting on my head. "You're welcome."

I knew it was time to pull back, but I couldn't bring myself to let go. His hug transcended the years apart, our devastating breakup, the craziness of today. It was just us—two people who had known each other since diapers—comforting each other.

Everything inside me stilled, as it always did when he was near, and I wished I could bottle this feeling and take it with me. This is what I wanted to remember when I had been awake for twenty hours, trying to finish a shoot that had gone wrong. This is what I needed to have when I forgot what the sun looked like for weeks at a time because I was drowning in work.

Jack cleared his throat. "Vera, I should go."

Reluctantly, I pulled back but kept my hands on his strong forearms. "You are one amazing man, Jack Reeves."

A hint of red touched his high cheekbones. He laughed uncomfortably. "Thanks."

That damn blush. It made something in my chest knot, and I stood on my tiptoes and pressed my lips to his. He froze as I captured his bottom lip between mine. Before I could pull back completely, his hands sank into my hair and he angled my head, deepening the kiss.

We both inhaled desperately, as if we had been suffocating until this moment. His tongue met mine in a familiar slide that turned my knees to jelly. My stomach dropped and I was floating ten feet off the ground. I gripped the front of his shirt, trying to get closer to him.

Without warning, he broke the kiss, his chest heaving as if he just ran a marathon. My heartbeats stacked up too fast in my chest. He rested his forehead against mine. "That was a mistake." He pulled back and stepped to the side, breaking contact with me.

I took two steps back, gently touching my scorching lips. I had kissed hundreds of people in my career, some of them really good, some of them off the charts. But there was always something special about the way Jack kissed me, like he couldn't get enough. Like he was a dying man and kissing me was the only cure.

I walked over to the edge of the bed and sat down, looking at my pedicured, cherry-red toenails. I needed physical space to calm my clamoring heart.

He cleared his throat. "Vera...everything fell apart that year. Your mom, and then you left, then..." He put his hands in his pockets and rocked back on his feet, looking everywhere but at me. "Danny died."

I gasped so loud it echoed around the room. "Jack, no," I whispered. "I'm so sorry."

Danny, Jack's brother, had been two years older than me and three years older than Jack. He was the person we'd sneak out with, going to crazy huge bonfires and concerts where the smoke was so thick you couldn't see the stage. He was charming and carefree, free-spirited in a way that responsible Jack never was.

Jack ran his hands through his hair. "When you didn't come back for the funeral, I understood. But you didn't call or text or email or hell, send a message in a bottle. Nothing."

I winced. "I didn't have a phone for a few weeks and a computer for even longer. Dad told me to leave them behind since he paid for them." I picked at a loose thread on the comforter. "I think it was his way of trying to get me to cave to his demands." I laughed without humor. "Which, ultimately, I did anyway."

He laughed, but it sounded wrong. "I tried to call and email you but got nowhere. Your social media accounts had been deleted and no one knew where you had gone. By the time I figured out who Roni Vegas was, I was too angry at you to reach out."

There was nothing I could say that would make this better, but he deserved the truth. "It was too hard to be here after Mom died. We had just broken up, and Dad, Grandma, and I had a fight..." I ran my fingers through my hair and let out a slow breath.

A fight was a gentle way of putting it. I had screamed my throat raw and tried to destroy the house as they gave me the ultimatum to get help or get out. Grandma had tried to call the cops, but Dad didn't want anyone to know what was going on.

I sucked in my bottom lip then dragged my teeth over it. "I was so lost to my grief, I didn't care about anyone else's pain. Nothing mattered anymore."

He looked at his feet for a long moment. "You left your entire support system behind. You left me behind."

"We were over. You made that very clear." I rubbed my chest with the heel of my hand, trying to ease the echo of heartbreak at the memory.

He rubbed the back of his neck. "Vera, you were in a tailspin and I was only seventeen. I didn't even know how to begin to help you."

I threw my hands up. "I didn't know how to handle her death and you just left me alone."

"You were trying to bring her back from the dead with as much alcohol and bullshit as you could!" he shouted, then pushed his fingers against his lips. We were both silent for a long moment as we listened to see if Grandma stirred. When the house remained silent, except for the ticking of the grandfather clock in the living room, he lowered his hand.

"You're right," I admitted. "It wasn't your job to fix me." I let out a long breath. "I ran away from dealing with...everything. I didn't want to get over the pain. I just didn't want to feel anymore." I shook my head. "Ironically, I ended up dealing with all my bullshit the moment I pulled out of the driveway."

There was a long beat of silence. "Why didn't you come back? Even to visit? Why cut off everything and everyone?"

I dug my toes into the soft carpet then studied the dents they left behind. "Honestly, I thought about it after a few weeks. Vegas in the summer is stifling. All I could think about was swimming in the creek and drinking iced tea on Grandma's porch. My apartment had more roommates than fruit flies and I was ready to come home."

I swallowed hard. "I still didn't have a computer yet, so I went to the local library to email Dad to apologize and see if I could come home. I probably should've called, but I was too afraid." I cleared the old memories from my throat. "The first email I opened was Dad's telling me about Grandma and something in me just...snapped. I couldn't come back. It was too painful. So, I deleted everything that had anything to do with Vera Tompson and started over."

I hadn't even read Jack's emails. I wished more than anything I hadn't done something so profoundly rash. But grief made people do crazy things.

When he finally looked at me, his eyes were glassy and hard. "I'm sorry. I wish I knew why your dad did what he did. If he'd never sent that email..." He shook his head. "I'm glad you got your life together away from Grenadine, and it's really good to see you."

I smiled ruefully. "But..."

"But I can't do this again, Vera. It's only been in the last couple of years that life has started being livable again for a lot of us."

He looked over his shoulder and down the hall, toward Grandma's room. "She lost her daughter and then her granddaughter, her son-in-law bailed, and then she lost a kid she'd treated like her own grandson." He shook his head and ran a hand over his face.

"She's the strongest person I've ever known." I looked down at my chipped nail polish, picking at the edge of my pointer finger. "I'm sorry, for everything. I'll stay out of your way. Promise."

Without a word, he walked out of the room, shutting the door softly behind him.

FIRE TRUCKS, GARTER BELTS, & MY PERFECT EX

HERE'S the thing about small towns: everyone knows everything in approximately eighteen minutes. The doorbell was ringing by eight the next morning. Not only had Grandma Bea's long-lost granddaughter returned home, but said long-lost granddaughter was also a successful porn star who'd just dropped three thousand dollars on her ex-boyfriend at yesterday's fundraiser, and then proceeded to rear-end Cynthia—Edie's dragon of a mother—which apparently made her a hero to half the town and enemy number one to the other half.

So you could say that my tenure in Grenadine was going...not great.

At least people were dropping off free food with their visits. Gertie Haninky, Grandma's best friend, was the first to arrive with coffee cake. I forgave her for making me get out of bed the moment I took my first bite. The fact that I followed that first bite with over-the-counter painkillers probably also helped.

Everything hurt, especially my left side. I had talked to my doctor last night after Jack left, and she didn't seem to be overly worried. All the pain felt like normal post-accident pain, but to be fair, I didn't know what accident pain felt like. I'd never been in an accident before.

By nine, we had been visited by ten different women and had enough food for a fifty-person gathering. I groaned, rubbing my neck with my hands and stretching from side to side. "You think I have time to take a shower before the next visitor?" All I wanted to do was get under the hot water and soothe my muscles.

Gertie was dipping her spoon into a breakfast casserole that Mrs. Patterson had brought over. It had way too much plastic cheese and dead animal for my taste. "I'm sure Bea and I can handle the crowd for now. But if you leave us alone for more than half an hour with the vultures, we will physically remove you from the bathroom."

I laughed, standing slowly and taking my dishes to the sink. "Half an hour, you got it." I turned to face my grandma. "Don't you have to work today?"

She shook her head. "We're closed on Sundays, remember?"

"Ah yes, small town hours. I keep forgetting. How often do you work?"

"About three days a week. Catherine McConnel—you remember her from Sunday school, I'm sure—is the best manager I've ever had. Now that her kids are off to college, she wanted to get a little extra income."

I frowned, trying to place Catherine, then balked. "You mean my Sunday school teacher?"

Grandma waved me off. "Yes, her."

"A Sunday school teacher is managing your sex toy store?"

She clucked her tongue at me. "Just because a woman is right with the Lord does not mean that she can't also enjoy pleasure. Maybe something to think about. Now, church starts in an hour. Father Wright finally moved mass later when Ray decided he wasn't going to open until nine on Sundays. You can just imagine what would happen if people went to church without their breakfast."

Gertie made the sign of the cross and looked Heavenward. "Amen."

"I'm not expected to go to church, am I?" I asked, trying to rub the throbbing above my eyebrow away.

"Unless you want people to continuously walk through that door today, it would be best if you just saw them all at once at church." Grandma got up from her chair and started to put away the food. "Also, my house, my rules. We go to church on Sunday."

"So..." I folded my arms. "You think it's a good idea for your long-lost granddaughter, a porn star who has had a lot of premarital sex with both men and women, to casually walk into church with you? In a small town. After she rear-ended the town busybody's car."

Gertie clapped her hands and squealed like a fangirl. "This may be the most fun in church I have ever had."

Grandma looked at her, eyebrows raised. "Really? What about that one time you and that altar boy—"

"Chicks over dicks!" Gertie sang.

FIFTY MINUTES LATER, I was doing something I hadn't done in eleven years except for weddings and funerals. I was walking into church. For the record, I did not burst into flames. Not that I thought my mere presence in the building would cause me to spontaneously combust—I tried to be a good person whether or not I spent my Sundays in church—but I was pretty sure that a few people were seriously considering lighting me on fire by the looks I was getting. Thankfully, they restrained themselves.

I had thought, naïvely, that we would just take up a pew near the back to avoid bringing attention to ourselves. Nope. That was absolutely not what happened. Grandma marched Gertie and me right up the center aisle to the front.

Clearly, I had underestimated my grandmother. Again. We were three rows from the pulpit. There would be no sneaking out or hiding behind my hair, which I had purposely left down because it created a really nice curtain. ~~Dammit~~ Darn it. (Swearing in church was probably frowned upon, even internally.)

Gertie and Grandma were whispering to each other, and from the snippets of conversation I heard, I realized they were taking bets on who would come over first. I leaned over. "Isn't gambling in church frowned upon?"

Grandma waved me off. "As long as no money exchanges hands until you're out the church doors, it's not really gambling."

I pinched the bridge of my nose. Crazy ran in the family. It was only a matter of time before it got me. I made the sign of the cross; maybe I really did need to start praying a little bit harder. I briefly looked around and saw my dad in the front row on the opposite side.

As if he could feel my eyes on him, my anger about his lie pelting him, his shoulders slumped. But he never looked at me.

The first person to approach us introduced herself as Amy LeMarks. I vaguely remembered she was on some PTA or Girl Scout board with Mom. She made a show of greeting everyone in the surrounding area before turning her attention to us.

She reached out her hands and Grandma took them. "Oh, Bea, I was so thrilled to hear you and Vera had reconnected!" She leaned forward as if to have a more intimate conversation, although her voice didn't get any quieter. "You know I would've been by first thing this morning, but with Cynthia's accident and all, I needed to go take care of her first. Surely you understand." She gave me the side eye.

Wow. Amy's passive aggressiveness was almost as good as my grandma's.

Grandma released Amy's left hand and patted her right one. "We completely understand. I've been around much longer than Cynthia, and I need less looking after. What matters is that you came by now."

Gertie shot me a look, and it took everything I had to keep a straight face. Battleship sunk. They exchanged comments about the perfect August weather we were having before parting.

I leaned over to Grandma and whispered, "That'll do pig, that'll do." It was a quote from the movie *Babe*, which had turned me into a vegetarian at five.

She elbowed me in the side. "Behave." Then she turned to Gertie. "You owe me twenty."

Gertie muttered something about extortion. "Lucky guess."

As the church bells pealed their final warning to all latecomers, I wished I could look around the church to see if Jack was there. I wasn't brave enough to look behind me. Gertie leaned over and tapped my arm. "Jack's not here. His truck wasn't in his driveway this morning, which means he's working."

I closed my eyes. She'd said it loud enough I was pretty sure someone standing outside the church could've heard her. This was going to be a long morning.

The organ started and Mass began. I remembered enough about the service that I didn't look completely ignorant. While a couple of lines had changed here and there—seriously, what happened to "and also with you?"—I basically was pulling it off. By the stares burning into the side of my head, it escaped no one's notice that Father Wright had spoken about forgiveness and welcoming lost souls home.

My suspicion that my grandmother was somehow involved in the sermon was confirmed when she dropped a stack of bills into the donation plate as it passed by. The look she gave me as she handed over the plate was a warning. *Do not screw this up,* it said.

I put in two twenties just to make her never look at me like that again.

The man sitting next to me took the donation plate from my hand, over-reaching on purpose so he brushed the side of my boob. I tensed. If I were anywhere but church, I would make this man cry. Thankfully, yet again, I had underestimated my grandmother.

The next time we stood up, Grandma put her hands on my hips and pulled me in front of her, then to her opposite side. She grabbed the man's arm and whispered something that made him pale. A few parishioners looked over, but I kept my eyes down. This wasn't an unnatural occurrence. Porn stars were often treated like pregnant women's bellies; strangers thought they could just randomly walk up and touch you without asking, as if they had earned the right just by being in your vicinity.

Despite the fact that this church was so old it didn't have air conditioning, and the ceiling fans overhead were fighting a losing battle against the mass of bodies, I pulled my shawl tighter around my shoulders and crossed my arms. Okay, it wasn't actually a shawl. It was a crocheted table runner that Grandma used for Easter. I had not packed any "church appropriate clothing," since I had not envisioned actually attending a service on my vacation. My best dress that didn't have a plunging neckline was a cornflower blue sundress with very thin straps. Grandma, who sold an astonishing array of dildos for a living, would not let me walk in church without my shoulders covered.

Welcome to small-town life.

When church ended, I sagged in the pew in relief. Grandma elbowed me. "Get up. We still have to make it out of the church, mingle on the sidewalk for five minutes, then we can go home. That should keep the vultures away for a few days. I have enough food in my house to feed us for a week. And the best cooks already came by this morning."

I impressed myself by not rolling my eyes. When we stepped out into the morning sunshine, the crowd split into two distinct categories. To the left, Amy and several other women about her age had crowded around the beautiful blonde woman I had rear-ended last night. She didn't have a scratch or bruise on her perfect face, and she wore heels as high as the ones I wore to shoot in. Guess they were only slut shoes when they were on a porn star.

To the right were several of the women who had stopped by this morning, along with some new faces. Some I recognized as people my grandma used to have over, but several others I didn't know. A man about my age and height was watching me carefully. He stood a few feet away from the others, playing with a ring on his hand and talking to a man whose face I knew almost as well as my grandma's.

Franklin Barwell, a barrel-chested, middle-aged man with curly hair and a bushy beard, stopped talking mid-sentence and opened his arms. "Vera, you're a sight for sore eyes!"

I practically ran to him as we caught each other in a tight hug. "Franklin, I've missed you more than words can say. How are you? How's the band?"

He released me and stepped back, puffing out his chest. "Playing a show next week about a half hour away. Please tell me you'll be there. I need someone with rhythm singing along!"

"If I'm still here, I'm one hundred percent in! All depends on when I get my car back." His daughter, Fiona, and I had been setting up the stage for the band since we were strong enough to carry the instruments. She had left for school the year before I graduated, and I had lost touch with her after I deleted everything Vera Thomson related.

"I'll give your grandma a call later with all the details." He patted the man next to him on the shoulder. "And, it's Franklin Senior now."

"Senior?" I asked. Franklin and his late wife, Mala, only had one child. I looked at the beautiful man next to him. He had Franklin's amber eyes and Mala's beige complexion. There was a small gold hoop in his right nostril, just like Fiona used to wear.

The young man smiled shyly and something about that look comforted me. I swear I knew that smile. "I changed my name to Franklin Junior when I transitioned. I go by Franky now," he said, his voice light, but deeper than I expected. He smiled huge. "Hi, Ra-Ra."

Only one person in the world ever called me that. Warmth spread over me and I smiled so hard it hurt. "It's so damn amazing to see you, Franky."

"Damn straight." He opened his arms. "Can I give you a hug?"

"Duh, you loser." I practically jumped as I wrapped him in the tightest hug I could manage, and we swayed back and forth, just like we used to as kids. "I'm sorry I didn't keep in touch after you left for college. I just—"

"No, loser, it's okay. I get it. I sucked too," he said, squeezing me tighter until I inhaled a sharp breath, my shoulders aching. "Sorry." He pulled back, those familiar eyes looking me over. "You look phenomenal, despite the face-punch look. Please keep the red hair."

"Right?! It feels like my natural color. And I feel sassier."

Grandma clucked her tongue. "This girl does not need to be sassier. She's got that in spades."

"Thank goodness!" Gertie chimed in. "We wouldn't want her to be an absolute bore."

"I heard that you didn't make a whole lot of friends your first day back," he teased.

I snorted. "That's quite the understatement."

He laughed. "So ladylike, as always."

Our reunion was interrupted when someone started shouting. "And then she hit my car! I swear, she must have been drunk. I told Caden to arrest her, but he was useless."

We all looked over to see Cynthia holding court on the other side of the sidewalk. I leaned over to Franky. "This is about to turn into a mostly white version of *West Side Story*, isn't it?"

He started snapping.

"And I know for a fact she didn't even acknowledge her own father this morning!" the dragon continued.

I saw red. She was damn right I didn't seek out the man who had lied to me about my own grandmother dying. I searched the crowd and saw him touch her arm and shake his head before turning and walking away toward the parking lot. I charged forward—toward Cynthia or Dad, I wasn't sure—but Franky's arm clamped around my shoulders. He could always read me too well. He leaned close to my ear and whispered, "Don't show your hand. This is like a social media argument; you will never win."

I tried to shrug him off, but he held on tighter. "Ra-Ra, pull it together. Don't let them smell your weakness. This is a town full of sharks. Trust me; I know."

The fight went out of me. Of course he knew. Being a biracial, transgender person in a small town was probably like being a captured superhero in a movie—people either wanted to study you or feared you intensely.

"Let's get back to my place," Grandma said. "I have enough cobbler and pie to get the taste of ignorance out of our mouths."

We quickly dispersed, and I hummed to myself to keep from hearing what else Cynthia was saying. As I climbed in the back seat of Grandma's 1989 red Cadillac—which she would never let me drive—I saw Jack's parents walking away from the crowd surrounding Cynthia. I swallowed hard, trying not to let it bother me. Looked like I hadn't won any points with them today, either.

CHAPTER EIGHT

MOM'S BUCKET LIST #4: VISIT AUSTRALIA WITH MY BEST FRIEND. PET A KANGAROO

FRANKY and I were lying on my bed head to feet, just like we used to do when we were teenagers. "Perks of being old," he said. "You don't have to leave the door open when you have a boy in your room."

I cracked up. "I literally make money having sex. I think that ship has sailed."

He let out a thoughtful noise. "That's probably true. I can't knock you up anyway."

I groaned and tossed one of Grandma's decorative pillows at him. He caught it and threw it back. "Be nice to me." I laughed. "I was in a car accident yesterday."

He pushed up on his elbows. "I heard! Can you not do that shit anymore?"

I mirrored his position. "What, getting into car accidents?"

"Car accidents, disappearing, trying to die, you know." He said it in a joking tone, but his eyes were serious.

I sat up and crossed my legs, rolling my shoulders to try to loosen them up. "I'm sorry our friendship got trampled by my drama."

He sat up too and grabbed my hands. "What happened between you and your dad? Why didn't you come to live with your grandma?"

It was the obvious question, the one that Grandma and I had yet to talk about. "I was a fucking mess after Mom died. I was stripping in a shady-ass place, stealing drinks from the bar, taking whatever pills the girls would give me." I bit my bottom lip at the memory. "She and Dad told me I needed to get it together, sober up, and find a less dangerous place to work, or I needed to get out."

His mouth fell open. "I don't believe it. The sober part, I get. But why was your grandma upset about you stripping? She sells sex toys for a living."

I shrugged and smiled sadly. "I know." I sighed and looked out the window. "It wasn't the stripping, at least not entirely. We'd been robbed twice in eight months and there was always a fight going down."

"Huh. Can't imagine why people who loved you wouldn't want you to work someplace you could drink underage, get high, and then —hey, bonus!—maybe you're physically assaulted or shot."

I rolled my eyes. "Tell that to eighteen-year-old me."

"So you left."

I nodded. "And after Dad sent that email, I stayed gone. But you came back?"

He nodded. "My dad is the best, and he needed help with the bakery. It was a no-brainer. Plus, the business degree helps." He raised his eyebrows. "So, porn?"

I winked at him. "It's pretty good money."

"You didn't do it for the money," he said, quietly, yet again proving he knew me better than almost anyone on the planet. Except for Jack.

"Fuck me, I missed you."

He released my hands and booped my nose. "Sorry, Ra-Ra, you're not my type."

I huffed and crossed my arms. "What do you mean, *not your type*? What the hell type am I?"

He laughed quietly. "Emotionally unavailable yet still secretly crazy about their ex."

I opened my mouth to argue but then nodded. "Dammit. I concede."

"Anyway, women as hot as you are usually crazy." A loud female cheer erupted from the other side of the door, followed by a lot of swearing by Franklin. "And it runs in this family. Why did Dad think he could beat your grandma at cards?"

"There's crazy in the water here. It's not just passed down through our genes," I confirmed. "Also, most of the women in this town, and men for that matter, are ridiculously hot. When did that happen?"

He shrugged. "Everyone knows the hotter you are, the crazier you are."

"God, you must be a lunatic!" I laughed, elbowing him.

"Says the dime in the room."

"Just calling it like I see it."

"So, you crazy enough to stay around for a while?"

I shrugged, grabbed a pillow, and scooted back to the headboard. "I never wanted to come back. It was like, as long as I kept this place locked away in the recesses of my mind, I would be okay. I love my life in SoCal. I built my dream company there. But now that I'm back, and now that I know Grandma is alive, how can I leave? But how can I not?"

He leaned against the headboard, too, playing with his ring again. "You know that your grandma's going to call you every day, no matter where you live."

"Twice a day."

"That's probably more accurate." He reached over to the nightstand and grabbed two chocolate chip cookies off a plate, handing me one. "And Jack?"

I shoved the entire cookie in my mouth. In the last twelve hours, I'd eaten more junk food than I had in years. But reunions with ex-boyfriends and undead grandmas totally deserved cookies, in my opinion. "Jack? He doesn't factor into my decision at all."

"I like how you think you can get away with lying to me. It may have been eleven years, Ra-Ra, but I can still read you like a map."

My heart clenched. I had missed my friend more than I had realized. "He told me to stay away from him. So, I'll oblige."

"You really think you're going to avoid Jack the entire time you're here?" The laugh in his tone earned him a poke in the ribs.

"I mean, how hard can it be?"

"Uh, he literally lives next door."

I waved him off. "Grandma has bushes I can hide in if necessary."

Franky laughed, then put his arm around my shoulders and kissed the side of my head. "Well, then, I would like to formally reinstate our friendship. You won't need to hide in bushes to avoid me."

I smiled up at him. "Friendship reinstated. I'm still just as dramatic as ever."

"Good." He tugged playfully on a chunk of my hair. "Come visit the bakery when you're ready to brave the town. First pastry is on me." Franky and his dad still ran the only bakery in town, that the late Mrs. Barwell had started.

"I'm there." I patted my stomach. "And I need to start running again." It had been days since I worked out, and as soon as it didn't hurt to move, I needed to avoid gaining ten pounds. Why were carbs so delicious?

"Now give me your phone. I'm putting all of my contact information in so you have no excuses." He held out his hand.

I sighed dramatically and handed him my phone. "You're gonna put Jack's number in there, aren't you?"

He smirked. "It's like you know me."

FOR THE FIRST time in many, many years, I was bored, and it was only Wednesday. I was still too sore to do my normal workout routines, but I needed to stop sitting on the couch watching cooking shows. I had tried to help Grandma do stock at Happy Endings, but she had none of it. I had gotten a lecture about how I needed to do my own job and that old people needed to have something in their lives that they looked forward to, or else they died. I did not bother to correct her by saying everyone died.

After fixing myself a late lunch, I went searching for something to do. The lawnmower wasn't in Grandma's shed and her flower beds were completely clear of weeds. We still had more food than a restaurant from people bringing over covered dishes, so I didn't need to prep dinner. I considered picking a book from one of Grandma's shelves but sitting still for another few hours would make me crazy. I was an active person! Forced rest was worse than my forced sabbatical.

I stuffed some snacks, a water bottle, and my wallet into my backpack and gingerly placed it on my right shoulder. Part of me wished I had accepted the car rental from my insurance company, but I couldn't turn my neck very far in either direction. It was far safer for me to walk than to drive.

I didn't have a key yet, so I opened the garage door and walked out into the immaculate one-car garage that Grandma's Cadillac could fit inside with very precise maneuvering. There was a keypad that would allow me to open and lower the garage door as needed, which was perfect unless the power went out. That would be just my luck.

I checked the sky for impending weather but was nearly blinded by the sun in the cloudless sky. August was one of my favorite months in Michigan. It was less sticky than July, but still juggled hot and milder days. Today was a perfect mid-seventies.

Armed with tinted sunscreen on my face and a giant pair of sunglasses, I stepped out into the afternoon and went to close the door when I noticed the bike and bike helmet against the side wall. With some effort—and a lot of swearing—I got it off the wall one-armed and managed not to hurt myself. Confirming that the helmet was spider and stink bug-free, I snapped it into place and climbed on the bike.

After getting hit in the face and side with an airbag, I had no desire to try to bike three miles to the store without at least minimal safety gear. I didn't want to imagine how hard cement was on my face. All I needed was a concussion or, you know, a cracked skull. I ran five miles a day when I was home, so biking shouldn't be that much harder.

I would remind myself of that on my way back.

Without the ability to turn my neck without searing pain, I kept my bike on the sidewalks, slowing or stopping for passersby and baby carriages, or in one case a dog in a wagon. Crosswalks proved to be the most taxing because I had to dismount and physically move my body in each direction to look both ways.

Finally, I pulled up next to the front door of the shop, leaned the bike up against the glass, and attached the helmet to my backpack strap. When I walked in, Grandma looked up from the shelf she was going through and smiled so wide even *my* face hurt. Totally worth the annoying ride.

After a quick tour and an introduction to her staff, I tucked my bag into her office and walked around with my water bottle and cell phone. Each aisle was stocked and clutter free. This store was like a hybrid of old school and new school: novelty gifts and bachelorette party decorations tucked between DVDs and high-quality toys. There was a little something for everyone, whether they wanted to spend twenty dollars or several hundred.

"Hey, want me to autograph my DVDs while I'm bumming around?" I called to Grandma.

"Grab a Sharpie from Kim and sign away. Maybe I can sell them for double."

I raised an eyebrow. "No one buys DVDs anymore, Grandma. My streaming videos make triple what DVDs do."

Grandma's cashier, who looked to be in her twenties with bright pink hair, snow-white skin, and an amazing full-color Harry Potter tattoo on her left arm, dropped a pink Sharpie and a black Sharpie in my hand with a smile. "People here are old school. We have to reorder DVDs every few months."

My eyes widened. "Seriously?" She nodded. "Well then, I better get signing." I gestured at her arm. "That's one really bad-ass tattoo."

"Thanks! Clearly, they're my favorite books."

We high fived.

I grabbed a stack of DVDs and walked over to the register, jumping up onto the counter.

Grandma clucked her tongue and shook her finger. "This is not a pub. We do not sit on counters like we are shameless and offering our wares."

I laughed but jumped down. "We *are* shameless and most definitely offering our wares."

Her response was to drag a stool out from around the counter and set it down next to me. I sucked in my lips so I didn't laugh and got to work writing a message in pink and signing *Roni Vegas* with the black marker. When I was finished, I took a selfie with me and the DVDs and with Grandma's permission, I posted it to social media with the shop's contact information and a promise that they could ship.

"You should do more of that," Grandma said, waving her hand at me.

"More of what? DVDs? Posting?"

"Why don't you make little posts about your favorite products around the store? Pick out a few of your favorite dicks. But try to do the mid-to-high end ones. Better sales."

I put my hand over my face. "So many responses."

Grandma clucked. "Because I don't want you to sell cheap dick?"

Kim silently laughed while pretending to rearrange a stack of batteries. I looked up to the ceiling like it had the answers. "It truly runs in the family. It's no wonder I turned out the way I did."

Grandma laughed. "It's a good thing you got your mother's nose and sense of humor." We both looked at each other and winced. My father's nose was wide and long, which he could pull off as a tall, robust man. I would've looked like a horse, and not in the cute way.

I shrugged and looked around the store. "I'll start with picking lingerie and work my way over to the more daring things."

"Chicken," Grandma muttered, but then turned her attention to a pair of women who had just walked in.

I pulled a few of my favorite outfits, including my trademark cherry red garter set, and then went into one of the dressing rooms. It was lush and clean, just like it had always been. Tiffany-blue upholstered furniture, spotless mirrors, beautifully subtle white patterned wallpaper, and a table that would hold my phone for recording. Memories tickled at the corner of my mind. Mom in Grandma's garage reupholstering chairs with a matching fabric. I didn't know how often chairs needed to be reupholstered, but for a moment it felt like Mom had just left the room and would be right back.

Starting with the lingerie had seemed like the best idea, but it proved to be much harder than expected with my inability to move like a regular human. After several failed attempts to unhook my bra, I gave up. What I really wanted was chocolate.

I huffed out of the dressing room and Grandma pursed her lips at me. "Well, I could've told you that you shouldn't start with something that requires you to take off the bra you had me hook for you this morning."

I held up my hand. "You can keep your logic over there, thank you." I hung the pieces back up on their corresponding racks.

"You know your mom decorated those dressing rooms." I nodded and stilled, wanting to soak in as much of the story as I could, even though I knew it. There was something special about Grandma reliving the memory. "She did the wallpaper and found those chairs for a few bucks at garage sales. She searched all summer for those pieces."

I swallowed hard. "I remember her reupholstering them."

Grandma smiled and sighed. "She was born to decorate." She tapped the oak shelving next to her. "They don't make them like this anymore. Solid oak. She used floor stain so they'd last."

I ran my fingers over the wood, recalling how Mom sanded and stained them. "How often do you have to refinish them?"

Grandma looked to the side, trying to remember. "Only a few

here and there needed touch-ups, especially the one with faster moving product. But most of these are still the original finish she did." She gave me a long look. "Your dad helped."

"My dad can go to hell," I snapped.

Grandma touched my shoulder. "We all fuck up with our kids. Some worse than others."

I didn't respond and she didn't say anything else. She just turned around and walked away.

I called out to Kim. "Where's your chocolate?"

She pointed behind me. "Back wall. Chocolate body paint, body butter, lube, and penis-shaped candy. We'll sample out whatever you use."

I gave her a thumbs up and made my way to the back wall. Despite the fact that fake chocolate things were usually disgusting, I had high hopes that one of these items would satisfy my cravings. The top shelf contained a variety of body butter and paint. I was pleased to see there was no sugar in them.

I pulled out the butter, the paint, the penis-shaped candies—that were about the size of a snack-sized bar—with a plan. That was, until I got to the flavored lube and started cackling. Not only were there the typical chocolate and strawberry flavors, but also crème brûlée, bubble gum, frosted cupcake, and bacon. I shit you not, *bacon*.

I shoved the chocolate items back on the shelf, except the candies because I had a feeling I was going to need them. This first video was going to be about trying different kinds of flavored lube. Thankfully, Grandma had the foresight to get sample packets of the full bottles, which was perfect.

I grabbed a packet of each and walked over to Kim. "You didn't tell me about the treasure trove of flavored lube!"

She laughed. "And ruin the surprise?"

I held up the lube packets like a deck of cards. "Have you tried any of these?"

"I tried a few. They taste artificial, but not bad. I rather like the frosted cupcake one." She poked at the bacon. "I have no idea why your grandmother ordered bacon flavored."

I spread them out on the counter. "So, what you're saying is I need to test them?"

"Yep! Especially the bacon."

I scrunched up my face. "I'm a vegetarian."

Kim smirked. "Don't worry. I'm positive it's all chemicals and no actual animal products."

With a sigh, I lifted my phone to her. "Want to do a live video of me?"

She squealed and clapped her hands. "Absolutely. Come on this side of the counter so you can see the high-end sales wall behind you. And it's better lighting." She pulled out her own phone. "I'm going to record one too, just in case."

I nodded at her, impressed. "Sounds good!"

We set up the shots, I pulled my shirt lower, and she hit record on both devices. We could see the parking lot so we could always pause if a customer drove up. Besides, tasting four lubes really shouldn't take that much time.

After introducing myself, I held up the five packets, explained why one would want to use flavored lube, and how to select a flavor. "The most common flavors are berries and vanilla, which taste a bit artificial but aren't bad. But I'm going to try the chocolate, crème brûlée, bubble gum, frosted cupcake, and bacon. Because I'm clearly a masochist."

I opened the chocolate and put some on my finger and rubbed it a little bit then gave it a good, sexy suck. Giving the viewers what they wanted. I bobbed my head back and forth. "The chocolate isn't bad. It's not hot fudge, but it's better than unflavored. Don't be tagging me asking why you can't use the chocolate syrup in your pantry, either! You do not want sugar below the waist. Yeast infection city." I pointed at the camera. "Don't do it."

I wiped my hand with a piece of paper towel and opened the bubble gum—not terrible—then the frosted cupcake. I clucked my tongue around in my mouth and pursed my lips. "That was surprisingly...delicious. Good if you're on a diet and need a hit of cake."

The bacon was bound to be worse than the crème brûlée, so I figured I'd get it out of the way. I dropped a bit on my finger, closed my eyes, and sucked. I gagged a little but managed to swallow it down. I couldn't cover the small cough that followed. "That was not good," I wheezed. "But I haven't eaten bacon since I was five, so try at your own risk."

Kim was silently laughing so hard the camera was shaking.

"Now, for the pièce de résistance, the crème brûlée. I expect this to either be insanely good or really disgusting. My bet is on insanely good." Dab, suck. Nothing could have prepared me for my body's response.

My eyes went wide and started to water. I pulled my finger out and put my palm against my mouth, bending over at the waist. It burned like really strong whiskey but tasted like a cocktail that had used rancid fruit. I don't even know how, there was no fruit in it. I coughed and wheezed and coughed again. Tears were streaming down my face and I was helpless to stop them.

Kim was laughing so hard she couldn't breathe. I was honestly concerned she was going to need CPR soon. I hit the counter with my palm and shook my head, trying to find some inner strength. The chocolate penises were on the edge of the counter and I reached for the bag, ripped it open, and shoved two in my mouth. As they melted, they eased the burning and offensive taste.

I wheezed and gasped for a lung full of air. I wiped my eyes and turned back to the camera. "Official recommendation—stick with the berries, vanilla, chocolate, and frosted cupcake." My voice sounded strangled around the dicks, but at least I could inhale again. "This is Roni Vegas, signing off."

When I looked outside the window to check for customers, I saw the official Grenadine Fire Department pickup truck driving by slowly. The triple honk confirmed what I had already suspected. Jack had totally been watching the live feed.

CHAPTER NINE

MOM'S BUCKET LIST #6: CLIMB TO THE TOP OF THE GRENADINE WATER TOWER AND WATCH THE SUNSET.

THE GRENADINE WATER TOWER WAS, like every landmark in town, bright cherry red. It was guarded by a six-foot chain-link fence and waist-high grass. I stuffed a bottle of water, a granola bar, flashlight, my selfie-stick, and my cell phone into my backpack and threw it over my right shoulder.

I was sore, but thanks to a couple ice packs and a few anti-inflammatories, I was feeling more like myself. I had lain low the rest of the day after leaving the store, recovering from crème brûlée poisoning, catching up with Grandma, and not obsessively watching Jack's house next door. I mean, it wasn't really obsessive if I just casually glanced to see if his truck was in the driveway, right?

I bent down and double knotted the laces on my shoes, fastened Grandma's eyeglass chain to my sunglasses, and climbed over the fence. My left shoulder burned a bit. I should probably have waited to climb the tower until I was 100% pain-free, but I didn't know how long I was going to be here.

Chieka had called and explained while she could do the work on my car—apparently, she had gone to Ferrari school once upon a time and could fix almost anything—she needed to special order a lot of parts. I wasn't too upset about the delay because I wasn't ready to leave Grandma. Being back with her, realizing I still had a family, was *everything*. We shared stories and cooked meals together, and those were moments I couldn't put a price on.

It was only half an hour until sunset and I had to make it to the top of the tower before then. I looked up at the ladder built into the side of the tower. One hundred and sixty-five feet didn't seem all that tall until you were staring up at it. A twinge in my gut warned me that this might not be my brightest move. But I was never one to back away from a challenge, especially one I set myself. Honestly, I don't know if that made me brave or just stupid.

I grabbed the bottom rungs of the ladder and hoisted myself up. I leaned back, testing my shoulders and making sure they could support my weight. There was some slight discomfort on my left side, but nothing I couldn't deal with. I basically had to be an expert yogi to have sex in some of the positions the directors wanted. If I could film a scene on a fire escape of an LA loft and not fall, I was pretty sure I could do anything.

I sang to myself as I climbed up the tower. My hands hitting the rungs set the beat, and I had made it almost all the way through Sorry Charlie's "Almost Home" by the time I reached the top. The skyline was breathtaking. I could see the entire town, blanketed by green trees that reached up to a pink-tinged sky.

I sat down in the middle of the catwalk, safely staying away from the edges. I wasn't necessarily afraid of heights, but I was still pretty freaked out to be this high up without a harness. I pulled out my selfie-stick and attached my camera, first taking video and then a panoramic photo. Finally, I took an overhead selfie and sent it to the group chat.

Me: I got really high today!

Jas: Ha! Looks so bad ass. Where R U?

Me: Top of the Grenadine water tower

Payton: Are you fucking insane? Also, not funny.

Payton: When are you coming home?

Payton: I'm seriously starting to get worried about you

Jas: Calm down Mom

Jas: But 4 real, txt when U get down

Jas: Google says it's 165 ft tall

Jas: Now I'm worried

Payton: Finally, I'm rubbing off on someone

Payton: DO NOT make a rubbing one off joke

Jas: *crying emoji*

Me: I promise to text when I get down. Xo

The cicadas sang me a song as the sun went down, the sky turning from soft pink to bright orange to purple. In the fading light, I pulled out the journal and put a check mark next to the entry. Sunset on the water tower, accomplished.

I put my phone and selfie-stick back into my bag and pulled out my flashlight. Taking a deep breath, I gripped the end of the ladder. Going down was going to be terrifying. No, that wasn't right. It was taking that first weird, turnaround step that was the scariest.

I stepped onto the top rung. Then I moved to the second rung. And that's when everything went wrong.

As soon as I put my full weight on the rung, it snapped. I started to fall, the flashlight tumbling out of my hands. I scrambled for purchase, my heartbeats colliding as I gripped the top rung as hard as I could, preventing my chin from smashing into it. My feet were dangling and my left palm stung and throbbed, slipping on the metal. I must have cut my hand.

The flashlight hit the ground hard and went out. I closed my eyes. "Please don't let me end up like the flashlight," I prayed. I tried to reposition my aching palm to grip the ladder better so I could lower myself past the broken step, but the moment I squeezed the bar, white-hot pain shot up my arm. My hand grew so slippery from blood I nearly fell again. *Shit.* There was no way I could climb down without a functional hand.

I was breathing so hard I was shaking. Or maybe I was just fucking terrified. Praising my personal trainer for always kicking my ass, I pulled myself up with my right hand until I could put my elbows on the rung.

It took all my core strength to then hoist myself up so I could get a knee on the rung and lever myself back to the catwalk on top of the tower. I laid down, panting. "You'll be fine in five seconds," I told myself. I counted backward and willed the shaking to subside.

Sitting up carefully, I dug my phone out of my bag and turned on the flashlight app to inspect my hand. My palm was smeared with blood, a lot of blood. I put my phone in my lap and slipped the backpack off. I struggled to get my shirt over my head, leaving me in a sports bra. I rolled the shirt then wrapped it around my palm, knotting it with my teeth.

Okay, so doing this at night had been a really fucking stupid idea. I should've done sunrise instead because at least then it would be getting lighter instead of darker.

I needed to make a plan. The longer I sat there, the darker it got, the more freaked out I became. There was a spotlight on the front of the tower at night, but all it did was throw me into greater shadow. I took a deep breath to settle my nerves. A panic attack wasn't going to get me off this tower in one piece.

Carefully, I picked up my phone and winced at the red low battery. I dialed 9-1-1 and prayed that I had enough battery for the call to go through. As soon as the operator asked what my emergency was, I rushed out, "My name is Vera Eastman, I'm stuck on the top of the Grenadine water tower, and the ladder is broken. I cut my left hand and I think it needs stitches. And my phone is dying."

There was a long pause on the other end as she took in the information and I tried to comfort myself with the thought that this was probably not the craziest thing she'd heard today. To her credit, the operator didn't laugh. She just explained help was on the way and she promised to stay on the line with me as long as my battery held out.

I was really proud of myself for not freaking out, at least, not until a blur of sirens and spotlights approached. My stomach squeezed as one very pissed-off Jack was fitted with a harness and climbed into a basket attached to the end of a ladder. The ladder didn't make it all the way to the top, so Jack hooked up the harness to the water tower's ladder and started climbing.

He was in control of his movements, constantly aware of his surroundings. Cool, calm, and assured that he was going to complete this rescue. When he reached the catwalk, his eyes assessed me, lingering on the shirt wrapped tightly around my hand.

Anger and something close to concern flashed across his face. "Are you hurt anywhere other than your hand?" His voice was detached and professional, but his eyes never left mine. I shook my head. He walked toward me with a second harness and explained how we were going to get down.

"You're lucky I was on duty," he said in a tone that sounded too calm. "I'm the only one besides Dad who has had experience in search and rescue, and he's too old to be doing this. The closest search and rescue team is an hour away. This isn't as easy as getting a cat out of a tree."

He strapped me in and said nothing else except directions on what we were going to do next. After securing me into the harness and then onto the rope line, we started to move down the ladder, carefully skipping over the broken rung. I was handed into the cart and passed off to Cassie.

By the time we reached the ground, the ambulance was already waiting for me. Sharon and Jack helped me onto a gurney as Jack went over all my information. He told her to take me to Burton General, the nearest hospital. I opened my mouth to argue, but the look on his face warned me to keep my mouth shut.

I was eternally grateful that we drove with the sirens off. Sharon took my vitals and made notes, not even flinching at the bumps in the road. I chewed on my thumbnail, choosing to ignore the fact that it was probably covered in flakes of lead-based paint and years of filth. I didn't know where my backpack or my phone were, which wasn't great because I didn't have my insurance cards.

When we got to the hospital, I was carted through the emergency room and into a curtained-off section. A flurry of people and stitches and one very uncomfortable tetanus shot filled the next two hours, and I would've given almost anything for a granola bar. I had fallen into a light doze when heavy footsteps signaled someone walking into the room and a chair scraped against the linoleum floor.

I sat up, surprised to see Jack sitting there, running his hands over his face. I groaned and laid back down. "We have to stop meeting like this."

"Nothing would please me more," he returned. He lifted my backpack and set it down in the chair. "Your friends Payton and Jasmine were blowing up your phone. I charged it for a few in my truck and answered it the twentieth time they called. I told them you were fine and would call them tomorrow."

I put my hands over my face. "Dammit. Payton's going to fly out here and kick my ass."

"Good. Someone should. I'm so angry, I don't even know—" He stopped. "Wait, Payton Spade? Like, *the* Payton Spade?"

I turned to him and smiled apologetically. "Yes...that Payton." I was a medium star in the porn world, but Payton was a superstar. "I'm one of the Payton's Playhouse co-founders."

He sighed and pinched the bridge of his nose. "Please tell her not to come to Grenadine. She will cause a riot."

I winced. "Yeah...this place doesn't know how to act chill."

"Apparently, neither do you."

That was fair. I held up my hands in surrender. "Please don't yell at me tonight. You can yell at me tomorrow, I promise. Right now, I'm just hungry and want to go home."

Jack scooted to the edge of his chair. "Me too. I just got off shift."

Guilt smacked me upside the head. "How long are your shifts?"

He yawned. "We just switched from twenty-four-hour shifts to twelve-hour shifts. I was on my way out when your call came through."

I pulled the sheet up over my head. "It's like the universe wants me to be the biggest asshole to you of all time."

"I don't think that's the universe." I heard him stand and walk over. I jumped a little when he patted the top of my head. "I'm going to go find a vending machine and coffee. Then we'll try to spring you. Just...stay in this bed until I get back. I don't have it in me to do another rescue."

I lowered the sheet and looked up at him. His earth brown eyes were tired and turned down at the edges. "You're taking me home?"

He shrugged. "I refuse to tell Grandma Bea that you tried to get yourself killed. Again." Frowning, he looked at his watch. "It's after midnight. Sunset was three and a half hours ago. Where does she think you are?"

I pulled the sheet back over my head. "Don't be mad."

He grabbed the sheet and pulled it down, searching my face. "Why would I be mad?" He said each word slowly as if the question were a warning.

I chewed some more on my thumbnail. "It's possible that I told her that I was going out on a date."

"Uh-huh. There are like five guys talking to you in town right now. Ray, who's too old, Franklin, also too old, Franky, who's smart enough to not get involved with you, Caden is taken, and…" He stood up straighter and pointed his finger at me. "No. No, you did not tell your wonderful, sweet, trusting grandmother that you were out on a date with me."

I opened my mouth to argue, but I couldn't. I had, in fact, told my grandmother that I was on a date with Jack. "She would've worried otherwise! They canceled bingo tonight because of the butter sculpture festival at the senior center, which made it harder to sneak out of the house. I thought one little white lie wouldn't hurt."

He raised his fist and pressed it against his mouth. Without a word, he turned around and walked out of the room. This, admittedly, may not have been my best plan. I bit my lip, wondering if maybe I should hold off on number 26 of Mom's list: swimming in Grenadine Creek under the stars. It would be my luck that I would try to drown or something and Jack would have to come to my rescue again.

CHAPTER TEN

GRENADINE ORDINANCE 4-15-89: IT IS ILLEGAL FOR COWS TO BE KEPT ON MAIN STREET WITHOUT A PERMIT

BY THE TIME we pulled into Jack's driveway, it was nearly two in the morning. The hospital had given me a scratchy, disposable scrub top to wear and I couldn't wait to get it off. The ride back had been awkward at best, both of us choosing to listen to sports talk radio and pretend to be interested in which team needed to work on their defense rather than talk to each other. Jack leaned back against his seat and ran his hands over his face. "What else is on your mom's list? How many more times am I going to get calls to rescue you?"

I continued looking out the passenger window. "I've already decided that I'm not running with the bulls, and I'm pretty sure Payton would cancel my insurance if I tried to skydive. But I would like to spend a month in Italy and learn to make pasta and see the Cliffs of Moher in Ireland."

"I meant, what else do you plan to do in Grenadine?"

I looked down at my backpack as if I could read the list through the fabric. "There aren't many more dangerous ones left in Grenadine. I'll probably cull the list."

He tilted his head to look at me. "The key phrase there is 'aren't many more.'" He reached out and gripped the steering wheel as if moving the tires while parked would change the direction of our lives. "Life is so fragile and so short. How could you take such stupid risks for a list that's not even yours? Especially now that you've reconnected with your grandma?"

I ground my teeth together. "This coming from the man who spends his life rushing into burning buildings to save people. Are you going to tell me you don't risk your life on the job?"

"The difference between me risking my life and you risking yours is that I'm doing it to save lives. You're just doing stupid shit in an attempt to bring your mother back. News flash, Vera! You've done this before. Finishing that list won't bring her back. But it might kill you in the process."

He shoved out the door, slamming it behind him. I scrambled out, anger ripping a hole through my self-restraint. I grabbed his arm and he spun around to face me but took a step back. "I know you're pissed at me for leaving. I know that you can't conceive how I left everything behind. But I did what I thought was best at the time. I was a fucking idiot eighteen-year-old with a few hundred dollars in the bank and no clue what I was doing."

"Why didn't you come talk to me? You know my parents would've taken you in. We would've figured it out!"

"Yes, twenty-nine-year-old Vera knows that. But eighteen-year-old Vera wasn't ready to face her demons. I didn't want to sober up and deal with it."

"You said goodbye in a text message! We had been telling everyone we were getting married since we were six." He raised his hands as if he wanted to touch me, but he turned away. "How do you think that felt? To not even get a real goodbye from the girl I had loved my whole life?"

"You broke up with me a month after my mom died!" I stomped over to face him.

He shoved his hands in his hair and started pacing. "I had to do something, Vera! You were killing yourself and you wouldn't listen to anyone." He released his hair and stilled, his hands moving down to cover his face. "I did the best I could."

His words were a kick to the stomach. I was being incredibly unfair to him, and I wasn't someone who blamed other people for their mistakes, at least not anymore. *Be the badass woman you are.* I counted backward from five to calm myself down.

"I know," I finally whispered. I put my good hand on his wrist and tugged. He let me pull his hand away and let the other one drop. "I know you did." I slide my palm against his cheek, his beard soft against my palm. He flinched but he didn't pull away. "None of this is your fault."

"If I had talked to my parents about what was going on…maybe we could've gotten you the help you needed. Maybe—"

I shushed him. "You know as well as me that thinking like that is poisonous. I don't regret leaving and making a new life for myself. But if I could go back and do it differently…" I shook my head and pulled my hand away. "Jack, let's make a truce. We forgive each other and just try to be friends."

He pursed his lips. "Friends?"

I smiled. "Or something like it."

"My friends aren't nearly this high maintenance."

I held up my hands in protest. "I swear, I am not this much trouble in SoCal."

The corner of his lip twitched up just a little. "I don't believe that for a second."

I smiled. "Seriously. I wake up, work out, do mountains of paperwork, have sex, and try not to fall asleep in board meetings. Every second and fourth Saturday, I meet up with Payton, Jasmine, and Jasmine's husband for game night. That's my life."

He quirked an eyebrow. "What exactly does a porn star game night entail?"

I laughed softly. "Darrin—Jas's husband—has an entire room dedicated to his board game collection, from Candyland to Shadows of Brimstone. I didn't even want to look at Shadows, let alone touch it, when I heard how much he paid for it."

"Tell me."

"Over two thousand dollars." I pursed my lips and nodded. "I was so afraid I was going to spill something on it that I stayed in the kitchen the entire night."

Jack gave me a smile so real, sparks shot down my spine. "This coming from the woman who just dropped three thousand on her ex at an auction?"

"Ha-ha." I rolled my eyes. "At least I helped save the shop."

"Yeah." He studied me for a long moment and something about his look made my skin warm. "What game are they playing this week?"

"Monopoly, which is one of the only games I ever have a chance at winning."

He chuckled softly. "But you hate that game."

I nodded. "I really, really do. I'm getting decent at Settlers of Catan, but we only get to that one twice a year or so."

He took a step closer and the air between us went electric. "Too bad they don't let you play card games, although we usually just ended up naked."

"They're smarter than that." I gave him a devilish grin. "How do you think I got the money to start a company with Payton?"

"Strip poker? Seriously?" He shook his head in disbelief. "Vegas wasn't ready for you." His voice was like gravel.

"I wasn't allowed to strip on the casino floor, but a few private games padded my bank account nicely."

He blinked a few times and took two steps back, clearing his throat and making it a point to look at his watch. It was a move meant to break the spell we were under, one that poured all the distance back between us. "I need to get to bed. Come on, I'll walk you home."

Panic tightened my throat and I grabbed his forearm. "Jack, wait."

He looked away from me as he gently removed my hand from his arm. "Vera." His voice cracked on my name. "I can't do this again.

You've only been back for a few days and it's already making me crazy. When you leave again…"

"Let's just see where it leads," I whispered, taking a step toward him, then another. "It doesn't have to be all or nothing." He closed his eyes but didn't answer. "I don't want to stay away from you." I put my forehead against his and he inhaled sharply, as if the simple contact was painful.

"Vera," he breathed, the one word full of our history, our memories, the whispered promises we had made to each other in the back of his old truck while we made love under the stars.

He'd been the love of my life since I learned what love was. I had been in relationships since Jack, but I never got that twisting in my gut, the feeling of *home*.

"Vera," he said again, taking a step back. "It's not worth the pain. It's like getting into a car that's already on fire. I don't even know if we can be friends."

"Jack—"

"I barely held my shit together when you left last time. Every memory of us leads to that moment that you disappeared, then Danny was gone. It was the worst year of my life. I can't knowingly open myself up for that darkness again." He gripped my shoulders. "You'll go back to your fabulous life in California, but I'll be the one left with a hole in mine. Again." He swallowed hard.

"I won't just leave like last time," I promised, starting to panic. Something about this felt too much like goodbye.

"I can't only be friends with you," he said in a low voice, as if the admission cost him. "You feel too much like home." The last word was so quiet I could barely hear it. He released my shoulders and shoved his hands in his pockets.

Home.

The word knocked the breath out of me. He felt it, too. For just a few moments, I imagined what life would've been like if I had come back after only a few weeks. We'd be married, probably have a few kids and dogs. He'd be the one to kiss me goodbye before I left for work. Even in my imagination though, I still went off to a film set. If I stayed, would I have ended up a successful porn star? If I had stayed, would Jack and I have made it?

We just stood there, staring into each other's eyes, searching for answers we'd never know. Then, I heard the clinking of metal on metal before something jumped against the back of my knees, sending me tumbling into Jack. He swore, wrapping his arms around me and taking the brunt of our fall onto his concrete driveway.

Whatever was attacking me jumped on my back and a small, terrified scream escaped from my mouth. "Play dead!" I whispered, recalling all those sayings about surviving wild animal attacks. I put my head against his neck and went completely still. Jack laughed.

"Taco! Down!" he choked out.

What looked like a dog jumped off my back and onto the driveway. It licked Jack's face and whined in excitement. I rolled off Jack, allowing him to sit up and calm the beast. "Vera, this is Taco." He scratched behind the dog's ears. "Such a good boy."

I just sat there, confused. Taco bounded over to me, nuzzling my hair and face. I laughed as his wet nose tickled me. He looked like a pit bull mixed with a greyhound and like four other animals. He was simultaneously the cutest and ugliest dog I had ever seen. "Okay, easy there, Taco." I looked up at Jack. "Is he yours?"

Jack scooped up a black and orange cat, whose beady green eyes had been watching us from the edge of the grass. "He's really more hers," he explained.

I frowned. "Who is that?" Taco took advantage of my distraction and climbed onto my lap.

"Um, Grandma Bea's cat?" Jack whistled low and Taco immediately stepped away and sat on the driveway. "Didn't you notice she had one?" He reached out his hand to help me up and I took it, hanging on just a little longer than necessary.

I let go of him and blew my hair out of my face. "Yes, I knew she had a cat. But I've yet to meet said cat."

Jack nodded. "Makes sense. Waffles hates new people. They've been staying at my house since you arrived."

He held out the cat and I tentatively reached out to pet her under her chin. She didn't bite me, which I took as a positive sign. "Waffles...and Taco...stay together at your house?"

He nodded again, as if this were the most logical pairing in the world. "Sometimes they'll stay at Grandma Bea's. She looks in on Taco when I'm on shift."

"The dog and the cat are a thing?"

"Yes. They've been inseparable since the day I brought Taco home." He shrugged. "The heart wants what the heart wants...and apparently the heart wants a cat and a dog named after food."

I pressed the back of my hand to my forehead. "I forgot how weird this town was. I think I'm living in a fever dream."

Jack smirked. "Wait until you hear about Mr. Donovan's cow and Francesca's teacup pig. Now that's a love story for the ages."

I sighed. "There needs to be a better word for..." I motioned my hands around to indicate everything.

The front door of Grandma's house opened, and she stepped out onto the porch, wearing a babushka over her head and a long, white housecoat. "I see they've found you! They woke me up, begging to be let out."

"Thanks for getting Taco tonight," Jack called.

She waved him off. "I'm going back to bed. I'll be wearing earplugs and have a sound machine. Please continue canoodling."

She went back inside the house and I groaned. "I feel like a teenager again."

"You are out past curfew," Jack teased, but his tone didn't match the serious look on his face. "Seriously, Vera. You need to be careful, okay? I was fucking terrified when I got the call tonight."

I leaned toward him and gave him a chaste kiss on the cheek. "Thanks for saving me. I'll try to stay out of trouble."

He smiled, but it didn't reach his eyes. "That's the biggest lie you've ever told." He gestured for me to start walking toward Grandma's. He set Waffles down and then opened the passenger door on the truck, grabbed my bag, and followed behind. "Goodnight." He handed me my bag and I took it from him with a nod of thanks.

I opened the screen door and stepped inside, but then I couldn't move. My heart was screaming at me, telling me to stop being an idiot and to turn around immediately and leap into Jack's arms. "Jack," I whispered, trying to figure out what to do.

I looked over my shoulder to find him leaning against the porch railing, his head lowered, and his eyes closed. "Go in the house, Princess. Lock the door. Get some sleep."

Swallowing hard, I moved to close the front door. He stayed at the bottom of the porch until I slipped the lock into place.

CHAPTER ELEVEN

MOM'S BUCKET LIST #11: PLANT ROSE BUSHES. GIVE THEIR FLOWERS TO THE PEOPLE I LOVE

AS I HAD PROMISED JACK, I laid low while my hand healed, and I was going insane. There were only so many planks and sit-ups I could do. By day two, I was going so stir crazy I reorganized Grandma's cabinets. Spoiler alert: she was not thrilled. She was even less happy when she heard about my water tower adventure through her gossip network on day three. I didn't get any cookies that day and she wouldn't let me come to the store to help out.

On day four, Chieka called and said my car repairs would be delayed even more because the parts were on backorder. I was midway through ranting to Grandma about it when she finally crossed her arms and sighed. "You are absolutely terrible at relaxing. You're on vacation! Read a book or go watch hummingbirds fly around or do a puzzle!"

"A puzzle?" I asked, confused.

She gave me a long look. "You used to do them all the time when you were a kid. There's some in the guest room closet."

While she went to some widow society luncheon, I started working on a puzzle that was a collage of ice cream sundaes. At first, I just really wanted ice cream. But then, something magical happened. I actually started to relax. And it was, dare I say, fun.

Grandma helped me finish the puzzle after dinner and I immediately started another one that depicted a log cabin on the lake. Day five found me staring out the window as a shirtless Jack washed his truck. It was...he was so...*gah*. It took me way longer to get the new puzzle done for...reasons.

By the time I got my stitches out on day eight, I had finished all of the puzzles in the house, rewatched all of *Hart of Dixie* (#TeamZade Forever), and sorted all of my email into different subfolders. I was getting good at this relaxing thing.

Once the doctor told me I was good as new, I took a long, hot bubble bath then looked over Mom's list, trying to figure out how to complete more of her items without ending up in the hospital. Again.

Me: Thinking about doing another bucket list item. What's the likelihood of me ending up in the back of an ambulance?

Payton: VERY HIGH.

Jas: Have U met U?

Payton: If you end up back of said ambulance, will Jack be there?

Jas: Such a sexy voice. If you end up in the hospital again tell him to call me

Jas: Have U fucked him yet?

Jas: As UR besties, we need a pic

Jas: Preferably naked, but not picky

Payton: Maybe just shirtless. I get too many unsolicited dick pics already *puking emoji*

Jas: Ew, no one likes dick pics

Me: Only solicited ones

Jas: Yes, true, but UR avoiding the question

Jas: *eggplant emoji* *cherry emoji*

Me: No. There shall be no fucking. Because then there will be *heart eye emoji* and then *crying emoji* and you both know how I feel about feelings

Payton: I give it a week

Jas: 3 days

Me: Your faith in me is astounding.

Jas: *Shrugging emoji* *Kiss emoji*

Payton: But seriously V, what's next after Grenadine? I think the sooner you leave, the easier it'll be

Me: TBD. Still don't have my car

    I stared at the text message, uneasy about Payton's question. Why did it feel like I was failing a test? We had been each other's rocks for a decade. We had started Payton's Playhouse in an attempt to create a safe, welcoming, feminist environment for every porn star we worked with. We had created a porn empire from the scraps of strip club tips and casino winnings we had begged, borrowed, and stolen.

I loved my job. I was proud of my work. We were not only making better, respectful, and high-quality videos, we were changing the porn industry as a whole. There would never be a person in our company who was forced to work with someone or do something on their "No List."

When we talked about starting the company, Payton made me promise to always have a backup plan. She had been doing amateur porn on the side for a few months and often bragged about how much money she was making compared to the strip club. She didn't have to pay the house a percentage of her earnings at the end of the night. She didn't give up any of her money because she didn't get the required number of lap dances or sell the right number of drinks. But she had seen the industry as an exaggerated beauty contest—the younger and more beautiful you were, the more successful you'd be.

"Porn isn't forever. Pay your rent, take care of your skin, hit lingerie sales, invest the rest. Get out before you're bitter and lost."

I wasn't bitter, but I was starting to realize I was no longer following any kind of roadmap. I had expected to do videos for another five years, maybe. But now, the thought of getting into my car and driving out of town made me nauseated. I could always come back and see Grandma every few months. I would see Jack when I came to visit, of course. I would go back to having sex with a lot of fun people.

But I'd miss the small moments. I'd miss the way Waffles chased after Taco before they collapsed on the porch for a mid-afternoon snooze. I'd miss the way Grandma put curlers in her hair while watching *Criminal Minds* and eating peanuts out of the jar. I'd miss the hugs, the endless supply of hugs that she gave whenever she left and came home. I'd miss doing puzzles together on lazy days.

I was still waiting for my car to get repaired, which was a blessing in disguise. I didn't actually have to make a decision until I had my car back. I shook off my melancholy, determined to finish as much of this list as possible and then have the right answer present itself. Because that's how hard decisions worked, right? The answer just magically appeared when you least expected it? Even I laughed at myself as I slipped into a sports bra, a tank top, and yoga pants, and headed out the door.

THE OAK TREES that lined my childhood street had grown even taller since the last time I had been home. Trees were like people, in that way. You might not notice the changes from day to day, but you definitely noticed them after a long time apart. The sun flickered through the leaves, casting highly contrasting shadows on the asphalt. The air was heavy with the late August heat, one last humid hoorah before fall moved in.

Each house I passed held a different childhood memory. On the corner was the bungalow that seemed to be for sale every two years. Jack and I had been convinced it was haunted, although I remembered my dad talking about water issues in the basement. Haunted would've been way cooler.

A few doors down was a brick ranch with the beautiful white gazebo. They used to hold a neighborhood-wide picnic every Fourth of July, complete with sparklers, a full dessert table, and an adult bonfire every kid tried to sneak into at least once. By the paint peeling off the gazebo and the weeds growing in the flowerbeds, I guessed the owners had moved.

The house next door to the party house had the best circle driveway on the block. I had skinned my knees and elbows more times than I could count trying to see how fast I could go around it on my bike. Mrs. Centro was always ready with antiseptic cream and bandages. She also gave full-size candy on Halloween, making her one of the most popular stops.

Across the street was Miss Jeanne, who had the first indoor pool in the neighborhood. Jack, Danny, and I used to take turns mowing her lawn or shoveling her driveway to get an invitation to swim. My mom used to call us a school of fish. I wondered if anyone still swam in her pool.

And then there was my house. While most of the structures on the block were bungalows or ranches, the telltale sign of the neighborhood's 1950s upbringing, we'd had several remodels done to the house, making it a slightly lopsided but very charming Cape Cod. It was white and navy blue, with just enough ornate trim around the porch and roof to make the house look like it was something from a fairy tale. I would always love this house from the outside. The inside was impossible to bear after mom died.

I swallowed hard, trying to get my heart out of my throat before I choked on it. It was the middle of the day on Thursday, and my dad should be at work. I looked around, making sure I didn't see any curtains moving or neighbors suddenly interested in getting the mail. Two squirrels ran across the street, chasing each other, and a hawk cried overhead, but otherwise, I was completely alone.

I made my way up the lawn and around the back of the house where my mom's beautiful rose bushes were still flourishing after all these years. I pulled out my phone, taking a few minutes to capture photos of the flowers. I swore I could hear my mom's laughter on the breeze. When we had planted these bushes, she was too sick to help. Dad and I had made such a mess trying to dig the holes and plant them exactly where she had wanted. I was covered in mud and Dad had to spray my sneakers twice to get them clean. It was one of my favorite memories.

I pulled out a pair of pruning shears, gloves, and a reusable grocery bag. I took some clippings from the white bush first, then the baby pink bush, then the red bush. Each flower had a slightly different shape, and I wished I remembered the names. I had just finished gathering a few more clippings from the bush with the hot pink flowers when someone cleared their throat.

I screamed and jumped back, dropping the shears and stumbling backward. Caden, the police officer from the accident scene, caught me by the elbow to steady me. "Excuse me, Miss Eastman, but do you make a habit of going around to stranger's homes to steal their roses?"

Shit. "Is it really a stranger's house if the stranger is my dad?" I gestured to the roses. "And these were my late mother's roses. I helped plant them. So, you see, it's not really stealing."

He searched my face for a long moment before sighing heavily. "Miss Eastman—"

"Vera, please."

"Vera, I'll admit I'm new in town and I don't have the luxury of knowing offhand who the previous owners of this house were. I do know Lance Tompson does not live in this house. Judging from the panicked call from the nanny who's home with the kids, I would say he hasn't lived here for a while."

His words were a kick to the gut. Dad had moved? And didn't tell me?

Of course, how would he have told me? Why would he have told me? But why didn't Grandma tell me? Or Jack?

"I'm going to have to ask you to come with me to the station."

My ears burned with embarrassment as I put the pruning shears into my backpack. My eyes stung and I blinked several times to try to clear them. I couldn't believe Dad could sell this house and leave the roses behind. But hadn't I done the exact same thing, more or less?

I handed the backpack and reusable grocery bag to Caden. I cleared my throat, not looking directly at him. "Please be careful of the flowers," I said quietly. It would be great if the ground could swallow me up right now.

He nodded, loosening his hold on the bag. His free hand gripped my elbow and he guided me to the car. I climbed in the back seat and pulled off my gloves, studying my chipped manicure. I used my thumbnail to pick at some flaking cherry red polish off my pointer finger, resisting the urge to look back up at the house.

It wasn't my house anymore. Hadn't been for a long time.

Caden slid into the driver's seat and we pulled away from the curb. "How many neighbors are watching right now?" I asked.

His eyes met mine in the rearview mirror. "No one has actually stepped outside, but there's a car sitting across the street with someone inside."

I looked up as we passed a silver sedan. I squinted as we drove by, the man in the car looking away from me. But I'd know that profile anywhere. That was my father.

I counted backward from five once, then twice. No, it didn't matter. He didn't want to talk to me and that was his prerogative. I wasn't going to waste time thinking about him.

We were silent until we got to Main Street, where Caden took a right instead of a left. "Where are we going?" I asked. "Isn't the station on Main and Cooper?"

"That was before my time. Rumor has it, the station moved next to the fire house after the Great Pipe Burst of 2015, which led to the Great Asbestos Discovery of 2015."

My eyes widened and I could feel the blood drain from my face. "What? Tell me you're kidding."

He shook his head. "They were remodeling to expand, and it all went to hell, I'm told. They still talk about it around town. Luckily, the post office had already moved to the other side of Main Street, so we bought up the space. It cost less to move than to deal with the repairs."

I rubbed my hands over my face. "Of course."

We pulled up to the police station and into a parking spot front and center. Caden grabbed my bags before opening my door. As if he had heard my thoughts, Jack started walking across the parking lot from the fire station. *Shit.* I leaned into Caden and whispered, "How fast can you run?"

"I can't run and not crush your flowers," he admitted.

"Dammit."

Jack stopped right in front of us, shaking his head. He crossed his arms. "I knew this week had been too quiet. I should've checked in on you this morning."

I narrowed my eyes. He hadn't talked to me in eight days, but now he thought he could just show up and save the day? I counted backward from ten. "This has nothing to do with you, Jack. I've got it handled."

Caden and Jack exchanged looks. Jack gestured to the front door of the station. "Caden, lead the way." He pointed at me. "We are going to talk about this list."

I huffed, indignant. "You keep telling me to leave you alone, but here you are, inserting yourself into my life. Make up your damn mind. I've been trying to stay away from you like you asked. It's only fair that you do your share here."

"That's true. You literally hid behind a bush by the front porch when I came home from work yesterday." Jack's eyes danced with amusement.

"It's a small town! I was trying to be helpful." Caden laughed so hard he startled a squirrel that was foraging in the nearby grass. I crossed my arms and glared at Jack. "Seriously, there was just a misunderstanding. I've got it handled."

Jack just gave me a long look. "I'm beginning to realize that staying away from you is an impossible task, Vera Eastman." He lifted his chin to Caden. "Let's go. I'll be a character witness or whatever."

CHAPTER TWELVE

"IF ASKING NICELY DOESN'T WORK, TRY BRIBERY." - GRANDMA BEA

THE NEW HOMEOWNER, Joslyn Bellini, had accepted my apology and I was let go with a warning. Since Jack was still on duty after his character witness heroics, I had to call my grandma. Having her pick me up from the police station was actually the least embarrassing part of my day. Unlike the time she had to pick me up from the station when I was sixteen after I'd been caught drinking underneath the bleachers at one of Jack's football games, she found this whole situation hilarious.

"It's like the universe doesn't want you to stay away from Jack," she mused.

I huffed. "I don't understand why it has to be such an asshole about it."

Grandma's warm laughter filled the car again. "You are the most stubborn person I know, except for your father."

I picked at the hem of my T-shirt and looked out the window until we pulled in the driveway. "Grandma, you know that I'm not staying, right?"

Grandma shut off the car and looked over at me. "Mm-hmm. That's what you tell me. But I'll be honest, I really like the company.

And you've been away for so long, I'm loving the time to catch up. Honestly, don't I deserve more time with my grandbaby?"

She climbed out of the car, and I jumped out after her. "Did you just guilt trip me because I didn't know you were alive for the last decade and now you want me to stay longer even though I have a bucket list to finish and a job to get back to?" I stopped dead as something dawned on me. "You paid Chieka to take longer on my car, didn't you?"

Grandma climbed the front steps and lifted one shoulder. "I don't have any idea what you're talking about. I would never stoop to such subterfuge."

"I can't believe this." I tilted my head back and looked up at the sky, letting out a long, steadying breath. "You paid Jack to pay Chieka to stall. You are an evil genius."

Grandma leaned back out the front door. "No. I had Jack do it because then I didn't have to lie. And you know I don't tolerate lying."

"No, of course not. Just lots of passive-aggressive manipulation."

She waved her hand at me, dismissing the accusation. "It's a long-standing personality trait passed down from generation to generation. Now get your bags out of the car. We need to get those roses in water before they die."

Silently counting in my head—this time from fifteen—I grabbed the bags out of the car and went inside.

As if I hadn't thought about Jack enough today, Taco came barreling at me the moment I walked through the door. He jumped up on my thighs with a sad puppy look, begging for attention. My stupid heart melted. "Hey, buddy, how are you?" I cooed. Humans turned into such idiots around cute animals. I was coming to terms with this.

We didn't have any pets growing up because my mom was allergic. Payton had a cat that her housekeeper took care of when Payton was traveling, but I was gone from home too much to be fair to the animal. Now I was thinking I might need a dog in my future. But maybe one with like half as much energy.

While I was giving Taco scratches behind the ears, Waffles came up to me and put her front paws on my knee and meowed, demanding attention. This was like a vortex of cuteness, one I knew my grandma had somehow arranged when I couldn't escape. Every time I tried to move, they would both make these cute little noises, and I was such a sucker.

It wasn't until my calf started to cramp that I finally found the strength to pull away. I put the flowers in a small vase Grandma had set by the sink, and then promptly locked myself in my room, away from meddling grandmothers and cuteness vortexes. First things first: figure out my car situation.

I dialed Edie's Auto shop and Tamicka answered. "Hi, Tamicka, it's Vera."

"Hi, Vera, what can I do for you? Your car's not quite read—"

"Cut the shit. We both know my grandma's paying Jack to pay you to stall on my car."

There was a rustling sound and then Tamicka laughed so loud I had to pull the phone away from my ear. "Who had today in the pool?" she shouted.

I heard one cheer, followed by several expletives. I pinched the bridge of my nose. "Who won?"

"Girl, you couldn't have waited until tomorrow? Although, Rosa won and she needs the money for her family, so it's cool."

That made me feel a little less annoyed. "How much?"

"Two hundred."

I shook my head. "This entire town is insane. Small-town-itis apparently is very real and completely incurable."

"We're like a fungus. You don't want to love us, but we grow on you and then you can't get rid of us."

I burst out laughing. "I've never heard a more apt description in my life."

"You know that's right." She chuckled and then I heard the sound of a keyboard in the background. "I need until Monday morning though. Edie's got some shit going on and Chieka is backed up. I'll throw in a wash and a detail for free."

"I'm sorry to hear about Edie. Tell her I'm thinking about her." I ran my hand over my hair and sighed. "Monday morning is fine and thanks for the detail. But for real, Monday I want my car."

DESPITE BEING ON VACATION, Payton had been texting me, making sure I had seen the dozen emails she sent about upcoming events, the latest Payton's Playhouse drama, and a few potential new headquarters staff. In between her frantic messages, a producer and a director reached out about doing new scenes and they weren't thrilled I was on sabbatical. These were the days I missed having an agent.

I was one of three people exclusive to Payton's Playhouse—Payton and Jas were the other two—so it made sense to part with my agent, except now I had to deal with bookings myself. When Grandma knocked on my door and told me dinner was ready, I was startled to see it was past six.

"Sorry I didn't help with dinner," I said when I slumped into a kitchen chair. "I got wrapped up in work."

"That's okay. I know you're busy. Sorry we're eating a little late today, I took a short nap when we got home." The smirk on her face made me narrow my eyes. She passed me a bowl of salad just as the sound of a lawnmower started in her backyard.

I glanced out the sliding door to see Jack pushing a mower across her lawn. Shirtless. "Grandma, I could mow the lawn for you. Why are you having Jack do it?"

"And miss having dinner and a show?" she scoffed.

"But why is he doing it shirtless?"

She leveled a stare over her glasses. "How should I know? Probably because he always does it shirtless when it's this hot. I pay him in cookies; it's a good arrangement."

"You pay him in cookies to mow your lawn shirtless?"

She play-hit me with a dish towel. "No. I pay him in cookies to mow my lawn. The shirtless is just a bonus. I also happen to give him more cookies when he does it shirtless. What he does with the information is up to him."

I laughed. "You do have the best cookies in Grenadine."

"That's not entirely true. I won second place in the Grenadine So You Think You Can Bake competition this year. But I broke my finger two days before and I just wasn't moving fast enough to get my cookies in the oven at the right time." She leaned across the table as if whispering secrets in a crowded room. "They were a little too chewy."

My fork hit my plate as her words sank in. She'd broken her finger, and I wasn't here to help her. I didn't even know. Grandma had won first place in the SYTYCB competition every year since its inception, according to the trophies in her living room. But I had failed to notice that this year's trophy was silver.

It was the little things that stung the most, the everyday occurrences that seemed so innocuous yet would make the best memories. The way my grandma laughed when she baked. The way she sang while doing the dishes. The smell of her hand cream or the way she looked out her kitchen window while she drank a cup of coffee in the morning. There was always a pint of mint chocolate chip ice cream in the freezer and apples on the counter.

"I think I've lost you," she said, startling me out of my thoughts. She reached over and cradled my hand with hers. "What's wrong?"

I blinked away the sting in my eyes. "I've missed so much," I admitted. "How am I supposed to get in my car and just drive away? I've lost eleven years of memories with you. I don't want to lose any more. But everything I worked for—my entire career—is back in SoCal."

She squeezed my hand. "You don't need to figure it all out today.

You don't even need to figure out tomorrow. I've missed you too, more than I can ever say. I've missed so much. You've missed so much."

I bit my lip and glanced out the window, my eyes blurry. "You didn't tell me Dad moved."

She shook her head. "I didn't want to bring it up yet. To be honest, sweetheart, I haven't really talked to your dad in years. I decided I would just pretend he doesn't exist until I got over the urge to bury him in my garden where no one could find him."

I laughed softly. "Probably a good plan. They'd pin it on me, anyway."

She leaned back and chuckled. "That's true. You have apparently ruffled some feathers since your arrival."

"That's the understatement of the decade."

A knock at the door interrupted our conversation, followed by someone calling a greeting. Gertie hurried in, walking over to the window. "Did I miss the show?"

I raised my eyebrows at Grandma. "Seriously? Did you at least sell tickets?"

Gertie lifted up a plastic container. "I made fudge."

"Acceptable form of payment," I agreed.

Grandma grumbled. "Gertie, pick one side or the other. We can't see if you're blocking the entire door."

"I'm less than five feet tall and weigh a hundred pounds soaking wet. I think you can see around me."

"You make a better door than a window."

Gertie looked over her shoulder at me. "She gets no fudge. Go hide this in your room." She handed me the container.

I cradled it to my chest. Grandma huffed. "Oh, for Pete's sake, grab yourself a plate of food and come sit down before you have a stroke. You haven't seen a man shirtless in so long, you're liable to drop dead."

"Says the woman who hasn't had a date in over twenty years."

"Not true! I had a date last month with Earl."

"You just agreed to a date with him because he owns the pub and you wanted free food."

She shrugged. "Best nachos this side of Kalamazoo."

I stayed silent, watching them volley the accusations back and forth, which reminded me so much of my text messages with Payton and Jas. Even while arguing, Gertie fixed herself a plate of food and came to join us at the table. When Jack made a pass really close to the back porch, Gertie ran to the door, opened it, and waved for him to come in. He held up his pointer finger to let her know he'd be a minute. I put my head in my hands and shook it back and forth.

Gertie touched my shoulder. "There, there. I'll keep your grandma busy tonight if you want to take that one for a ride."

Grandma rolled her eyes. "They're in the 'we're going to pretend the other one doesn't exist so we don't risk hurting ourselves when Vera leaves again' stage."

Gertie nodded. "Ah, yes." She turned to me. "Stop worrying about tomorrow. You can't plan for these things. One of you could up and die tonight! That's what happened to my Jimmy. One day he was here, the next day"—her hand hit the table—"dead as a doornail. I miss that son of a bitch every single day. I would trade every day I played hard to get for one more minute with him."

I narrowed my eyes at her. "If you're both going to sit here and get gushy on me, I'm eating this fudge right now." I opened the container and shoved a small square into my mouth. It had been so long since I had eaten fudge that the moment the smooth chocolate coated my tongue, my eyes nearly rolled into the back of my head. "Oh my God, this is the best thing I've ever put in my mouth."

Grandma laughed. "I find that hard to believe. You had Gray Lorde's co—"

I held up my hand. "I love that you watch my videos, but it's a little weird—"

"It's not like I didn't see you naked all the time growing up. Don't be ashamed of your—"

"I'm not ashamed of my body, oh my God. I just don't want to think about you and me and cocks when I'm eating a delicious piece of chocolate."

"What about a chocolate c—"

"I walk in on the most interesting conversations," Jack said, making us all jump. Like three meerkats, we all looked over at the sliding door and tried to look innocent. Sadly, he was now wearing a shirt.

"Jack!" Grandma said as if she were surprised to see him. "Grab yourself something to eat and drink and come join us."

"Thanks." He winked at me before going to the cabinet and grabbing a glass. While he was filling it with water, Gertie chimed in.

"We were just comparing blowjobs to fudge. Vera says my fudge is better."

Jack's glass fell into the sink but thankfully didn't break. I put my head down on the table and banged it a few times. "I need to go buy an airplane ticket to anywhere else," I grumbled.

"Uh, I see," Jack said, clearing his throat.

"Well, you've had a blowjob from Vera and eaten my fudge," Gertie continued. "Which one do you think is better?"

This was how I died, wasn't it? A heart attack, right here in the middle of the kitchen.

He set his glass down on the table and sat down next to me. "This is a trick question. There is no answer I can give here that wouldn't offend at least one of you."

I could feel him looking at me, but I kept my head down on the table. I pushed the fudge over to him. He took a piece and put it in his mouth, and the moan that came out of him made me melt into the table. That was not a fair moan. How was I supposed to stop thinking about eating fudge off of him with a moan like that?

Apparently, Gertie and Grandma decided this was their cue to leave. Gertie stood up and gathered the dishes while Grandma put the food away. I watched all this from the corners of my eyes. Grandma bent down to kiss my cheek. "We're going to book club.

Read a really spicy book by Shelly Bell and I can't wait to pick it apart!"

Gertie laughed. "Ethel is going to lose her shit over that book. I can't wait."

"Leave the dishes!" Grandma called from the front door. "I'll do them when I get home. You kids have fun."

I stayed face down on the table until I heard the door close and lock. I rolled my head to face Jack. "Well. I think I need to have them both committed."

He laughed uncomfortably, his ears turning red. *Ha! Welcome to the club.* He ran a hand down his face. "It's very likely." He took a long drink of water and I did *not* stare at his Adam's apple. "Okay, let me see this infamous bucket list. Let's try to avoid you battling the emergency services of Grenadine for at least one of them."

I pouted. "I took a picture by the Grenadine sign without any problem."

He rolled his eyes. "That's because you weren't technically *in* Grenadine yet."

I pursed my lips. "Fair point. I concede." I walked to my room, grabbed Mom's beaten-up journal, and brought it back to the table. Jack's eyes were on me, on my legs. I was wearing tiny shorts—but in my defense, I didn't know he was going to be coming over.

He lifted his chin. "That's gorgeous." His eyes were focused on the ink on my right upper thigh.

The side of my mouth lifted. "Payton's late sister drew it for me." My leg sported a watercolor style tattoo of a cherry tree with fruit in different stages of ripeness.

Jack reached out like he wanted to touch it, but then pulled his hand back and cleared his throat. He nodded to my shirt. "I keep seeing you in those shirts. Some kind of sponsor?"

I looked down to see what I had on—his hands were really distracting—and smiled at the white tank with bright yellow lettering that read #SayYesToConsent. "This is my new clothing line. It's still in the infancy stages, but I'm really excited. All the profits go to funding sex education and consent programs, especially in low-income cities."

"That's really awesome." He leaned on the table and shook his head. "Every time I tell myself I'm going to stay away from you, I turn into a liar. It's like there's an invisible force pulling me into your orbit."

"I get it," I whispered. I handed him the book to break the tension. He flipped through it, and I knew he was seeing the progression of her cancer, the clear script becoming garbled and shaky.

I looked away, not wanting the memories. "A-at the end." I cleared my throat. "I made a list of everything she wrote."

He flipped to the page that was bookmarked and scanned it over once, then twice. He put the book down on the table and tapped his hands against the edge. "You're going to do everything on this list?"

I shrugged but nodded. "As much as I can."

"And there's a reason you have to do it all right now?"

I breathed out slowly and ran my finger along the wood grain of the table. "After my surgery, a switch flipped in me. I've been in a rut for a long time and I needed to stop planning and start doing. Payton let me take a sabbatical to heal and to work on the bucket list. Call it ten years of vacation rolled into one trip."

He leaned forward and put his hand on mine, stilling it. "Surgery?"

Dammit. I wasn't going to tell him about that. I hadn't even told Grandma yet because I knew it would just stress her out. "You can't tell anyone. Not even Grandma."

He nodded, searching my face. Worry creased his brow and I wanted to reach up and soothe it with my fingers, but just him holding my hand was enough to make my heart start racing. "I'm okay; it was benign," I began. His grip on my hand got tighter. "I had a biopsy when I found a lump and they removed the mass." I looked over his shoulder to watch the golden glow of the sun dip behind the trees.

He leaned back in his chair and pinched his lips together before pulling his hand away and nodding. He crossed his arms as if he needed to fold in on himself for a moment. "That must have been terrifying."

I nodded, tapping on the table. "Yep. Had a panic attack during a scene right after I called and made a doctor's appointment. Thankfully, it was with Jas and her husband. She calmed me down enough to get through filming and I took a long-earned vacation after that. Came back here after surgery."

"To do your mom's list."

I nodded, although it wasn't a question. "I still am freaked out. Like they'll call me back and say, 'Just kidding, it was cancer!'" I ran my fingers through my hair and piled it on top of my head, grabbing the elastic from my wrist and tying it up. "I realized I had become an insane workaholic. If I wasn't filming, I was going over paperwork, or shoot schedules, or business ideas with the team. If I'm not busy with those, I'm on social media making posts or editing teasers. I was in back-to-back board meetings for my twenty-ninth birthday and didn't even remember it until Payton showed up at the office with a cupcake."

Jack studied me quietly but didn't interrupt. He was so good at listening. I chewed on my thumbnail for a moment before he reached out and grabbed my hand, smoothing it under his. "Are you going to go back to Cali? Keep filming and everything?"

I lifted one shoulder. "It's been a hell of an outlet for my exhibitionist side and I love running this company," I admitted. "I love most of it. But it's hard on the body—I'm not twenty anymore. When I'm filming, I have to bend my neck like a giraffe to make sure my mouth is in frame. And my hips could live a much longer and happier life without another pair of stilettos. I'm always in the office early and home late, there's always a crisis, another event to plan for..."

I turned my free palm upward, inspecting it for answers. "When you're a top company, you have to fight to stay on top." I sighed. "But I don't know if I want to continue being this woman who never takes a day off unless she's literally concerned about dying. I don't want to not come home for a decade at a time. But I don't know what else I would love doing."

He made a sound of understanding and squeezed my hand before releasing it. He grabbed the journal again. "Okay, so. This is how I'm going to help you."

I lifted an eyebrow. "I thought you wanted me to stay away from you?"

He leveled me with a look. "I can't leave you to yourself. You'll end up dead or in jail."

"Ha ha." I searched his face, trying to figure out what was going on. "What changed? Why do you suddenly want to be around me? I've been doing my best to respect your wishes."

He shrugged one shoulder. "Friends, remember? Friends don't let friends get arrested for stealing flowers." I bit back a smile. "I can't help you with 'eating macarons in Paris,' or 'seeing the Northern Lights in Iceland,' but I can help you with...this one. Number thirty-seven." He closed the book and shoved it back at me. "We can do it Sunday night. I just took Mom to Costco last week. I have so much toilet paper."

I grabbed the book and flipped to the list. 37. *Toilet paper Grenadine High School.* "Let's see if I can get arrested twice in one week."

"Ah, but you won't get arrested if I'm there. I'm the secret ingredient."

I rolled my eyes so hard they hurt. "Sure, Jan." I stood and walked over to the roses on the window sill. "Mr. Secret Ingredient, want to help me plant some roses? The internet says I can grow bushes from clippings. Let's see if it's right."

He stood and nodded. "Do I have to do it shirtless?"

"Do you really want me to make you cookies?"

He shook his head slowly. "Absolutely not. Please don't ever bake. The talent truly skipped your generation."

I put my hands on my hips. "Excuse you, I baked for the freshman bake sale and sold every single brownie!"

Jack winced and then gave me a sad smile. "There's something I have to tell you."

I pointed at him. "Jack Reeves, what did you do?"

He put his hands up, trying to placate me. "I may have...switched your brownies out with some that I made. For the safety of everyone at the sale."

My hand flew to my chest in indignation. "Excuse me?!"

"Vera, seriously? You cannot bake. You can do a lot of really amazing things. You are gorgeous and incredibly intelligent and are one of the kindest people I know."

I opened my mouth, but he held up a finger. "But," he continued. "You. Cannot. Bake. Please don't in the future. Just let me or your grandma or Gertie do it, okay? For the safety of yourself and everyone around you."

I crossed my arms and pouted. "You're a jerk."

He raised an eyebrow. "Remember how I told you I chipped my front tooth playing basketball?" I nodded. "That was a lie. It was on your brownie. I just didn't have the heart to tell you."

My mouth just hung open. "I am aghast. Speechless. Affronted. Insulted."

He booped my nose. "Come on, Thesaurus, let's go plant some roses. I'll even happily take one or two for my yard."

CHAPTER THIRTEEN

GRENADINE ORDINANCE 2-16-73: TRASH TALKING ANY MICHIGAN TEAM IS PROHIBITED ON THE WEEKENDS, WITH THE EXCEPTION OF A UNIVERSITY OF MICHIGAN VERSUS MICHIGAN STATE GAME.

WHEN I WALKED into the house, it smelled like spaghetti and cookies. I took a deep breath, savoring it. "I would like to come home every day to a house smelling like this!" I leaned over and gave Grandma a kiss on the cheek. "What can I do to help?"

She waved me off. "It's almost done. Just set the table."

I dropped my bag in my room, changed my clothes that were a bit sweaty from the bike ride home from the store, and went to set the table. "Got another awesome video on buying good products today. Your Saturdays get really busy! Met a few more fans today."

"Good. Is it going to go viral like the lube one?" she asked hopefully. I groaned. "What? Our phone orders have tripled since you filmed. I'm going to have to get the website updated so it can take inquiries."

I pulled down plates and bowls and carried them to the table. "I'll take care of the website. Give me all the info and I'll send it to my designer."

She waved her wooden spoon at me. "You don't need to do that."

I put my hands on my hips. "But I'm going to and you're going to deal with it." My voice was firm and for once, she didn't argue.

FIRE TRUCKS, GARTER BELTS, & MY PERFECT EX

"Well, alright. If you insist." She pointed to the fridge. "Get the salad out, too."

She brought dinner to the table and we savored the meal. My diet and exercise routine in California was very strict. I needed to keep my body in constant athletic condition to help combat the wear-and-tear, as well as look good on film. We had actors of all body types, but I had built my brand on the way my body looked and that's how I wanted to keep it.

However, since returning to Grenadine, I hadn't had a single protein shake or meal replacement bar. Grandma was a big believer in homemade foods. If she could make it, she did. What was I going to do, not eat it?

Instead, I avoided stepping on the scale in the bathroom. I also avoided looking at it because I knew it was judging me. When I'd showered this morning, I'd put my slippers on top of it to hide it from view.

I started on the dishes right after dinner, purposefully not looking out the kitchen window to see if Jack's truck was in his driveway. Nope, I was not interested in his whereabouts. Grandma took out a cookie tin and started piling in double chocolate chip cookies. I dried my hands and reached for a cookie, but she slapped me away. "Ow! Rude."

"These are not for you!" She finished stacking them in and closed the lid. "These are for Jack. Go take them next door."

I blinked hard and stared at her. "These are payment for him mowing your lawn shirtless, aren't they? I will not be part of your tomfoolery."

She stared at me. "Tomfoolery? Are you eighty years old?"

I rolled my eyes. "This was your deal with him. You go take him the cookies."

"I can do no such thing!" She put her hands on her hips.

I mirrored her posture. "And why not?"

"Because it's almost dark and I could trip and fall."

I looked outside then at the oven clock. "The sun doesn't set for two more hours."

She motioned to the floor. "I could trip and fall. Break my hip and ankle just like poor Winnifred did last month. Then you'd feel really guilty. You'd have to stay and help me, or hire a nurse, and I'm told they're really expensive."

I pinched the bridge of my nose. "Fine. I'll take him the damn cookies."

She grabbed my upper arms and kissed my cheek. "You're the best granddaughter I have."

"I'm your only granddaughter."

She shrugged. "Naw, I count Waffles, too."

I leveled an incredulous look at her. "You mean the cat is competition?"

She waved her hand. "Don't worry. You beat her out for first place when you came back to Grenadine." She walked into the living room and turned on the television. "Don't hurry back! It's time for my stories." By stories, she meant reruns of *Criminal Minds*.

I walked out the back door and down the porch, crossing the grass to Jack's driveway. I stopped short when I realized there were four cars parked out front. I looked back at Grandma's house and narrowed my eyes. She'd planned this. I didn't know what her end game was, but this was clearly a Grandma Plot™.

I looked down at my ragged jean capris and off-the-shoulder T-shirt—another one from my collection—that showed the strap of my teal bralette, then shrugged. Whatever. Who was I trying to impress?

With a deep breath, I straightened my shoulders and continued to Jack's front door and knocked. I could hear a group of men cheering and shit talking each other. They were probably watching sports. Sports were good; it would mean they would all be distracted, and I could make a quick and easy getaway. Even if that meant I wouldn't get a cookie.

Jack opened the door and I was not prepared for the scene in front of me. There were four other men inside, two on a big black couch and two in matching armchairs, facing the large flat screen.

What I didn't expect to see was that they all had sewing machines on small folding tables in front of them. I tilted my head to the side as I took in Jack, who had a piece of fleece slung over his shoulder like it was a dishrag.

"Grandma sent me over with these," I managed, keeping a completely straight face.

One of the men shook his head and gestured to the television. "Why would he use that fabric? That's not going to lay right with those pleats."

My plans for a quick escape were replaced by my avid curiosity. The man in front of me sighed and opened the door wider. "You might as well come in, then."

I gave him a quick smile and stepped through the door and onto his beautiful light blond hardwood floor. Taco let out a quiet bark in greeting but went back to napping on his dog bed with Waffles sleeping on his back. The guys were so involved in their projects and with their show, they didn't even notice I was in the room.

I took a moment to look around, utterly charmed by his house. While it was the same layout as Grandma's, he had knocked down a wall, making the living room and kitchen the same space. An island stood in the center of the kitchen with a pot rack chandelier over it. He had double ovens and a beautiful gas stovetop. Behind his kitchen table was a picture wall, each photo matted and framed. My eyes caught on a picture of me, him, and Danny, and I smiled.

Jack reached for the remote and hit pause, a chorus of confusion following. When they all finally looked over, they sat up straighter. A couple of them had red stains on their cheeks. "So," Jack started. "Every other Saturday is Project Runway night."

I nodded. "I see."

"This month, we've been making fleece blankets for the Grenadine Animal Shelter. Each animal that's adopted gets one." Jack pulled the fleece off his shoulder and draped it over the empty sewing machine. "It relieves stress and helps the community."

My stupid heart did a little tap dance. "And Project Runway?"

He shrugged. "Baking shows made us want to eat all the time. At least this way, we just want to sew more."

"Although after this, we're going to switch to knitting hats for the newborn unit at the hospital," a handsome, fair-skinned man with blue eyes and blond hair said. "Hi, I'm Michael. I'm Kristyn Taylor's younger brother."

"Oh yeah! How is she?"

He smiled. "Married, three kids, teacher, and has a chronic volunteer habit."

"So, awesome then." I laughed. "She was always on every student-run committee she could fit in her class schedule." He laughed and agreed.

Another man stood, burly and bald, and walked toward me. He had a salt and pepper bushy beard and a tanned complexion from years in the sun. It took me a minute to recognize him as Paul, Jack's best friend from the football team. With an excited greeting, he lifted me off the ground in one of his patented hugs. He was a beast and therefore gave all-consuming hugs.

Sam, another one of Jack's friends from high school, stood and gave me a really tight squeeze. He was a few inches shorter than Paul but still gave great hugs. I loved a guy who wasn't afraid to hug platonically. "You got married!" I exclaimed, checking out the gold band. "To Kristy?" They had started dating the year I graduated.

He smiled. "Yes, in July. Too bad you missed it! There was a lot of drama." He fake-whispered, "We had to change the old Grenadine ordinance that a black man couldn't marry a white woman before we could set the wedding date."

My mouth just fell open. "Say what?"

He scrunched his nose, his glasses moving with the gesture. "They haven't enforced the law in a long time, but Kristy made it her mission."

I beamed. "I always liked her."

"That wasn't even the most dramatic part!" Paul called out.

Sam shook his head dramatically. "Sadly, he's right."

I widened my eyes. "Spill."

"A lot of Cynthia drama," Franky said, then stood to give me a kiss on the cheek. "I stopped by Grandma's earlier, but she said you were at the store."

"Yeah, I was doing more live videos."

Sam cracked up. "Kristy watches the lube video on repeat."

I groaned. "The bacon was bad, but that crème brûlée..." I shuddered.

Jack opened the cookie tin and passed them around. I happily took one. He raised an eyebrow and shook the container at me. I bit my lip and took a second one. It was like he knew me.

Hey, guess what? He does know you, my brain yelled at me.

Shut up, brain.

"Michael and I were driving back from getting the Petersons' cat off the roof, again, when I stumbled on the video," Jack explained.

"I almost drove off the road," Michael confirmed. "It was one of the funniest things I've ever seen."

Just the thought of the video made the memory of the aftertaste resurface and I shoved one of the cookies in my mouth to ease the pain. It helped.

Franky reached into the tin and paused, looking sheepish. "Vera, you didn't make these, did you?"

"*Et tu, Brute?*" I exclaimed through a mouthful of cookies.

Jack shook his head. "I'd never do that to you, friend."

With a wink, Franky took two cookies. "Okay, Vera, I'm so glad you're here, but"—he gestured to the television—"I need to know if the guy with the weird-shaped head is going to pull this off or not."

I opened my mouth to respond but realized I had nothing. "Carry on." I walked over to the only open seat in the room, which was of course on the love seat next to Jack. He hit play on the DVR and resumed sewing his blanket.

Watching these men sew, talk light-hearted shit about the fashion competition, and compliment each other on their good work made my ovaries almost explode. This was the Jack I fell in love with. I got up and snagged another cookie. Cookies could stop people from falling in love again, right?

Jack looked over at me while I tried to chew. He just threw his head back and laughed. He grabbed a pair of scissors and pointed to a bolt of fabric sitting on the coffee table next to a ruler and an index card. "When you're done, Cookie Monster, can you please follow the measurements on that card and cut us some more fabric?"

I gave him a thumbs up.

"So, Sam," I said as Jack fast-forwarded through a commercial break. "Tell me about the Cynthia wedding drama."

He groaned. "You remember Kristy's cousin, Edie, right? Owns the auto shop?"

Franky leaned over. "She just hit Cynthia's car. She knows who Edie is."

Paul let out a deep belly laugh. "I can't believe I forgot about that already!"

Sam chuckled. "Right on. So, Cynthia announced she was engaged to Edie's ex, Will, at our wedding."

I just looked between him and Franky, wondering if they were pulling my leg. "Come again?"

Franky smirked. "That's what he said."

I groaned and put my head in my hand. "But for real? Cynthia did that?"

Jack cleared his throat and held up his phone. "I got video."

Sam sighed. "Of course you do."

I looked at Jack and shook my head. "I thought my family was messed up."

Jack let out a low whistle. "No kidding." He gave me the kind of smile that made my stomach squeeze and I couldn't look away. Damn Jack Spell™.

"Hey, Jack! Too far," Michael called, gesturing to the television. Jack fumbled with the remote to stop fast forwarding well into the show. I swear I didn't smile at the fact that his ears turned a little pink.

CHAPTER FOURTEEN

MOM'S BUCKET LIST #37: TOILET PAPER GRENADINE HIGH SCHOOL

AFTER THE SUN set on Sunday, we launched our mission. His gaze moved up and down my body as I approached his driveway. I was wearing black leggings, a long black T-shirt, my hair was piled in a bun, and I had one of Grandma's powder blue scarves tied around the lower half of my face. He threw his head back and laughed.

"Wha-what are you wearing?!" he wheezed. "Is that one of Grandma Bea's babushkas?"

I slapped his arm before walking around to the passenger side of the truck. "Yes, jerk. We need to keep our faces covered so we don't get caught."

He was still laughing as he climbed into the driver's seat. "With something that everyone in town knows is your Grandma's? She's had that longer than you've been alive."

Okay, so he had a point. I shoved it off my face and folded it, putting it in the door compartment. "Make sure I don't forget that. She'll kill me."

He was still chuckling as we backed up out of the driveway and took off toward the high school. It was all of a two-minute drive and we could have easily walked, but if we needed a quick getaway, his truck was ideal. We could always pretend we were arriving to the scene to help, too.

He shut off his headlights as we pulled into the parking lot. The school was one long, U-shaped building that looked fairly innocuous at night. I swear I could smell teenage hormones and anxiety pouring off the bricks.

Jack reached into the back of his truck and pulled out a bag of toilet paper. "Let's get to work."

I didn't need any more prompting than that. I grabbed a roll, held the end tight, and tossed the toilet paper onto the roof. Or, at least I tried. It missed and just rolled along the sidewalk until it hit the front door. I groaned. "Dammit."

Jack was laughing again, but quieter. "Here," he said. "Let the ex-quarterback do it." His roll, of course, sailed smoothly over the roof line, making a beautiful arch of white paper.

"I hate you just a little bit right now," I grumbled.

"Here, let me help," he said, handing me another roll and stepping behind me. He placed his left hand on my hip and ran his right hand from my shoulder to my fingertips. My stomach did a somersault and tingles chased after his fingertips. I may have leaned back against his solid chest just a little bit.

He pulled my arm back and we launched the roll of paper through the air and over the roof. The tail broke free from my hand and flapped in the light of the full moon as if it were a bird on a mission. Careful to stay as close to me as possible, he grabbed another roll and helped me toss it, then another, and another.

By the time we reached our last roll, we were laughing so hard we made a terrible throw. It bounced into the bushes, rolled back out the bottom, and hit us in the feet. I had to pull away from Jack because I couldn't catch my breath. My arms were wrapped around my cramping stomach and tears streamed down my face. I took one deep breath, then another, trying to calm myself, but it was wasted effort when Jack went to throw the roll and it dropped behind his head.

I had to kneel down on the sidewalk, unable to stand upright because the laughter wouldn't stop. "It-it-it..." I tried, gasping. "It is just like..." I wiped fresh tears from my eyes. "It's j-just like the game aga-against—"

Jack wheezed out, "If you s-say Saint F—"

"Saint Francis!" I snorted, giving up and rolling onto my back. I was laughing so hard I was pretty sure I was in danger of peeing my pants. Which would be super unattractive, but possibly worth it.

"I had just come back from a shoulder dislocation!" he defended, indignantly.

I couldn't help it. It made me laugh harder. Still, I pushed myself up to standing, clumsily grabbed the escaping roll of toilet paper, and did a really terrible imitation of how he went to throw the football and it fell behind him, all those years ago.

He grabbed me by the waist and threw me over his shoulder in a firefighter hold. I was still laughing so hard I couldn't even tell him to put me down. He picked up the toilet paper roll and tossed it over a row of benches. "You are so irritating," he grumbled. His hands went to my butt pocket and he pulled out my phone. I was disappointed he didn't give me more of a butt grab, but at this point, I was too far gone.

He took a picture of our handiwork, then a selfie of me over his shoulder then tucked it back into my pocket. "Alright, Looney Tunes, we're done here." He had turned us around when someone walked around the side of the building. We froze and the laughter evaporated from my lungs. All my years of contorting for the camera paid off as I maneuvered myself to peek over Jack's other shoulder to see a trio of teenagers under a parking lot light giving us that patented "why are these old people acting like loser kids" look.

They turned away and headed to the playground, as if we were beneath their notice. "Think we have anything to worry about?" I whispered.

"Naw," he answered quietly. "Did you see how much disdain the striped-shirt kid exuded with that eyebrow lift?"

"So much shade!"

We were meandering back to the truck—and by that, I mean Jack was carrying me back to the truck—when we heard the first siren. The teens ran off, back the way they came. Jack swore and ripped open my door, dumping me inside. I buckled up as he jumped in, hit the start engine button, and took off like a shot. "Go, go, go!" I chanted.

We pulled out of the parking lot with no headlights and went into the nearest neighborhood. I looked behind us, my heart in my throat and a smile so big my cheeks hurt. He took one turn after the other, leading us around town the back way. We pulled down a dirt road that connected to a series of local farms and pulled into a field next to a fence.

He leaned back in his seat and rubbed his hands over his face. "Jesus, you are a trouble magnet." He laughed, shaking his head. "I can't believe we almost got caught."

I turned to face him, taking in a shaky breath. "But you had so much fun, right?"

His smile matched mine. "Yeah, I definitely did."

The darkness was thick around us and the entire cab filled with a heavy tension. I was so amped up that my blood was singing. I wanted to put my hands all over him and take this night even further. As if reading my mind, he reached out and dug his fingers in my hair.

"Only friends," I whispered.

"Fuck only friends."

"Thank God." The minute the words left my mouth, his lips crushed mine in a frantic, needy, desperate kiss.

He'd never stopped being my favorite person to kiss, even after all these years. A whimpering noise escaped from my throat and he growled, pulling me tighter and deepening the kiss. The years fell away and in this suspended moment, we were just two naïve kids who were crazy about each other. This was how it was always supposed to be, grown-up us still making out in cars and laughing until we cried.

Except now, we didn't have a curfew.

My heart was beating, beating, beating so hard. His kisses

breathed life into long-dead feelings, feelings that clogged in my throat and came out in whispers of his name and small little gasps.

Home.

He was home.

Not my condo in LA, not Grandma's house, not even my old childhood home. He was my home. When I hung up my garter belt after a long day, I wanted to fall into his arms.

Unable to bear the separation any longer, I scrambled over the center console and straddled him. His arms went tight around my waist, pulling me down on his lap. We both moaned when I settled against his hardness.

The sparks we were sharing roared into a raging fire. My skin was hot under his touch and I grew restless from having so many clothes on. His hands moved under my shirt, palms against the skin of my back. I leaned into him, his touch a magic wand making me float high above the ground. Heat flooded through me and I broke the kiss only to get his shirt over his head. I needed, *needed* to touch him.

His hands went up my back to my neck, taking my shirt with him. He paused, looking at my heaving chest in my black lace bra, his eyes blazing. He leaned forward and gently nipped my breast above my bra. "So beautiful," he mouthed against the curve, his lips brushing against my sensitive skin.

"You told me to wear black," I gasped.

His lips kissed everywhere he could reach as if he couldn't decide on one particular area. Neck, jaw, shoulders. His fingers made figure eights along my collarbone, the barely-there caress making my head spin. His soft beard scraped against my skin, making me shiver with anticipation. I wanted to feel that beard between my thighs.

"Jack," I whispered, not even sure what I was asking for.

Always knowing what I needed, he pulled down the right cup of my bra and sucked me into his mouth. My stomach fell through the earth as electric heat raced a path from my chest to between my legs. I was throbbing with need, but desperate to keep doing this as long as possible. I gripped the back of his head and arched against him as his teeth and tongue concentrated on my nipple.

Adult Jack was so sure of himself, unashamed and unembarrassed by our desperation. There were no "is this right?" or "we should stop," just the need to close the distance between us. He unhooked my bra and pulled it down my shoulders, then sat back to stare at me in the moonlight. He just shook his head like he couldn't believe I was really there, then put his mouth back to my chest.

It had been nearly two months since I had last filmed, my breast being too sore and red to comfortably work after surgery. The break had allowed my desensitized body to find pleasure in simple touches again. Just his mouth on me was winding me tighter and tighter, hotter and hotter. This wasn't how I wanted to come.

I grabbed Jack's face and brought his lips to mine again. He pulled me against the hardness of his chest, the soft hairs brushing against my smooth skin, making us both let out deep, shuddering breaths.

"God, I've missed you," he breathed against the skin of my neck, shivers cascading from his touch. "No one else makes me feel like this." He lifted his hips and slid me along his hard length.

"Jack," I cried, desperate for him. I tried to move to take off my leggings, but my elbow went back too far and hit the horn.

We both froze, our chests heaving, waiting to see if the horn had alerted anyone to our presence. Five intolerable seconds later, I gave up. I needed to taste him again, needed to memorize every inch of his skin before I left.

My mouth sucked and nipped and licked under his jaw, down his neck, and across his shoulders. Gone was the teenage softness. In its place was solid muscle, strong enough to save lives. A burst of pride I had no right to feel surged through me. The man he had become was incredible.

And that man wanted to make love to the woman I had become. Not because I was a famous porn star, not because I was some teenage fantasy, but because I was *me*. *Be careful Vera,* my head warned, but my heart gave her the middle finger.

Honestly, I couldn't remember the last time I had sex with someone outside of work. I didn't really date anymore—I didn't have the time or energy. The sleeping with other people as my day job also really freaked a lot of guys out. But right here, right now, I didn't have to worry about my makeup, the camera angle, or sucking in my stomach. I didn't have to project my pleasure to make sure the boom mic picked me up. I just had to savor the man in front of me. Under me.

"Jack," I begged. "I need you. Please."

"Anything, Vera. Anything for you." He pulled my mouth up to his again and kissed me deep. I struggled to unbuckle his belt because I refused to move off his lap. His mouth moved down my neck. "I just had my annual physical. Healthy and no STIs."

His hand moved to my left breast and he gingerly traced the small scar with his fingertips. "Does it hurt?" I shook my head. His mouth followed after his fingers and I nearly hit the roof. There was something so intimate about him kissing my scar.

My entire body throbbed. I was soaking through my leggings. I needed him *right now*. "Had two tests since I last filmed, everything was negative," I gasped.

He reached down between us and undid his belt because I was failing to do so miserably. "Birth control? Do we need condoms?"

"IUD." I kissed him hard, distracting him from his task, but I couldn't help it. "No condoms." The sound of his zipper filled the cab, making me shake with anticipation. I was about to have this amazing man again.

His hand moved beneath the waistband of my leggings and my underwear, cupping my smooth skin before thrusting a finger inside of me. My eyes rolled into the back of my head.

A rumble left his chest. "So smooth," he whispered against my neck. "So wet."

Thank you, electrolysis. I could do little more than moan in response. He added a second finger, but it wasn't enough. I ground down on his hand, not wanting him to stop touching me but needing more. "You," I forced out. "Need you." He pulled his hand out and I brought it to my mouth, licking myself off his fingers.

His head hit the back of the seat as he let out the kind of groan he usually saved for when he was inside me. I smiled. I couldn't wait to hear that sound again.

Then I heard a sound louder than my heart hammering in my chest.

Jack stilled. "Did you hear that?" he whispered, his eyes huge. I nodded. Slowly, we both turned to look out the foggy driver's side window. He wiped the condensation off with his hand.

I screamed.

Then I launched myself off his lap, over the center console, and into the floor by the passenger seat.

Jack shushed me but was too busy redoing his pants. "That's the creepiest fucking thing I've ever seen."

"Why are they all just staring at us like that?!" I was an exhibitionist, sure, but this was something out of a horror movie. Next to the truck, on the other side of the fence, stood a dozen cattle.

One of them mooed.

The rest just looked at us with their beady eyes through the partly foggy window. Chewing. Chewing and judging.

Jack shook his head. "I now understand your fear of cows." He grabbed my shirt and tossed it to me. "Seatbelt."

"You're still shirtless," I reminded him, but he didn't care. As soon as my own shirt was on, I was off the floor and in the seat, buckling in. "Buckled! Go!"

He started the truck and we were pulling away seconds later. He handed me his seatbelt and I snapped it as we hit the main road. "I forgot cows like full moons," he said. "I would've never parked there."

I turned to stare at him. "You're saying a lot of words that should mean something to me but don't." He laughed and I nearly moaned at what it did to my heart. I wanted to eat that laugh with a spoon and a cup of coffee.

He lifted his hands halfway off the steering wheel in a kind of shrug. "Cows—well cattle, collectively—generally graze in the morning and late in the day. But they love full moons, apparently. They probably saw the pickup truck and thought food."

I just blinked at him. "I know I should have a response to this, but I don't. Fucking small-town-itis."

We drove in silence for a few moments before Jack softly mooed.

I almost peed my pants.

We were still laughing when we pulled up into his driveway. He leaned over and kissed me sweetly. "Vera."

"Jack." I kissed him back, nipping his bottom lip.

"I know you're just passing through and I know I told you to stay away, but you're irresistible. Please, let me take you out?"

I pulled back, searching his face. "Like on a date?"

He nodded. "Like on a date. In fact, you paid for one at the fundraiser."

My heart thudded hard. "I really, really want to," I admitted.

He narrowed his eyes. "But you're not saying yes."

I smiled apologetically. "I'm saying maybe." Because a yes would complicate everything. It would make leaving so much harder for both of us, even though saying yes would make staying so much easier. But if we went out, the chances of us having sex were very high. But having sex would only make everything even more chaotic. I loved chaos. I was pretty sure by Jack's smile he could see the entire argument playing out on my face.

He kissed me again. "I'm good at waiting."

CHAPTER FIFTEEN

@GRENADINEUNOFFICIAL GRENADINE HIGH SCHOOL WAS TOILET PAPERED OVERNIGHT. TOO BAD THEY DID A PRETTY CRUMMY JOB. BEFORE YOU ASK, KIDS, YOU'VE STILL GOT SCHOOL TODAY. #SORRYNOTSORRY

THE NEXT MORNING, I was in a heinous mood. Despite a quiet explosion between my sheets last night, a few swipes of my hand couldn't calm the fire that Jack had started. Grandma knocked on my door to tell me she was heading to the store for the day and I barely managed a grunt. She added on that there were blueberry muffins and coffee, and I'll admit that tamed the beast a little.

I missed sex—real sex, not porn sex—and I hadn't realized it until last night. The intimacy, the urgency, the risk of sharing a piece of your heart. It was thrilling, like a roller coaster, just before the first drop. But I also missed filming. I loved being on camera and bringing people what they needed to pleasure themselves. When all the bottom of my cup of coffee did was make me crankier, I knew I needed to do something.

I grabbed my phone and opened a text box. Franky had added Jack's number into my phone, and I was about to use it for the first time.

Me: Are you as cranky as I am this morning?

I knew I was playing with fire sending that, but my better sense was still back in that field of cows. I shuddered. Cattle freaked me out.

Jack: Vera?

Me: Got it in one

Jack: Yes. So cranky. Need to take a long shower today

Me: Want to shower together?

Okay, so that was a little beyond shameless flirting.

Jack: I would want nothing more, but I am at the grocery store right now. Thankfully there's a cart in front of me.

I burst out laughing.

Me: I'll let you get back to squeezing melons

Jack: *eyeroll emoji*

I cleaned up my breakfast dishes, then locked myself in my room with a new mission. I needed to film, and I needed to get off. Thankfully I was prepared for most eventualities on this road trip, even with only one suitcase.

I set up my selfie-stick as a tripod and attached my cell phone. I wished I had my laptop and webcam, but I hadn't expected to make videos on vacation. At least I brought my favorite toy, which was a bright pink dual-action vibrator. It had a dozen combinations of speed and vibration and was made of the highest quality silicone on the market.

I pulled the toy out of its lint-free bag, rinsed it off, and then put my fancy bottle of lube on the nightstand. It looked like an old potion bottle and was much more attractive than a sticky bottle with a hand pump.

After setting up my gear, I found and put on a cherry red lace bra, garter belt, and stockings, which looked badass with my new hair color. I was going to leave my bra on for this one since I wasn't ready to show off my new scar, no matter how small it was. I didn't want to answer questions from fans just yet.

I turned on eighties rock, which always got my engine revving. Once I had on enough mascara and concealer to look like a person, I started the video.

I talked about why I liked the toy and how to keep it in good condition. Then, I gave myself one hell of an orgasm while thinking about Jack's hands and mouth all over me. I chased a second orgasm quickly after, this one quiet with its fierceness. Breathless, I blew a kiss to my viewers and stopped the recording. I laid back on the bed and sighed. That was fun. I needed to do more of those.

I reached for my cell phone and took a selfie that showed my bra and up. My face was flushed from pleasure, my hair disheveled, and my smile mischievous. I opened a text message box to Jack and typed, **Not feeling so frustrated anymore!**

Jack: You don't play fair, woman.

Jack: I need to get my mouth on that bra, too.

Me: I'm pretty sure that can be arranged

I bit my lip. I was practically offering myself up to him on a silver platter while still not sure what the hell we were doing. *Stop playing with the man's feelings and decide!* my brain shouted.

I winced. I did need to actually stop shamelessly flirting with him unless we were for sure going to do this.

Me: I'm just realizing I'm being an asshole. Don't mean to play hard to get.

Jack: Princess, stop acting like I don't know you better than anyone else on this planet.

Jack: I'm good at being patient.

Me: But what about what you said? Avoiding pain when I leave, etc?

Jack: It hurt just as much to stay away

I ignored how fast my heart started beating.

After cleaning up and hopping in the shower, I was even more excited to get the video posted. I sat at the desk wrapped only in a towel, adding a Payton's Playhouse frame to the video, the needed intro and outro, and adjusted the color and audio. I loved how amazing our cell phone app was. I uploaded it to draft videos for approval, then grabbed my phone.

Me: Just uploaded a cell video. Want to do more like these. Approve?

Payton: Will check it out

Payton: Foundation meeting this afternoon, 2pm, PST. Dial in?

Me: Wouldn't miss it. Send me info

I did the time difference match and added a reminder to my calendar to check in for the meeting. Payton and I had created The Kaitlin Elizabeth Foundation after one of our dear friends passed away from domestic violence. Our mission focused on preventing domestic and sexual violence through education. Under the umbrella, we donated to women's shelters, shelters that welcomed transgender and non-binary individuals, and shelters that welcomed men and children.

I closed down my computer and walked to the dresser to pull out clothes. Grandma knocked on my bedroom door and I told her to come in. Except it wasn't Grandma.

"Jack!" I squeaked, startled. I shut my dresser drawer too fast, catching the edge of my towel. When I stepped back, my towel stayed in the same place. It was like watching a magician pull the tablecloth out from under the dinnerware. Except the dinnerware—or my clothes in this instance—dropped everywhere. Which left me completely naked.

Jack's eyes widened and he turned around, half shutting the door. "Sorry!" he sputtered and shook his head as if trying to clear it. "Uh, Grandma Bea called and said you needed a ride to Edie's to pick up your car."

"Oh, yes, today's Monday." I grabbed my towel and wrapped it back around me. "Sorry, clothes. Right."

Jack made a painful noise. "I finally was able to walk like a person and I think this just undid all that hard work."

I snickered. "Hard."

He groaned. "I'm going to the kitchen, unless you want to pick up where we left off last night. When you're clothed, come find me." He stopped. "Don't say 'come' in that voice," he warned, closing the door.

"Sex puns are the best!" I called.

"YOU DON'T WORK TODAY?" I asked as we drove down Main St.

He shook his head. "Only work four days a week. This is one of my days off."

"Cool. Well, thanks for driving." I tried to be casual, but to be honest the sexual tension was making it hard to breathe. I lowered the window a crack.

When I saw the sign for Barwell Bakery, I gasped. "Wait! Stop!" I ordered.

"What? Are you okay?" He immediately pulled into a street parking spot. That was just like Jack; he was blessed with some magical parking fairy dust to always have a parking spot available at his every whim.

I smiled sheepishly. "Sorry, I promised Franky I'd stop in for a free pastry."

Jack rubbed his forehead. "You could've led with that instead of trying to give me a heart attack."

"But where's the fun in that?" I grabbed my purse and jumped out of the truck. Jack followed behind me and grumbled. I was so lost in my own little world, I forgot this was the first major town outing I had done besides church. When I opened the door and stepped in, the bakery fell quiet.

Everyone turned to stare at me, and then at Jack as he walked in behind me. I turned around and put my hand on his chest, trying to push him out the door. "I changed my mind." He rolled his eyes, caught my left hand and slid it into his. Then he took the lead, pulling me to the counter.

Franky walked out of the back with a smile on his face. "Indhira, I got this," he said to the young woman at the register who was giving me a curious glance. He cleared his throat and gestured to the entire seating area. "Show's over. Get over it or get out," he called to his customers.

Everyone made a show of returning to their conversations and eating their pastries. I blinked at my friend. "I can't believe that worked," I whispered.

He shrugged. "I make the best pastries within an hour of the city limits. And I hold a grudge." He said it light-heartedly, but I didn't miss the shadow that passed over his face.

I leaned on the counter and batted my eyelashes at him. "You are my hero."

He took the towel off his shoulder and play-hit me with it. "You need to put your wiles back in your purse. That look is potent."

I mimed pulling off sunglasses and tucking them in my front pocket.

Jack laughed. "Potent is right. I lasted less than three weeks before it did me in."

My heart beats tried to step over each other. I really needed to see a cardiologist soon if that was going to keep happening. *Here lies Vera Eastman, dead from feelings.*

Franky smiled. "Now that two of my favorite people are here, let me grab us some coffee and pastry. Go find a table."

"No nuts," I begged. I despised nuts in dessert. They took up room that other ingredients, like chocolate chips, could inhabit.

He looked at me with a serious face. "But you love to eat nuts."

I hit my face with my palm. "I walked into that one."

Jack let out a belly laugh. "It's good to have you home," he said quietly as we walked to a four-top table in the back corner.

He sat next to me, not releasing my hand. I bit my bottom lip and considered pulling away. As if he could read my mind, he tightened his grip. I leaned over and whispered, "You know everyone is going to think we're dating."

He shrugged. "We were dating for more of our lives than we weren't. It's nothing new."

"Jack," I said more urgently. "I come with a lot of baggage. Tabloids, online trolls, competitors. This isn't going to be as simple as dating me in high school."

"Are tabloids worse than Gertie running around with a cell

FIRE TRUCKS, GARTER BELTS, & MY PERFECT EX

phone camera catching people in compromising positions then posting them on @GrenadineUnofficial social media pages?"

I opened my mouth to argue and realized I had nothing. Tabloids had nothing on small-town busybodies. "But I'm not staying." As soon as I said the words, my throat filled with a mix of emotions I didn't want to deal with. I swallowed hard to shove them back down.

He lifted my hand to his mouth and kissed it softly. "Babe, you've been mine and you'll always be mine. We'll figure it out."

"Jack!" I hissed. "I am inherently a realist—"

"With a heavy dose of pessimist."

I nodded. "Okay, yes, that's true. But, Jack, I'm not just going to give up my life in SoCal. And you're not going to give up your life here."

He looked at me, blinking hard once when something dark passed over his features. Just like that, his brown eyes warmed again and held me under a Jack Spell™. I stayed like that, lost inside of him, until Franky set down a tray with three coffee mugs and an assortment of cut up pastries.

"You two are disgusting. At least get it on film so you can post about it," Franky said.

I laughed and turned to face my friend. "Sorry, this is an eating establishment. We'll behave."

"Boring," he replied, sitting down and passing out the mugs. "Jack, I gave yours an extra kick so you can keep up with this one." He pointed at me. "You get decaf."

I gasped and put my hand on my chest. "RUDE."

"You've already had two cups today," he surmised. "But I added some chocolate."

I frowned but said nothing, accepting the mug. I had already had two cups. It was weird having people in my life who knew me so well. Payton and Jas knew me inside and out too—literally—but in a different way. There was something about people who had known you since you were practically born that you couldn't replace.

He motioned to the plate. "These are my four favorites. Vera, avoid the zucchini lemon because I added walnuts."

I mimed barfing. "Why would you ruin a perfectly good pastry with nuts?"

He shrugged. "Why did we ruin perfectly good penises with nuts?"

Jack choked on his coffee and I slapped his back. "Why do I forget that I can't drink anything around you two?" he wheezed.

"More like can't swallow," I whispered.

Franky threw his head back and laughed. Jack put a hand over his face and silently laughed. I smiled so hard it hurt. Sitting there, with my two favorite men on the planet, I didn't know how I was going to turn around and drive away. But I couldn't give up everything I'd worked for over the last decade.

My stomach squeezed. Once I got my car back, I had serious decisions to make.

CHAPTER SIXTEEN

"JUST LIKE WITH CARDS, SOMETIMES LIFE DEALS YOU A SHIT HAND. THAT'S WHY GOD INVENTED BLUFFING…" - GRANDMA BEA

THE SHOP WAS a mere two blocks from the bakery, so we went on foot. Jack continued to hold my hand and I continued to let him. There was just something about picking up my car that would change everything. All the decisions I had been putting off, all the "I can think about it laters" were about to turn into "right nows." The physical space between us stayed the same, but with each step forward, I felt the crevasse widen. I was losing him, I was losing us, and there was nothing I could do to stop it.

Jack gave a dirty look to a woman who shoved her child to the other side of the sidewalk when we got close, but I ignored them. It happened other places too. I wanted to scream that I wouldn't harm their kids, but they wouldn't care. All they knew was that I had sex for money, and that's all they wanted to know.

He shook my arm gently. "Hey, where'd you go?"

I blinked up at him. "What do you mean?"

He searched my face. "You're a million miles away."

I shrugged. "Just have a lot of decisions to make once I get my car back."

He squeezed my hand and we walked in silence the rest of the way to the shop. He opened the door and I was thankful we had to release hands to walk in. I put my hand in my pocket to keep him from grabbing it again. He sent me a puzzled look and tried to read my face, but I walked over to the office and ignored him.

When I knocked, Tamicka looked up. "Hey, Vera! Your car just got polished within an inch of her life. She looks brand new."

"Awesome. I miss her."

She pointed to the waiting room. "Hang tight there. I'll grab Chieka to go over everything." She stood and nodded at Jack.

We walked over to the area where several chairs and a loveseat were set up more like a parlor than a waiting room. To keep myself busy and not think about Jack, I pulled my cell out and snapped a few selfies of me, trying to get some of the shop in the background, and posted them on my social media. I looked at every photo and drawing on the wall. I teared up when I came across a letter from Edward to Mario about starting the auto shop when Mario got home from Vietnam. I snapped a picture of that, too.

This place was so cool.

Chieka walked up to me with a big smile. "Vera! Just took her out for a spin and she's purring. She's as good as new." She gestured for us to follow her. I held my breath, anxious to have my transportation back. The trapped feeling started to dissipate.

We walked through a bay door and I let out a long breath in relief at my baby glittering under the late morning sun. I stroked her, telling her how beautiful she was and how much I missed her. Her strong angles and rich red mirrors were all back in perfect shape. Her tires were new, and her engine ran like the day I got her. I *may* have leaned down and kissed her. Just once.

Chieka didn't look at me like I was crazy. She turned to Jack. "I would be the exact same way with that car." Jack just shook his head and leaned against the wall, smiling.

When I finished gushing, I smiled sheepishly and Chieka handed me the invoice. She went over what she'd repaired and the parts she'd ordered, then gave me my total.

I shook my head. "This is half the cost of what it would be in LA." I handed it back to her. "You can charge me more. Local shops like you are priceless."

Chieka studied me for a moment. "That's what I'm charging. But if you want to help, leave a review and tell your friends. We're trying to build a presence."

A lightbulb went off in my head. "I'll do you one better. I'm going to work on your marketing. You got a girl doing that?"

She smiled. "Let me introduce you to Rosa. She's been trying to get our Instagram up and running." She leaned closer. "She's a bit of a fangirl, just FYI."

I winked at her. "Fangirls are the best." Jack just shook his head and gave me a soft smile. Chieka walked ahead and Jack and I fell behind. "You know," I started. "I'm all set. You can go do whatever it is you have to do today."

He looked like I had punched him in the stomach. He checked his watch. "Yeah, I should probably go. Vera—"

Chieka called my name, cutting off his sentence. His lips pressed together, and he shook his head. "I'll text you later." He kissed my forehead and waved at the crew before walking out the door. I pretended that just watching him walk away didn't hurt like hell, even knowing it was temporary. I was so screwed.

When I turned to face Chieka, Tamicka and a young woman who must be Rosa stood there watching me. Tamicka shook her head. "Great. We have another one. I'm too old for this," she grumbled.

Chieka laughed. "You're thirty-five, T-money."

Tamicka held up a hand. "When you find that great love, you do what you need to keep it. End of story. Goodbye." She closed the office door with a little more force than necessary before she sat down at the computer and started playing loud music. Christmas music, to be precise.

Chieka let out a low whistle. "When the Christmas music comes out in early September, you know she's in a bad mood."

"Should I ask?" I whispered.

Chieka made a slice across her neck. "Let me introduce you to Rosa." She made formal introductions and I reached out to shake Rosa's hand.

She was adorable, with that early twenties pep and big, brown eyes and tawny skin. A blush darkened her cheekbones. "*Hola*, it's nice to meet you. *Me llamo* Rosa."

I replied that it was nice to meet her, too, in Spanish. Her eyes grew wider and her cheeks even more red.

"*¿Habla Español?*" she asked, excitedly.

I shrugged. "I can speak just enough Spanish, Italian, German, and French to get me in trouble."

Chieka laughed and gave Rosa a half hug. "Breathe before you pass out. She's only human, too."

I smiled. "Just think of me pooping. That's what I do when I go into fangirl mode. It helps me stay sane."

Rosa laughed and looked a little less star-struck. "Who do you fangirl over?"

"I once had backstage passes to meet Sorry Charlie and I nearly died when Charlie *herself* gave me a hug." I still had the T-shirt I wore that night, even though it was tattered and would serve better as a rag than a memory.

"Awesome," Chieka said. "They're a favorite around here."

"Then I think we're going to be fast friends," I said, and surprised myself by meaning it. "Now, Rosa, show me what you're working on. I'll work on a game plan before I leave town."

Chieka looked between me and Tamicka's closed door. "Ah, okay. I see."

"What do you see?"

She held up her hands. "Far be it from me to tell people how to live their lives." She motioned between Rosa and me. "I've got a transmission leak to deal with. Shout if you need me."

I followed Rosa back to the break room. If I hadn't known this was a shop of mostly women, I would've guessed by the impeccable, homey space. Stainless steel appliances, comfortable chairs, and a beautiful backsplash. It was like a home away from home, comfortable and welcoming.

Rosa and I went over her ideas and I gave her some pointers on hashtags and times of day to post. For a nineteen-year-old, she had a really good head on her shoulders. I always maintained that as much as I knew about social media, teenagers always knew more.

When we were done with business, we delved into personal stuff. Well, quite frankly, Rosa did.

"I can't believe you're going to leave Jack behind. *Chica, estás loca*. I love women, but even I would consider making out with him once." She pushed her Pop Socket up and down on her phone, pursing her lips as if trying to figure me out.

I pulled some lip balm out of my jeans and applied it, then spun it on the table. "My life is in California."

She shrugged. "My life was in Texas. Lives can change."

I made a noncommittal noise.

We sat there for a few moments, lost in our own thoughts, until a chicken appeared in the doorway and waddled over to peck at Rosa's foot. I tilted my head to the side as I watched her kneel down and pet the creature before taking his photo. This town just got weirder and weirder. *In today's news, a deadly outbreak of small-town-itis killed two women and a chicken at a local auto shop...*

Rosa looked up and smiled at me. "This is Sergeant Cornflakes. He's the shop's mascot."

I nodded as if that was the most logical thing in the world. I crouched down next to Rosa and reached out to pet the bird. "Hey, Sergeant. It's nice to meet you."

He turned his beady eye to me and then walked off, definite attitude in his step. I turned to face Rosa. "You have a chicken."

"Technically he's a rooster."

I laughed so hard I fell back on my ass. Rosa reached down to help me up. "I have an idea."

Rosa jumped up and down on the balls of her feet like only someone with teenager energy could accomplish. "Tell me, tell me!"

"Focus on Sergeant Cornflakes, but also have lots of photos of you ladies and him. Everyone likes hot girls and cock." I laughed at myself. "Him with cars, in cars, on cars. Make it look like he's fixing a car if you can. Take a group picture with all of you holding him for your main photo."

Her eyes went wide. "You're brilliant."

"Naw, I'm just really good at sex puns."

CHAPTER SEVENTEEN

GRENADINE ORDINANCE NO. 458-8-19: AT NO TIME ARE CHICKENS ALLOWED TO CROSS THE ROAD WITHOUT THEIR OWNER. ROOSTERS ARE EXEMPT.

AFTER GOING over the rest of Edie's Auto's online presence—and holy hell did they need my help—I called Grandma about lunch. I arrived at Happy Endings a half hour later with food for the two of us and Kim. While Kim tended the store, Grandma and I went into her office to talk.

She took a forkful of her chicken salad and looked at me casually. I tried not to look at her salad and think about Sergeant Cornflakes. "So, now that you have your car back, are you making plans to leave?"

That hadn't taken long. "I should probably do that," I admitted, picking at my veggie stir fry.

"But you aren't ready to leave," she surmised. I shrugged, not willing to admit anything. "Would that have anything to do with the fact that Jack was shirtless last night when he brought you home?"

My mouth fell open and I stared at her. "Seriously?"

"I can see his driveway from the kitchen window, dear. Settle down."

I put my fork down and leaned back in my chair. "I'm not quite this used to someone keeping tabs on who I'm making out with."

Grandma raised her eyebrows. "I think I have about fifteen

DVDs out there that say otherwise." She gestured to the showroom with her fork.

I balled up my napkin and threw it at her, both of us laughing. "You know what I mean. Jack walked into the bakery with me today and you would've thought I'd robbed a bank with the attention we were getting."

She nodded. "I heard about that."

I checked my phone. "It's been...two hours. How have you already heard about that?"

"This is Grenadine. I know when someone farts within fifteen minutes." She leaned back in her chair, mirroring my posture. "Don't string that boy along. He had a bad enough time of it when you left last time."

I threw my hands up. "I'm not stringing him along! At least, I'm trying not to. There's this...I dunno how to describe it, magnetism that just keeps drawing us together. I can't help it."

She leveled me with a look. "Yes, but it doesn't mean you have to be naked."

I crossed my arms. "For a woman who sells sex toys, you're sure acting like a prude."

She crossed her arms back. "There is a difference in being careful with yours and someone else's feelings and being a prude. I know what he went through when you left—"

I rolled my eyes. "Yes, of course."

"Vera Meredith," Grandma said in the voice she used when she was mad. I sat up straighter. "You will stop interrupting me right now. You will sit and listen to what I'm going to tell you."

Knowing better than to verbalize my answer, I nodded, my ears growing hot at her reprimand.

"As I was saying, I know what Jack went through. Losing you and then his brother was unbelievable to everyone, especially to the people who loved you both."

Her words were a kick to the gut. I had made so many mistakes that had lasting consequences.

Grandma sighed. "But I can't even imagine what *you* went through."

Surprised, I looked at her. I had pushed the memories of leaving, the months of nightmares and dirty, cheap rooms down where no one could ever get to them. After Dad's email, I had continued to spiral until Payton came into my life. She hated me at first—I was the coworker who was always too inebriated to do a perfect job—and eventually, we got into an all-out brawl.

After I bloodied her nose and she blackened my eye, she told me she wouldn't tell our manager about the fight if I played a game of Texas Hold 'Em with her. I had already been fired from two jobs and I needed to make rent that week, so I agreed. If I won, she'd quit her job and leave me in peace. If she won, I had to get sober. It was the only time I had ever lost to Payton, although I ultimately won my life back. I owed her so much more than I could ever repay. "What do you mean?" I whispered.

Grandma stood and walked to the window, staring out. It overlooked a small river surrounded by trees that shielded her from the building next door. "Jack and his family had an entire community to support them in their loss. They're never going to get over it, but they'll never be alone, either."

She looked back over her shoulder. "But your father's and my anger and fear shoved you out the door, all alone. I'll never forgive myself for that. I was so worried something would happen to you working at that shitty club. There was always a car being stolen or a creep hanging around, and then it was robbed twice. I acted out of fear and desperation to keep from losing you and ended up losing you anyway."

Two tears slipped out of the side of my eyes. I stood on shaky legs and walked up to this woman who had always seemed larger than life, until right now. I laid my head on her shoulder and wrapped my arm around her. "You haven't lost me. We just got separated for a while."

She patted my arm. "I missed so much of your life because of fear."

I swallowed hard. "Me too."

"But I fear now. I fear that you'll hurt Jack when you leave and that you'll hurt so much you won't want to come back. These bones ain't what they used to be, and they don't like airplanes."

I squeezed her just a little harder. "Jack or no Jack, I'd still come visit."

She patted my arm again. "I'm old and greedy. But I know you need to get back to your life in California."

I nodded against her, but whispered, "How can I be in two places at once? How can I never leave here but also be there?"

She *hmm*'d. "If anyone can figure it out, it's you. You made an empire with a few hundred dollars and a duct-taped Ford Escort. Don't forget, you also have airline miles."

I laughed and we both took a deep breath. "Okay, food now. Food will help." I released her and we sat back down in our chairs and resumed picking at our lunch. My head was full of too much noise to make good conversation.

WHEN THE FOUNDATION conference call wrapped up, Payton called me back on a private line and I picked up on my headset. "Baby girl, I miss you," she purred in her trademark voice. It was smoky and sexy, and it was a balm for my soul.

My throat closed up with emotion; I missed her so much. "Ditto," I admitted.

"That video you posted was great. We can get some toys from our sponsors and have you do a few more videos."

"Okay," I agreed. "That sounds good."

"Hold on a sec." I heard Payton talk to one of her assistants in the background and I thought about my own empty office. Payton was always the brains and was the true CEO. I was the talent with a dream and eventually, a bachelor's in both gender studies and media arts, as well as a master's in sexuality education.

"Sorry, I'm back," she said. "Listen, did you get your car back?"

It was a completely innocuous question, one I'd been expecting, but it still nearly brought me to my knees. "I got my car back this morning," I managed to say without wheezing. The knot in my chest twisted tighter.

"Great. I know you're on a sabbatical, but it would mean the world to me if you could cut your trip short, at least for now."

I swallowed hard. She wouldn't ask me if it wasn't something big. "What's up?"

"Remember that secret project I was working on with Kirkland Studios and REfocus?"

"Yeah." I stood up from the desk and paced the small length of the room. I had started sweating.

"We're ready to announce it. We're going to start making parody films—full feature length—of the biggest box office hits. We're going to focus on romcoms and action flicks, but I'm hoping we can get fantasy on that list if we can afford a good CGI team."

My mouth fell open. "Holy shit, that's huge, Pay!"

"This is what we've been working for. We'll need to immediately double our admin staff and when you get back, I want to talk about promoting Jas to VP."

"Of course! She should be, honestly." I swallowed hard. "This will be years of work. What about the films we have on the production schedule now?"

"We'll work around what we have booked and put a hold on the others until we cast the movies." She squealed. "This is going to make us one of the top porn companies worldwide."

Dread pooled in my stomach. I should be excited. I should be jumping for joy and screaming and crying. This was something we'd both dreamed of since we were barely old enough to drink. "I'm so proud of you," I said quietly.

"I'm proud of *us*, Vera. We did this together. Years of eating peanut butter from the jars and living in the shittiest studio apartments. It's all finally happening!"

My eyes watered and I blinked it away. Was it possible to have your dreams come true and be heartbroken at the same time? "Unreal," I whispered. My throat constricted and I fought to breathe normally.

"I know it's going to be even more long nights and weekends, but I can feel it all coming together. It's the best feeling in the entire world."

Long nights and weekends. That meant trips back home would be scarce. I sat down on the edge of my bed and rubbed at my temples. "I wish I was there right now to hug you."

"I'm giving you the biggest fucking hug right now!" She blew out a breath and laughed. "I can't believe it. Listen, can you be home by next Saturday? I want to tell Jas and Darrin together at game night."

"I-I—" I cleared my throat, giving myself a moment to think. It was twenty-three hundred miles home, which would take around three days. I'd have to leave by next Wednesday afternoon if I wanted to be a human by game night. *Wednesday.* A little over a week.

"I need you here, Vera. I know you needed time off, and I'm so glad you're okay and healthy, and that you've reconnected with your family. But I can't do this alone. You're my other half, my right hand, my Super-Vera."

I laughed quietly. "I'll be there by Saturday," I promised, wiping the tears off my face with the palm of my hand.

"I can't wait to see you." Someone spoke in the background and Payton swore. "Baby girl, I need to go deal with a diva meltdown. Love you! See you soon."

I hung up the phone and lay back on the bed. I bit back the sob burning a hole in my chest. This was everything we wanted. This was the dream.

Why did it feel all wrong?

I heard the back door open and Grandma call a hello. "I'll be out in a sec!" I called back, sitting up and wiping my eyes. Who would she say hello to when she got home when I was gone? Who would Jack make out with in his truck? Who would Franky give free pastry to?

When did nowhere start to feel like home?

I took a deep breath. I would have a meltdown later when the house was quiet. For now, I was going to go make dinner with my grandma.

CHAPTER EIGHTEEN

MOM'S BUCKET LIST #14: SKINNY DIP IN GRENADINE CREEK

I SAT IN MY CAR, staring out at the slow-moving creek. It was a cloudless night and the stars and moon reflected off the calm surface. I grabbed a bite-sized chocolate from my purse and shoved it into my mouth. I hadn't fooled Grandma for a moment. As soon as I had walked out of my room, she'd asked me what day I was leaving.

She kept up her smile until she went to bed, but I knew she had to be hurting as much as I was. Everything felt wrong. Every decision was like heading full speed down a one-way road in the wrong direction.

I got out of the car before I started crying and pulled my sundress over my head. The earth was still warm under my bare feet. The early September evening was fighting valiantly to stay warm. In the light of the moon, I could see the trees around me starting to turn yellow and orange. I loved the way the colors changed. It was like the trees took a long vacation and then started over when the time was right.

I placed my towel and cell on the hood of my car before shedding my bra and underwear. This place held so many memories. Picnics with my parents, swimming trips with my grandma, bonfires with

FIRE TRUCKS, GARTER BELTS, & MY PERFECT EX

Jack and Franky, drinking with Danny. Tonight, it was empty, which was fortuitous.

I walked up to the rope swing that still hung from the largest tree that rested on an incline along the bank. After tugging on the rope to check that it would hold me, I squared my shoulders and got a running start before I chickened out. It was second nature to let go of the rope at the perfect time and free fall into the water.

My heart was in my throat as soon as the cold water shocked me, but I broke through the surface, spluttering. Chills racked my body. I pushed my hair out of my face and started laughing. This was one of those moments where I was truly alive.

My nipples were so hard they hurt, and my teeth were chattering. But I still swam to the bank and jumped three more times before my limbs started to complain. Slowly I got used to the water, the coolness relieving the tired aches. I flipped onto my back and floated, watching the stars.

Trust yourself, I heard my mom's voice in my head. Or maybe in the stars.

"I'm trying," I whispered. "I don't know what to do." Admitting it to the dark helped, somehow.

You will.

"I thought I'd find you here."

I screamed, slipping beneath the water for a moment before pushing myself back to the surface. "Jack!" I admonished. "Are you trying to kill me?" I was treading water now, my naked body below the surface. By the look on his face, I had no doubt that he knew what I was doing.

He held up a battery-powered lantern that emitted enough glow for me to make out his hardened features. "No, but you're clearly trying to kill yourself, swimming alone at night."

"I have to finish the Grenadine part of Mom's list."

He stared at me and I saw the moment he read between the lines. I had to finish Mom's list because I was leaving. As he took in the news, it was as if his normally sharp features dulled. He set down the lantern, leaned against my car, and pulled off his shoes. "When do you leave?" His socks came off next.

"Next Wednesday. I got the call this afternoon that..." How did I explain that all my dreams were about to come true? Because they weren't. Not really. "A major project we've been working toward is finally coming together."

"That's great. I'm really proud of you, Princess." He pulled off his T-shirt and my mouth started to water. In the glow of the lantern, he looked like a hard-carved stone statue. "You don't sound as excited about it as you should."

"I'm excited!" I defended.

"But?" His hands went to his buckle and I shook my head, trying to remember what he was saying.

"But it means leaving. And a lot of working nights and weekends."

He set his clothes on the hood of my car. Had he walked here? It was only about a quarter mile, but still, it was dark. Said the lady in the water alone.

"So when you leave again, you're gone-gone," he surmised.

"Yep." I closed my eyes as he pulled his boxers down.

He chuckled. "Why are your eyes closed?"

"Because if you come near me naked, I'm going to finish what we started," I admitted.

I heard him walk into the water. "And what if I want to finish what we started?"

My eyes flew open at that. He half dove into the water, giving me a quick flash of his perfectly round ass and my entire body gave a hard throb. He surfaced right in front of me and pushed back his hair. Water droplets trailed down his incredibly defined shoulders and chest and my mouth went dry.

Need.

"Come with me," I tried, desperate. "Move to California with me."

He made a pained sound and wrapped his arms around my waist, pulling me against him. We both moaned at the contact, our skin slippery and so, so sensitive. "You know I can't. I can't leave my family. Everything I worked for is here. My life is here. And I couldn't separate Taco and Waffles."

I laughed softly, despite my heart breaking. "You're right, you couldn't separate them. It would be cruel."

He put his forehead against mine. "Stay," he breathed.

"I can't."

"I know. But I had to ask." He kissed me so softly, so gently, cherishing the moment. He pulled back and put his forehead against mine.

"I'm leaving," I whispered. "I don't know when I'll be back. If we do this, it's just for now. There's no happily ever after here."

He nodded. "I know." His voice was soft and resigned. "I would suffer through a lifetime of goodbyes for every stolen moment I can have with you."

I searched his eyes and nodded. "Me too."

His lips brushed mine carefully as if he were afraid if he pushed too fast, I would spook. His kisses savored me, tasting then pulling away. Top lip, bottom lip, small kisses on the corners.

He was melting me from the inside out. I wrapped my arms tighter around him, my tongue tentatively tasting his bottom lip. His mouth opened, pouring all his unspoken feelings into mine. I could hear every silent word as it twisted inside of me, my body desperate to yell them back. In the dark and under the stars, it was as if we had crossed into a secret world of magic. In this world, we could be just us, together.

For a long time, we just held each other. He had moved us to an area of the creek where he could reach the bottom, allowing me to float with him as my anchor. He kissed me leisurely as if we had all the time in the world. As if no sunrise would come that would chase us away. As if California didn't exist. As if we could stop time.

He grew hard between us and I let out a tiny whimper. The storm inside me roared to life, as big as a hurricane. Our soft kisses turned more desperate, our teeth clashing and tongues tangling. One of his hands tangled in my hair and the other one held on to my back as he dragged his lips down my neck. He stopped at the place where my shoulder and neck met and bit, then quickly kissed away the sting.

I ran my hands down his chest and waist, but he gently tugged on my wrists, pulling me away from him. "If you touch me right now, this will be over before it's begun," he warned.

I pouted, but he leaned forward and nipped my bottom lip. "Now," he said. "I need to make you come." In an instant, he let go of my hands and grabbed my waist, dragging me down the length of him before his hand slipped under the water and cupped me.

My breath hitched when he pushed two fingers inside of me. He kissed me, moving his tongue and his fingers in a slow, deliberate pattern. I was panting between kisses, my arms shaking as I hung on to him. He was so good at touching me.

He growled as I started to dip below the water line. I gripped his forearm as he pressed his palm against me and sucked my nipple into his mouth. "Jack!" I whispered, my voice shaking as I came apart in his arms.

"There it is," he said against my mouth. "The way you say my name when you come has haunted me. It's like a drug."

He ground his palm into my clit and pushed a third finger in. I swore, the cross between pleasure and pain was electrifying. "I need you to say it again." This time he wasn't gentle, and neither was I. I rode his hand, desperate for more. Anything and everything. The water splashed with the movement of his arm, which just turned me on more. I crested again, saying his name over and over again. He kissed me so hard, I couldn't breathe.

"Need you," he pleaded as he pulled away.

"Yes! Hurry," I begged in return. I didn't care if one hundred cows were watching us; I wasn't going another night without this man.

He kissed me and then moved us to shore. "Land," he panted. "I don't want us to drown."

"But what a way to go," I said, breathlessly.

The moment his feet hit dry land, he scooped me up into his arms. He carried me over to my car and set me down, facing it. He gently pushed down on my back and I bent over, placing my palms on the hood. He dropped to his knees and sealed his mouth between my legs.

His touch made me half collapse onto the hood. I almost came just from imagining what we looked like right now, me splayed on this beautiful car, his mouth kissing me in the most intimate way. I swore as he gently nipped my clit, making me grind into his mouth. He gripped my hips so hard I was certain he would leave bruises. *Good.*

My knees were useless as he continued to lick and suck and groan. His moves were familiar but perfected. Everything I had liked about us eleven years ago was ten times better right now. I was so wet I was dripping down my leg, and I didn't care. It was dirty and erotic as hell, and my body begged for more. "This is the hottest fucking thing I've ever done," I said, but it sounded more like a sob.

In response, he bit me again. I fell onto the hood, my breasts pushed against the sexiest car in existence, and I exploded.

He swore and immediately came up behind me, positioning himself at my entrance and pushing in mid-orgasm. We both cried out at the feel of being one again as I pulsed around him. I forced myself upright and he wrapped one arm around my breasts, reaching the other down to bring my knee to the bumper.

He pulled my back against his chest as he shifted his hips to go even deeper. I gripped the back of his neck, needing to get closer.

"Fuck," he moaned, pushing in so hard he lifted me off the car. "I missed you, so much." His face was against my shoulder as he moved in powerful thrusts, sliding his hand from my leg to my clit.

I put my hand on the hood to keep us from toppling forward and laid my head back against his shoulder. "Jack, Jack, Jack," I repeated.

My breath caught as his hand did a slow circle between my legs. "Harder, please, harder. I need more of you."

He grunted and pushed in again and again, harder and harder until I had tears of absolute bliss streaming down my face. Every touch made me want more of him. He kissed up and down my neck. "Hurry, love. Need you to come."

It was the way he said "love" in that voice that sounded like it had endured too much already. I fell apart and he cried out a few moments later, throbbing his release inside of me. My heart clung to his in a hold I knew I wouldn't be able to break. I didn't regret a single moment.

He kept moving us, even as our shaking subsided. When we finally stilled, he lowered my leg to the ground and moved his hands around my waist, burying his face against my neck. "Are you okay? You're crying."

"I'm perfect." I gripped his arms tight. "You're perfect."

"We're perfect." His words were the cocoon I needed right now.

I turned around and put my head against his chest. "Take me back to your house and make love to me again," I demanded. "Preferably on a dry, warm surface."

He chuckled softly and kissed me. "Your wish is my command."

CHAPTER NINETEEN

"THE BEST PART ABOUT GETTING OLD IS BEING RIGHT ALL THE TIME." - GRANDMA BEA

THE NEXT MORNING, Jack walked me home as the sun skated over the dew-blanketed grass. He kissed me at the back door until we were both ready to climb into each other again. "Don't go," he said against my lips.

"Don't stay," I returned, bunching his shirt in my hand and kissing him again.

We jumped apart when the back door opened to let out Taco and Waffles. This time, I didn't get knocked to the ground by Taco's overexcited greeting. "Alright, you two," Grandma said. "Vera, we need to get to the store to stock up for the party. Jack, you're not allowed over tonight! You've got Waffles and Taco duty."

I laughed as he gave me one more kiss before whistling for his dog. Waffles, true to form, followed along. I walked in the house and Grandma leveled me with a look. "Stop, I texted you that I was staying at Jack's."

She just shrugged and went back to drying her dishes. "I didn't say anything."

I rolled my eyes. "You didn't have to. I can hear it loud and clear."

She put her hands on the counter. "I just don't want you to regret anything."

I walked up and put my arm around her waist and my head on her shoulder. "I know. But I would regret not making the most of whatever time we have."

She sighed and patted my hand. "I understand. I was like that, too, with your grandfather. I still miss him every day."

I kissed her cheek. He had died when I was very young, but Mom had told me stories about their beautiful love. "Want help drying the dishes?"

She shook her head. "Go rest and shower. We're getting groceries at 8:30. We have a lot to do before the party tonight."

I frowned. "Party?"

"Well, it is the first Tuesday of the month. I always have my in-home sex toy parties from five to seven. I figured you wouldn't mind." She winked at me.

"Of course you have in-home sex toy parties."

She made a face at me. "Well, just because you and I are comfortable with our own pleasure, does not mean other people in town are. This allows them to come and check out the high-end toys without being seen at the store, and since it's a private residence, I circumvent the stupid law against selling sex toys in Grenadine."

"So, wait. You host parties to sell to people too afraid to buy the toys in the store, yet everyone knows you do these parties every month. How is that different?"

She shook her head at me. "Young lady, this is Grenadine. Appearances mean everything. Now, please go nap and shower. We are busy, busy, busy today."

WHEN GRANDMA SAID we would get to the store by 8:30, she wasn't kidding. One minute before, we were pushing a shopping cart into the grocer, which still looked almost the same as it had the last time I was there. It wasn't a big store, but the fruit looked amazingly fresh and there was an aisle that was labeled "Gluten Free." I smiled.

"They added that about six months ago when a few people in town discovered they couldn't eat gluten. The cookies aren't bad," Grandma explained as she bagged apples. "I'm going to do an apple crisp and a vegetable tray. We'll make some hummus. Go grab veggies."

I nodded and went off on my mission, selecting baby carrots, a bag of celery, cucumbers, and a rainbow of peppers. I picked up a container of hummus, but when I got back to the cart, Grandma clucked her tongue at me. "We make our own, dear. Go grab me some chickpeas instead."

I laughed and returned the store-bought hummus to the refrigerator before heading to the canned-food section. I stopped dead when I saw Pam, Jack's mom, with a can of baked beans in her hand. She was talking to my dad. His shoulders stiffened as he caught sight of me. I just stood there, staring at him. Without a word, he turned around and walked away.

Pam stood there glaring at me. I didn't want to acknowledge her, but I was better than a passive-aggressive cold shoulder. I swallowed hard and pasted on a smile. "Hello, Mrs. Reeves. It's good to see you again."

She set down the can and wiped off her hands as if she was completely offended by the beans. She nodded once. "I was hoping you'd left already. When are you leaving?" Her voice was as cold as ice.

I rocked back on my heels. "In about a week."

She looked relieved and I couldn't help but feel offended. We had so much history between us, but it didn't seem to matter to her. "Good." She picked up two cans and put them into her cart. "You are the worst kind of person for what you did to my family and yours. Stay away from my son. I hope you haven't sunk your claws into him too deeply. You tried to destroy my family once, but you'll do it again over my dead body."

I leaned onto the shelf, her hurtful accusations knocking the wind out of me. She walked past me and called back, "Maybe we'll get a Sunday miracle and you'll be gone by the time church starts."

She left me gutted, right there in the can aisle. I didn't know what I'd expected, but it wasn't such open hostility—as hostile as anyone in this town ever was.

Grandma turned her cart down the aisle. "You okay?"

I shook my head and plastered on a smile. "Yep!" I turned to the shelf next to me and grabbed two cans of beans. "Let's finish up!"

I followed her down the aisles, not willing to venture out on my own and risk seeing Dad or Pam again. I rubbed the heel of my hand across my chest, trying to ease the discomfort her words instilled there.

"What's wrong with you?" Grandma asked. "You feeling okay?"

"What?" I turned back around to face her. "Yep, totally fine."

She frowned. "Who said something to you? What'd they say?"

I waved her off. "No one." She just continued to stare at me, and I sighed. "It was nothing." But my grandma never met a staring contest she couldn't win. "Fine, I saw Dad talking to Pam Reeves. He walked off without a word and she basically told me she couldn't wait until I left."

Grandma *hmphed*. "Well, that's why that bitch isn't invited to my toy party tonight."

My mouth fell open. "I thought it was an open invitation?" I asked when I had recovered enough to make my jaw work.

"Yeah, but not for bitches who treat my granddaughter that way. They're lucky I wasn't in the aisle with you. I would've chucked a can of beans at both of their heads."

I cracked up. "You are fierce."

"I could make it really hard for her to hand out communion on the fourth Sunday of every month with a couple flicks of the wrist." Grandma held up her hand and mimed breaking the fingers.

By the time we got to the register, I was nearly doubled over in laughter. Grandma sweetly asked the cashier how her day was going like she hadn't just spent the last five minutes talking about doing bodily harm to Jack's mom. My laughter evaporated and I sobered at the realization that these moments would be too few and far between. How much time did I have left with her?

Days? Years? A decade? She was seventy-five and still acted like a younger woman. I could only hope that her youthfulness would give us many more years to catch up.

The cashier handed Grandma her bag and leaned over. "I can't wait to see you tonight," she whispered.

Grandma winked at her. "Me neither!"

I smiled at the cashier then took the cart from Grandma. I would enjoy today. Future Vera could make the harder decisions.

GRANDMA and I stared at the clump of dough in the bowl and then at each other. I tilted my head to the side. "I don't think that's supposed to look like that," I said slowly. "It's...uncomfortable looking." I held my breath, trying not to laugh.

She nodded slowly. "That is a very apt description." She blinked rapidly and sucked in her lips. Her phone had rung three times while we were mixing the cookie dough and somewhere along the line, one of us forgot to do something—most likely me because I was not a baker. I was a take-out-er.

I shook the bowl as if it would change the lumpy, unmixed dough to a perfectly smooth texture. Then I couldn't hold it in anymore. I put my head down on the table and started laughing. Grandma sat down next to me and joined in, dabbing at the edges of her eyes with a tissue. "I-It's like I've forgotten how to bake!"

I laughed harder. "That's l-like the Pope forgetting how to p-pray!"

We both looked at each other, made the sign of the cross the wrong way, and fell apart again. I leaned into my lap, covering my face with my hands and went silent. I couldn't breathe and my stomach hurt so bad, it was like I'd done ten-thousand ab curls.

Someone came through the front door, but I couldn't even bring myself to look up. Grandma just laughed harder.

"What is going on in here?" Gertie walked into the kitchen with her hands on her hips. "Did you light up and forget about your best friend?"

I managed to look up as Grandma pointed at the bowl then looked at me. A fresh wave of laughter washed over us. It really wasn't that funny, but for some reason it was. Gertie leaned over the table to peer in the bowl then looked back at the two of us before she joined in. "W-what did you do?"

"No idea," Grandma wheezed.

A knock at the back door startled us but just made us all laugh harder as a very confused Jack stepped in. "Dare I ask? I was just bringing over some gluten-free cookies for Edie and Joelle."

I took two deep breaths and waved my hands in front of my face. "C-c-cookies…"

He smiled, unable to resist, apparently. "Cookies?"

I nodded then shook my head. "Didn't work."

He leaned over the table to look in the bowl and then smoothed his hand over his face, trying to hide his smile. "Have you tried turning them off and then turning them back on again?"

Grandma, Gertie, and I went back into a laughing jag and I laid my head down on the table. The bowl disappeared. I shifted to watch Jack put the bowl into the microwave and hit a few buttons. We all stared, residual laughter bubbling up even as we tried to stay calm.

When the microwave beeped, he grabbed the mixing spoon and started folding the dough. When he finished, he set the bowl down with a flourish. The contents were magically smooth. "You forgot to melt the butter."

Apparently, our faces must have been picture worthy, because this time he threw his head back and laughed until he was wiping tears away from his eyes. Grandma excitedly started telling Gertie the story of how we failed to notice the butter wasn't melted.

I stood up and wrapped Jack in my arms. "You're my hero."

He was still chuckling and gave me a sweet kiss. "Spend the night tonight."

I just stood there, smiling like an idiot, as he walked out the back door, still under the Jack Spell™. I pressed my fingers to my lips and looked at my grandma and Gertie. Grandma pulled a twenty out of her pants with an expletive and handed it to Gertie.

I rolled my eyes. "Don't tell me. I don't want to know."

CHAPTER TWENTY

@GRENADINEUNOFFICIAL YOU KNOW WHAT AND YOU KNOW WHERE, TONIGHT AT FIVE. CREDIT CARDS ACCEPTED. BERNARD, REMEMBER TO TURN OFF YOUR HEARING AIDS.

THE LONGER THE party went on, the more I realized this was the social gathering of the month. The house was full of the ladies from Edie's Auto, several of Grandma's friends, Edie's older brother Jami, and Franky. Franky and Jami seemed to be there for the entertainment value, which I could appreciate. They kept the lemonade and iced tea flowing—it was a dry party because everyone had to work in the morning—while Grandma went over different external and internal toys.

At some point, the lube-tasting video was brought up on Grandma's smart TV—seriously her TV was better than mine—and I got to watch myself choke on fifty inches of screen. When Gertie pulled out sample packs of the crème brûlée, I ran out of the house and onto the porch, holding the screen door shut as Franky tried to shove a packet at me.

Everyone made five-dollar bets on who could swallow the nasty stuff and not make a face. "I am a survivor!" I yelled. "You can't make me go back to that dark place!" This just encouraged everyone to throw in and the pool got up to seventy-five dollars.

The reactions grew funnier each time. Table hitting, swearing, and watering eyes were the most common reaction. Gertie stumbled out the back door wheezing before pulling a flask out of her slacks pocket, guzzling whatever was inside. Grandma bowed her head and prayed for the Lord to take her. I had to go change my underwear after that one.

Rosa was the last to go. When she ripped open the packet, we started shouting, "Chug, chug, chug!" With a wink at me, she downed the sample while keeping a perfectly straight face. I was flabbergasted.

"Five seconds!" Chieka shouted, looking from the stopwatch app on her phone to Rosa's face. "Ten...fifteen seconds...thirty! Come on, *chica*, hold it, hold it...sixty seconds!" She raised Rosa's hand over her head like she'd just won a UFC fight. "Rosa takes home the pot!"

Rosa's composure broke and she grabbed for her lemonade, drinking it all down, nearly choking. Her eyes were still watering when she did a victory lap with the seventy-five dollars held high above her head.

I picked her up in a huge hug and swung her around. "How did you do that?!"

She laughed. "I have six siblings. They used to put shit in my food all the time. Can't show weakness."

I just shook my head, impressed. "You are a treasure."

Edie came up and grabbed her around the waist, spinning her around. "Yes!" she cried. "That was amazing."

Chieka came up and high-fived her before wrapping them in a group hug. There was so much sisterhood in their movements. Like they'd fight against the world for each other. It made me simultaneously wish to be included and wish to be home with Jas and Payton. Why couldn't I just pick up Grenadine and put it in California?

Then the doorbell rang, followed by a hard knock.

The celebrating went quiet as we all looked at the door. "Everyone knows to just walk in," Grandma said, confused. "Besides, it's almost seven."

She stood, but I waved her off. "I'll get it." I had a sinking feeling this wasn't a visitor. I opened the door to find Caden standing there in his police uniform, looking resigned. "Hi, Vera, I'm sorry to bother you. We got a call that there's underage drinking going on."

"Are you for real?" I asked, laughing. "The only things we're drinking are lemonade, iced tea, and lube."

A puzzled look crossed his face. "Is Grandma Bea here?"

"Grandma! Cops are here." The crowd went completely silent.

Grandma walked over to the door and held it open. "Well don't just stand there, Caden. Get in here and have some iced tea." Caden looked incredibly uncomfortable as he walked through the door.

I guessed it was the sex toys until I saw the look on Jami's face. Tamicka, who had come with the shop crew, grabbed the bowl of popcorn off the counter and stood there eating it, taking everything in. Rosa, Chieka, and Edie joined her, grabbing fistfuls.

Jami crossed his arms. "What are you doing here? It's girls' night with special guests Jami and Franky."

Caden looked between them. "I get why you're here" —he pointed at Jami— "because you're designated driver."

Edie held up her hand and waved. "Kristy and I pre-gamed, like a lot."

Tamicka snickered. "You're gonna love work tomorrow."

Edie threw a piece of popcorn at her and Tamicka caught it in her mouth.

Caden looked at Franky. "You're here voluntarily?"

"I was grandmothered in." Franky shrugged. "When Grandma wants you here, here you are. And there are cookies."

Edie raised her gluten-free cookie. "And Edie-safe cookies!"

"Made by Jack!" Gertie said. All the women *awww'd*. Desperation to keep him for myself slapped me across the face. I shook my head to clear it. So what if he made cookies and was incredibly thoughtful and smart and handsome and amazing in bed and—*Vera, focus.*

I walked over to Rosa and whispered, "Why is Jami so angry at Caden?"

"It's not angry so much as weird foreplay." She giggled. "They're still in the honeymoon stage of their relationship."

"Ah," I nodded. "Makes total sense." It was so very like Jack and me.

Caden cleared his throat, clearly incredibly uncomfortable. "I got a call that there was underage drinking at the party." He searched the room and winced. A good half of the occupants were collecting social security. "Which seems unlikely."

Rosa rolled her eyes and raised her hand. "I'm the only person under twenty-five in the room. I've had lemonade all night." She handed him her lemonade to sniff.

He opened his notes then looked up at her. "A neighbor heard the phrase 'chug, chug, chug' being shouted several times. Can you tell me about that?"

Jami grabbed the pile of lube samples. "We were betting on who could drink the crème brûlée lube and keep a straight face. Rosa won."

Caden looked between Jami and Rosa and then just shook his head. "Of course that's what you were doing," he muttered.

Grandma crossed her arms and tapped her foot. "Are you done harassing my guests now, Caden? You know that I don't serve alcohol at my toy parties. Who would be fool enough to make that call? I want to charge them with harassment and stalking."

"Ma'am," Caden started. "It was just a—"

"Don't *ma'am* me, young man." She shook her finger at him. "I sit in the pew in front of you every Sunday. Don't treat me like some common criminal from the big city. This isn't Chicago. We're all family here."

"Except the asshole who called the cops," Gertie added. "Neighbor, my ass. Virginia is right here!" Grandma's neighbor on the left waved. "Bernard across the street takes out his hearing aids so he can't hear us. That leaves who, Jack?"

Tamicka looked out the window. "You mean the Jack who has a

red sedan in his driveway?" She put another piece of popcorn in her mouth. "The same sedan that Edie just changed the brakes on."

"Aye, aye, captain!" Edie responded. "That's Aunt Pam's car."

Aunt Pam's car. Jack's mother had called the cops on the party. Her words from the grocery store swirled around my head and I saw red. In order to threaten me away from her son, she tried to implicate my grandmother in a crime? *Oh, I do not think so.*

Caden nodded and took a step back. "I'm sorry for interrupting. Obviously, there is no underage drinking here. Have a good night."

He turned to leave, but Edie cleared her throat. "Aren't you missing something there, Officer LeBlanc?"

He turned around to find Jami giving him a challenging look. Caden took a deep breath, walked back to Jami, and gave him the sweetest kiss. Everyone swooned a little, even me, and I was ready to make heads roll. "See you after work, babe," Caden said and then left.

Franky and Jami exchanged fist bumps.

Rosa fell into her chair, laughing.

But Tamicka's eyes were glued to me as if she knew I was fifteen seconds from losing my damn mind. Then I saw Pam looking over at us through Jack's window and I snapped.

Franky tried to stop me, but I had crossed over into the red zone. "Too late," Grandma warned. "She's ready to blow."

"Get it, girl!" Tamicka shouted.

Chieka walked fast behind me, a wicked smile on her face. "Yes!" she cheered.

I jumped off the porch, not bothering with the stairs, and stomped over to Jack's house. I banged on the door so hard it shook. It swung open and a startled Jack caught my arm in midair as I prepared for another round of knocks. "Are you okay? What's wrong?" He gave me a once-over and then stepped outside, shutting the door most of the way behind him. "Why do you have inferno eyes right now?"

"Caden LeBlanc was just at my door. Do you know why?"

He looked over at the house. "Is Grandma Bea okay?"

"Yes, of course." I waved him off. "It was because one of the *neighbors* called him because they were *concerned* there was *underage drinking*."

He frowned. "But everyone knows that Grandma Bea doesn't serve alcohol. Especially on a weeknight."

"Yeah, yet somehow Caden still showed up. Weird, right?"

Jack shrugged. "I don't know who would've called him. Virginia is a staple at the parties and Bernard takes his hearing aids out. That leaves me, and I didn't call him."

I crossed my arms. "But you're not alone in your house tonight, are you?"

He stepped toward me, closing the distance between us. "What exactly are you suggesting?"

"Your mother despises me, Jack. She had some things to say to me today in the grocery store."

"She doesn't despise you. She's just worried, is all." He rubbed the back of his neck. "She wouldn't do something like that."

"Really? Because after the shit she said to me…"

He frowned again. "What did she say to you?" His eyes searched my face and I deflated.

I didn't want to be the reason he and his mom got into a fight. "She just wants me to stay away from you, is all."

Jack put his hands on my shoulders and rubbed my upper arms. "Princess, she has a right to be worried. But I'm not going to go blame her for something she wouldn't do."

I let my arms uncross and hang at my sides. "Then who did, Jack? Who did? This was an intentional move to hurt Grandma and me and embarrass the women in there!" I gestured to the house. To be fair, no one seemed all that embarrassed. "There's only one way to solve this."

"I agree."

It seemed, however, Jack and I had different ideas on what that one way was. As I pushed open his front door to barge in and confront his mother, he wrapped me in his arms to kiss me. That's when Jack's mom screamed.

Jack pulled away and looked around, trying to figure out what was going on. His eyes landed on his mother who was crying into his father, Morris's, shirt. "Mom? What's wrong?"

"I can't believe you would hurt me like this," she wailed.

"Like...what?" Jack asked, genuinely confused.

She pointed at me, going from devastated to vicious in two seconds. "You, carrying on with that whore! I asked you to find a nice church girl and instead you find one that makes her living on her back! Even worse, it's *her*."

"It's a pretty good living, actually," I countered. "I made about a million last year alone." Morris, at least, looked impressed. Jack was still trying to catch up. I stepped over the threshold, but still stood in the entryway. "Pam, I get that we have our differences. A lot of them. So many, *many* differences."

"We get the point," Jack mumbled.

"But," I continued. "If you ever call the cops on my grandmother again, I will have my legal team serve you with stalking and harassment charges, so help me."

Jack looked between me and his still-blubbering mother. She would've been a natural in Hollywood. He pointed at me, ready to fight, but something about my face made him pause. He turned toward his parents. "Mom, did you call the cops on Grandma Bea?"

His mother nodded. "Of course I did." Jack looked like his mom had slapped him. "You know they were drinking and selling that garbage! No one in their right mind would buy something from that woman if they were sober."

Jack ran his hand through his hair. "I love you, Mom, but that was not okay."

"Jacky boy, watch your tone," Morris warned. "Your mother did what she thought was right."

Jack shook his head. "No, Dad, she did what she thought would hurt." He pinched the bridge of his nose for a beat and then looked straight at his mother. "If you ever do something like that again without talking to me first while you are in *my house*, you will not be invited back again." His voice was deep and steady, the cadence of a man who was calm and collected in emergency situations.

Morris looked affronted. "Now Jacky, you don't mean that."

Jack crossed his arms. "Unless there is an actual emergency and you need to call 9-1-1 to save a life, I absolutely do mean that. Grandma Bea is a wonderful neighbor. She is constantly sharing her food and her home with me, and she takes care of Taco. You will not, I repeat *not*, ever use my house to harass her or her family. And Vera is part of my life again. End. Of. Story. Are we clear?"

"Jacky—" Pam pleaded.

"Are. We. Clear?" he asked, each word sharp enough to cut. Both his parents nodded. "Good. You can get your things and go. I don't want to deal with you anymore tonight."

Pam took a step toward her son, all of her tears magically gone. "I was just trying to make sure the community was safe, dear."

"No, you weren't." He reached down and grabbed my hand. "You were trying to one-up Vera and push us apart. Guess what, Mom? You just did the opposite, on both accounts." He started pulling me out the door. "You can let yourselves out."

He led me down his front steps and across the yard to where fifteen people were crammed outside on Grandma's porch, eating from the mostly empty bowl of popcorn. "Fucking small-town-itis," Jack grumbled.

"I told you so," I whispered back.

With whistles and "look at the time" comments, everyone dispersed back into the house. Jack and I stood at the bottom of the steps and he gave me a really tight hug. "I'm sorry I questioned you."

"I would've questioned me too, I suppose," I admitted. "I'm sorry about what happened."

He released me and gave me a soft kiss. "I'm going to go for a drive to clear my head."

I cupped his face. "You okay?"

He nodded once. "Yeah. I will be. Just need some windows down and some music up." He grabbed my hand from his face and squeezed. "Listen, I just want to be alone tonight. Can we just start fresh again tomorrow?"

My stomach fell, but I kept my smile in place. "Of course." I gave him a soft kiss before stepping back and releasing his hand. "I'll see you tomorrow."

With a nod, he turned and walked away, taking my heart with him.

CHAPTER TWENTY-ONE

MOM'S BUCKET LIST #71: TELL MY DAUGHTER I LOVE HER EVERY DAY

WHOEVER WAS RINGING the doorbell had a death wish. Cleanup had taken forever—seriously, lube gets on everything and is so sticky—and I hadn't been able to shut off my brain until about three this morning. It was only 7:30. "Go away!" I mumbled, turning onto my stomach and pulling the pillow over my head.

The ringing blessedly stopped, and I slowly drifted back onto the verge of sleep. Then the knocking started at my bedroom door. I bolted upright and screamed, tripping over my sheets and tangling my arms in my long T-shirt. The door opened and Jack poked his head in. "Calm down, it's just me."

I was panting on the ground, adrenaline burning through me. "You're an asshole. Have you ever heard of a phone?"

He gave me a look. "You didn't answer your phone or the door and Grandma Bea is at her Women's League breakfast. I decided to just use my key."

I pushed my tangled mess of hair off my forehead. "Why are you trying to break in so early?" Except that I was whiny, and it sounded more like "eaaaaaaarly."

"Come to the kitchen and find out."

"Come to the kitchen and find out," I mocked.

He just laughed and started walking away. "I forgot how much of a morning person you aren't."

Without bothering to look in the mirror, I twisted my hair into a giant bun on top of my head and pulled on a pair of shorts. With a yawn so huge my jaw cracked, I made my way to the bathroom to wash my face and brush my teeth. Once I felt more like a human than a dead thing, I trudged into the kitchen and stopped.

I rubbed my eyes, pretty sure I was hallucinating. Jack had set the table with a fancy white tablecloth, white china plates, and crystal glasses. There was a colorful bouquet of sunflowers in the center of the table. I blinked at the table, then him, then the table again.

"You still needed to cross 'eating breakfast at Grenadine Manor' off the list. I figured you wouldn't enjoy being around Mrs. Simons after she was terrible to you, so I brought it to you." He gestured to the table. "This is totally their table setting though, and I promised we'd bring it back intact. So we have to eat carefully."

I was not going to cry. I was *not* going to cry. Dammit. I loved this man. L-O-V-E-D him.

I put my palm over my mouth so I didn't do something stupid, like say that out loud. Instead, I nodded and took my seat at the table.

The breakfast feast was in disposable aluminum containers, but everything was still warm and not soggy. He had to speed all the way here. We dined on French toast, waffle squares, poached eggs over salad greens with balsamic glaze, fried potatoes, and fruit salad. We drank fresh-squeezed orange juice and cucumber water.

I ate until I couldn't move, and we still had leftovers. "How did you do all this?" I wanted to ask why, but I didn't have the guts.

He gave me a huge smile. "I called them and threatened to tell the Grenadine Herald all about the time they kicked you out of their B&B even though you just wanted to follow your late mother's last wishes."

I gasped. "You didn't!"

He shrugged. "Maybe I did, maybe I didn't. But fuck anyone

who's going to treat you like shit." He reached out and grabbed my hand. "You and me against the world, remember?"

I squeezed. "Yeah." Neither of us mentioned the giant elephant that was sitting at the table with us...the fact that I was leaving in six days. "So, what are we going to do today? Do you work?"

He laughed softly and looked down, as if embarrassed. "I, uh, took a vacation day. We are going to do as many things on your mom's list as possible."

"Seriously?" I whispered.

He nodded. "Completely. Get dressed and grab the list. I'll clean up. We can drop off the dishes during our marathon."

I practically ran to my room, all my exhaustion pushed out of the way by excitement. I put on stretch jeans, sneakers, and one of my #SayYesToConsent T-shirts. With an application of tinted sunscreen, mascara, and lip gloss, I was ready to go. I quickly braided my hair, grabbed a hoodie and bounced my way all the way to Jack's truck.

"Read them off to me," he said, backing out of the driveway and turning toward town. I opened the journal to the list and started reading as he slipped his hand into mine.

"Go zip-lining, release a floating lantern, have a picnic in the Grenadine gazebo," I cringed. "So many food things."

He laughed. "We'll wait a few hours on those."

"Be nominated Cherry Queen for the Founder's Day Festival, add a heart to the bridge, and play trumpet with the Grenadine Marching Band." I rescanned the list. "That's everything that happens locally."

Jack nodded. "We can work with that. Although it's too early to run for Cherry Queen." He kissed the back of my hand. "I'll make you the paper crown, though."

I laughed. "You're ridiculous."

We pulled up to the B&B and gave them the middle finger, then laughed. Jack pulled out a pen from the center console and handed it to me. "You can mark off breakfast." He leaned over and gave me a kiss that I turned into something heated. He pulled away and cleared his throat. "I have to walk into a public establishment. Hold that thought." He readjusted himself and climbed out of the driver's seat.

I snorted and sighed, my eyes never leaving his retreating form. There was a small corner of my brain throwing out questions I couldn't answer. *How can you leave him behind again? Why do you have to choose between your work dream and life dream? His family hates you. Don't you think you're better off alone?*

I turned on Jack's radio and connected it to my phone. Scrolling through my streaming playlist, I played one of my favorite songs and started dancing and headbanging in the truck, not giving a single fuck what passersby thought. Today was going to be awesome and my brain could ask me those ugly questions tomorrow.

Jack was already laughing when he climbed back in. I looked up at him and smiled. He leaned into me, digging his hands into my hair and kissing me senseless. All of the air evaporated from my lungs as he deepened the kiss and let his fingers trail down my neck. I was ready to climb into his lap, despite being downtown and in public, when he pulled back.

His eyes were blazing as he licked his bottom lip. I let out an audible moan. "Forget the list. Let's find another field," I breathed.

"You make it impossible not to fall in love with you," he admitted quietly. He shook his head and pulled back, turning to his steering wheel. "Come on. We've got work to do." As he maneuvered out of the parallel parking space and merged with traffic, I just stared at him.

You make it impossible not to fall in love with you.

Did that mean he was in love with me?! I bit my lip and pulled out my phone but realized I didn't want to text Jas and Payton. I didn't want them to know how in over my head I had gotten. If I admitted having feelings for Jack, the questions about what my plans were would ramp up by tenfold.

I opened a text to Franky. **I think Jack just admitted he loved me...**

Franky: What did you say back?

Me: Nothing?

Franky: *selfie of his hand over his face*

Franky: I...okay. Start from the beginning.

I looked over at Jack who was smirking at me. "Instead of texting Franky, wait about forty-five seconds. We're stopping for coffee. I can't face teenagers without coffee and Franky's is ten times better than the B&B's."

My face was on fire. How did this man know me so well? "Coffee sounds great!" I said way over enthusiastically. I needed help.

We pulled in front of Barwell Bakery and I jumped out before the truck was off. Jack let me run ahead into the bakery. Franky disengaged from a customer and walked over to meet me at the edge of the counter. "He's right behind you, isn't he?" he chuckled.

"Shut up!" I whisper-yelled. "He told me I was impossible not to fall in love with and now we're spending the day doing things on Mom's bucket list and I'm freaking out!"

He nodded seriously as Jack walked in, waved, and then walked to greet a group of people he knew. I gestured toward him. "And he's perfect."

"Uh-huh," Franky said, clearly trying not to laugh. "That man has been in love with you his entire life. You are the love of his life. The sooner you admit he's the love of yours, the sooner it will all fall into place."

I just stared at him. "Come again?"

"Which part of that was confusing?"

"I cannot be in love with him!" I hissed. "I'm leaving in less than a week."

Franky rolled his eyes. "Dreams change, Ra-Ra. Did I think I was going to be running a bakery? No. I thought I was going to be the bassist in a band touring the world. But I wouldn't change a damn thing."

"That's your solution? Because my solution is to go back to SoCal and come back for holidays."

He put his hands on my shoulders and gave me a friendly shake. "You are overwhelmed, and I respect that. But today is all about you and your mom's list. Make this decision on another day." He narrowed his eyes. *"On another day,"* he repeated with emphasis. "Mom said worrying about tomorrow means you'll miss out on what's special today."

I bit my lip. "Your mom was wise."

He nodded. "Yes, she was."

I let out a deep breath. "Okay. Yes. Focus."

He smiled. "Let's start over. Vera, get coffee. Go spend the day with Jack. Trust yourself to figure it out."

He kissed my forehead and walked behind the counter to make me coffee. Jack came up and wrapped his arm around my waist. "Freak out better?"

I shrugged. "I mean, I guess."

He chuckled low, leaning down to whisper, "You're my favorite."

Franky just started laughing at whatever look crossed my face. "You both are my favorite."

Goddamn best friends.

I DID NOT EXPECT how hard it would be to blow a trumpet. It was...not the most embarrassing thing I've ever done, but let's just say it would give the crème brûlée a run for its money. But the high school band was excited to meet the football player who'd brought state-wide support for the band even years later, and even more to meet an IRL porn star, and so my terrible trumpet playing was counted as a win.

Quite frankly, I was surprised they even let me, a porn star, near the high school. But by mid-morning, everyone had started talking about Mom's list. In fact, our old art teacher, Mrs. Lyons, came by the band room and said she had something to show us.

I stared at Jack quizzically. "I may have tagged you in a social media post and also told your grandma. And Gertie."

"So basically, the governor knows by now."

He nodded and gripped my hand. "Yeah, expect a call of encouragement soon."

Mrs. Lyons took us down the art hallway where a watercolor landscape hung, with a plaque that said "In loving memory of Lauren Tompson (Eastman). Class of '76."

Unlike breakfast, this time I did cry.

Mrs. Lyons squeezed my shoulder. "Your dad made a donation to keep that on the wall and add a plaque. I just wanted to make sure you saw it." Some mixture of anger and sadness washed over me. I wanted to hate my father for what he did, for not being brave enough to even talk to me. But in moments like this, my chest ached with the need to be near him again. To dance while standing on top of his feet and watch home improvement shows together.

Jack took a picture of me with the painting and then gave me a huge hug. "Come on. We've got ice cream to eat."

I gripped my still full stomach but started walking with him. "There's always room for ice cream."

IT WAS BECOMING VERY apparent that nothing about the day was actually spontaneous. I didn't know how or when he'd done all of it, but when we walked into Mr. Moo's Ice Cream Parlor, there was a table set up with a "reserved" sign. At an ice cream parlor on a random Thursday at eleven thirty in the morning. On the cow-printed stool, there was a paper imitation of the Cherry Queen crown.

Jack pulled out the stool and placed the crown on my head,

giving me a kiss on the cheek, before sitting down across from me. A cheerful, college-age girl bounced over and set two bottled waters down in front of us. "Your sample spread will be out in one moment, your majesty!"

I just shook my head at Jack and smiled. "I don't know how you did all of this."

He shrugged. "Small town. People care."

A few minutes later, giant platters filled with twenty-five miniature scoops of ice cream were set on the table. I stared at the dessert then stared at Jack. "Holy shit. We're going to die."

He shrugged. "Probably. But it'll be worth it." He picked up his spoon and stood. "But we're not eating here."

I frowned at him. "We're not eating here?" I looked around like he was crazy.

He shook his head and smiled. "Nope. We're eating there." He used his spoon to point to the Grenadine gazebo next door to the shop. "Come on."

We walked out of the shop and over to the gazebo, which had a card table set up with two padded folding chairs. We sat down and talked only of ice cream for the next half hour, as if we were afraid to break the spell. Cookie Monster—a blue ice cream filled with a variety of cookie crumbs—was obviously my favorite and lemon lavender was Jack's.

While several groups of people walked by and waved, no one approached to interrupt. When we were finished, Jack reached over and cupped my hand. "Now that we've eaten enough dairy to actually turn into cows, let's take a walk and then get in the car. We have about a forty-five-minute drive to get to the zip-lining place, and we need to be there by two."

I rubbed my stomach. "Shouldn't we have eaten ice cream after?"

He laughed. "Yeah, but this was a bit more impromptu than I care to admit, so I'm working with what I got."

I frowned, uncertainty rushing over me. "Does this have anything to do with the fact that you feel guilty about your mom not liking me?"

He made a face. "No. It was something I was thinking about doing before that."

I smiled, sheepishly. "Okay, good."

He leaned over for a soft kiss.

ZIP-LINING WAS ABSOLUTELY TERRIFYING, and I couldn't wait to go again. Nothing compared to flying through the trees from a small, suspended wire.

Also, watching Jack's body flex as he made his way from platform to platform was making me crazy. I needed to get my mouth and hands all over him. We barely made it into his truck before I kissed him so hard my head was spinning. He pushed us apart, panting. "Wait, wait, wait," he breathed.

I gave an exaggerated sob and leaned back in my seat. "You're mean."

He laughed. "And we're in public." He ran a hand down his face. "Don't worry. Tonight, I'm all yours." His pupils grew wider as we stared at each other.

"Promise?" I whispered, running my hand from my neck, over my breast, and across my thigh.

He closed his eyes and put his head on the steering wheel. "*That* was mean."

I laughed and bumped his shoulder. "Sorry not sorry. But really, what's next on the adventure list?"

He started the truck and drove back to the highway. I put my hand on his leg and he covered it with his. "We've got a bridge to go defile, a biodegradable lantern to release, and dinner."

"And then naked time."

He laughed. "Yeah, horny eyes. Naked time."

My phone buzzed and I read the text.

Grandma: Going to a hoedown then sleeping over at Gertie's. Love you! *kiss emoji* *heart emoji* *winky face emoji* *heart eye emoji* *cowboy hat smiley emoji*

I looked at Jack. "You taught my grandma how to use emojis, didn't you?"

He smiled. "Absolutely. She sends the best texts."

I bit my lip, overwhelmed with emotions. "Thank you for taking care of her when I went rogue."

He kissed my hand. "Always."

I answered Grandma with a string of my favorite emojis and then turned to face Jack. "Is that why you moved next door? To take care of her?"

His thumb ran over my knuckles. "That was a definite perk." He negotiated around a merging semi-truck and gave me a quick glance before refocusing on the road. "I could tell you some story about property values, low turnover in the area, and so on. But now that I think about it, I think that having some connection to you, no matter how small, is what made that house feel like home as soon as I walked in. I had the bid ready before the tour was over."

"Jack..." What did I say to that?

"That wasn't the only reason," he defended. "That makes me sound like an insane person who was waiting for someone who might never come back. But when you lose someone important to you, whether from relocation or death or whatever, you start making decisions differently. It changes you. Your leaving changed me permanently, just like it changed you."

I laughed, although what he was saying wasn't funny. "Ain't that the truth."

"You have my word that I'll always take care of Grandma Bea. Don't let that be a factor in your decision. And I can always come out to Cali for long weekends."

I squeezed his hand and refocused on the road. Long-distance relationships were hard. But one without an end date? Even worse. Jack said he was okay with me continuing in porn, but was I?

I didn't date outside the industry because it was too hard. There was always jealousy that led to resentment. After spending a week having sex on camera, I didn't always want to do it when I got home. And how would Jack feel if I was off having sex all day while he was home waiting for me to Skype at night? Sure, we could be in an open relationship, but that wasn't Jack's style.

There was so much more to unpack here than just the distance. So many decisions I needed to figure out for myself. I ran my hand through my hair and sighed.

"I can hear you freaking out." Jack glanced at me. "Talk to me."

I shook my head. "Later. Today is for us." I took a deep breath and pushed all the thoughts away.

"For us," he agreed.

CHAPTER TWENTY-TWO

GRENADINE LEGEND: LOVERS WHO WRITE THEIR NAMES INSIDE THE GRAFFITIED HEARTS ON THE GRENADINE BRIDGE SHALL BE FOREVER BOUND IN LOVE. OR GO TO JAIL FOR DEFILING A MONUMENT.

AFTER WRITING our initials inside a painted heart on the old stone bridge on the edge of Grenadine, we went to an early dinner at Ray's. Unlike the last time I was there, we practically held court, like the Grenadine royalty we used to be back in high school. I snuck one over on Jack and slipped Celine my credit card to pay for everyone's meal in the restaurant, which was on my own bucket list.

As the sun set, we released a biodegradable lantern in his backyard, and he kissed me slow and deep as it floated away. That kiss turned the smoldering heat into a raging inferno. We stumbled toward Grandma's house and as soon as the back door closed, Jack pulled my legs around his waist and a strangled moan came from my throat when I felt how hard he already was. He carried us to my room and shut the door, pressing me against it, and pressing himself into me.

"I watched the video you posted," he growled. "Watching you pleasure yourself in this room? I nearly lost my mind."

His lips moved to the sensitive spot beneath my jaw and down my neck. I was already panting, and we had barely started. "Well, I still have that toy," I promised. "In case you wanted an in-person demonstration." He thrust against me as confirmation. We moved against each other for a few more moments, every inch of my skin heating. Setting my legs down on the floor, I immediately fell to my knees and put my hands on his belt. "Take off your shirt."

"That's not how I want you," he said before I unzipped his pants.

I looked up at him through my eyelashes, giving him the Vera Look™. "But it's how I want you."

He groaned and took off his shirt, putting his hand on the door to steady himself. I pulled down the waistband of his boxers and took him in my hand. He was hot and heavy, and a thrill went through my body from my hairline to my toes. The last time I had given him a blowjob, I was a fumbling eighteen-year-old. Now, I was a professional—I had won an AVN award for Best Blowjob Scene last year and Best Oral Sex Movie four years ago—and I couldn't wait to make him lose control.

I started out slowly, short hand movements and licking lightly. Then I pulled him as deep into my mouth as I could without deep throating. He moaned my name and gripped the back of my head with one hand, letting me set a lazy pace. I ran my fingers over his ass, then between his legs to the sensitive area he liked touched. He shook a little as I played with him, tongue and fingers caressing his length and cupping him.

"Vera," he pleaded. "I need to touch you."

I pulled him out of my mouth with a pop. "You're about to touch the back of my throat." When he groaned, I did my magic. I deep throated him in one move, licking his scrotum as I bobbed over him. The sound he made almost made me come right here. His abs flexed and I ran my nails down them, wanted to bite them and lick them.

I smiled as he fell hard against the door and fisted his hands in my hair. He started fucking my mouth and my eyes started watering. This was my new favorite memory of Jack— watching him lose control. I moaned and the vibration made him jerk harder. I gripped his ass and hummed again, looking right into his eyes.

He detonated with a hoarse cry as I swallowed him down. His

entire body tensed, his legs shaking with the effort of holding himself up. He was breathing like he had just run a marathon. "Vera," he whispered reverently before letting out a stream of profanity. "You're amazing."

I licked my lips and smiled. He bent down and kissed me hard, wrapping his arms around my shoulders and lifting me until I was pressed against him. "My turn," he promised.

My entire body throbbed in anticipation. I couldn't remember the last time I was this excited to have sex with someone. Sure, I was excited to work with some actors and shoot some scenes, but this wasn't a performance. This was just us, sharing and giving pleasure.

He picked me up and carried me to the bed, a bit awkwardly since his pants were still around his knees. "Undress," he ordered.

I pulled off my clothes so fast I heard the seams protest. I didn't care; I knew how to sew. Then I lay back on the bed, my legs spread. He wasn't fully hard again yet, but I had no doubt I could get him there. He finished taking off his clothes then looked around, grabbing a towel from the top of the dresser. "We're going to make a mess."

"Promise?" My voice came out breathless, my heart doing a somersault in excitement.

He gave me a wicked smile. "Oh, I promise." He laid the towel on the bed, grabbing my ankles in one hand and lifting me straight up so he could lay it under me. The brute strength made me shiver in excitement. "Where's that toy?"

He dragged his fingers from my ankle to my upper thigh and I gasped. "Top left." He pulled away and went to the drawer of the dresser, pulling out the toy and the bottle of lube. Watching him handle my toy was the sexiest thing I had ever seen. He tested it to make sure it had batteries—I had left them in after the shoot—and then brought the lube and the toy over to the nightstand.

He climbed on the bed, hovering over me but not touching. His shoulders and biceps flexed with the effort and I bit my lip to keep from crying out. I needed him. "We're about to play the 'how many times can Vera come' game," he whispered in my ear.

This time I didn't hold back the sound. He smiled and kissed me behind my ear. "I want to come inside of you, every hole." He put his weight on one hand and trailed his fingers over my hip. We had tried anal sex before, but I had a feeling tonight was going to be very, very different now that we both knew what we were doing.

I searched his eyes and nodded. Anal wasn't my favorite thing to shoot—really who liked enemas?—and I had added it to my "No List" a few years ago. I was successful enough without adding the extra wear on my body.

But I was desperate to do it with Jack, to have him so intimately connected to me. "Please," I begged. "Please."

He captured my lips with his and lowered his weight against me, every part of our bodies touching. His cock moved against my opening and I cried out, needing him to push inside. "You're so wet," he said against my skin. "I could take you right now with just a tilt of my hips." He rotated his hips and pushed in just a few inches and then pulled back out. I clawed at his back. "But I think I'll wait."

I nearly cried as my abdomen clenched at the emptiness. He gave me one more kiss then sat up, putting my legs over his shoulder and sealing his mouth over my clit in one smooth movement. I shoved my fingers into his hair, pulling it, as he used the flat of his tongue to taste me. He moved his head back and forth and I pushed into him.

It was raw and desperate, both of us trying to get me to my first orgasm of the night. It didn't take long. The pleasure burst through me. "I'm coming, I'm coming, don't stop," I begged, barely above a whisper. He didn't stop. He eased up but kept licking, tasting, and savoring.

I was limp and a little bit sweaty. Honestly, I could've been done for the night and just stayed in his arms. But Jack had different plans. He gripped my hips and flipped me over, taking his time kissing me from the back of my neck and all the way down my spine to my butt. He kneaded, bit, and kissed my cheeks and the fire in my body grew from a smolder to a bonfire. "I love this ass. I want to make love to this ass."

I couldn't do much more than say please a few times. He lubed his fingers and slowly ran them over my tight opening before pushing in the first one and then the second. Just from his prep, I was pulling at the sheets. When he added a third finger, I grabbed the lube off the nightstand and shoved it at him. "Hurry," I ordered.

"Move over." I flipped over and moved to the side. He lay down on the bed and coated his very hard length in lube. I couldn't look away. Every part of him was perfect.

His cheeks and neck were growing red with need, an image I would never forget as long as I lived. I loved the way he wore his desire on his skin. I loved the way I could still make it happen.

I loved him.

I swallowed down the words, wanting to wait to tell him sometime other than when we were about to have sex. That was way too cliché. But when he looked up at me, his eyes softened, like he could read it on my face. *Dammit.* He knew me too well.

"Come here."

I obeyed. Slowly, crouched over him and facing away, I took him inside of me. I almost had an orgasm right then. I forgot how much I loved this position.

He helped me lie down so my back was against his chest and I was the happiest I had been in years. He was all around me, everywhere. His heart and my heart were racing together as he kissed my neck and shoulders. His hands played with my breasts and skated over my body with loving touches.

He moved slowly, purposefully, as if we had all the time in the world. This buzzing filled me, this feeling of being loved and cherished and needed climbing into my soul. Our skin was growing sweaty, but I didn't care. I never wanted this moment to end.

Our legs tangled and his arms held me tight as he coaxed another orgasm from me. "I want you like this forever," he whispered against my neck. "Mine. My Vera. My beautiful, amazing Vera."

"My Jack," I managed. He thrust harder in response and I bowed off the bed with a spike of pleasure.

Then he stilled and reached over to the nightstand, grabbing the toy. He put a thin layer of lube on it, then handed the toy to me. "You up for using this, too?"

I shuddered hard, excited. "Yes." I took the toy from him and he opened our legs, pushing in a little deeper. I was starting to shake from all the feelings swirling inside of me, and he had to help guide my hand. Slowly, so slowly, I pushed the toy inside. The feeling of Jack behind me, the toy in front of me, and external vibration on my clit was overwhelming. My breathing grew shallow in anticipation. I was so full, so ready.

"Turn it on," he ordered, his voice so gravelly and deep I felt it to my soul.

I flipped the switch. We both cried out loudly. "Oh God, it's too much," I cried, but still moved the vibrator in and out, pleasuring myself. He started to move in and out of me, opposite my thrusts, and my vision blurred. Never had anything felt as intimate and special as this moment.

A strangling, desperate wave of pleasure crashed over me, then another one on its heels. Jack grew rougher with his thrusts, his touches. He bit my shoulder and gripped my breasts in his large hands. It was everything. "More," I sobbed. "Harder."

Three, four, five more orgasms, until they were nearly continuous. Tears were rolling down my face and I was sobbing. My hand was shaking too bad to continue holding the toy. Jack took it out of my hand and laid it down on the towel before pulling out of me. I cried out in protest, but he shushed me and kissed me sweetly.

He climbed over me, putting a pillow under the towel and under my hips, then centered himself between my legs. He thrust again into my backside and leaned down to kiss me, long and sweet. He moved slowly, languidly, my body still on fire everywhere, but I was finally able to catch my breath.

My eyes flew open when I heard the vibrator turn on again. Keeping his eyes locked on mine, he placed the toy at my entrance and pushed in. I arched off the bed. "Do you want to keep coming?"

he asked. "Because if you say yes, you're going to keep coming until I come."

I nodded so hard my neck hurt. "Yes, please," I choked.

He kissed me hard then nipped my bottom lip. "Good."

Then he fucked me. I came again, then again. The pleasure was burning on the knife edge of pain, as he and the toy moved inside of me. I couldn't tell when one orgasm ended and the next one started. I was lost on this plane of pleasure, even as he shoved the toy aside, gripped me hard, and came inside of me, with a cry of my name that echoed around my room.

He pulled out and collapsed beside me, scooping me into his arms. His fingers trailed over every inch of my skin that he could reach, his lips leaving small kisses over my face and hair. "You are the best thing in my life," he whispered as I fell over the edge of sleep.

I WOKE up to being lifted off the bed. I snuggled into Jack's chest as he carried us to the bathroom and stepped into the filled tub. The water was warm enough to sting, but it felt soothing. He settled me between his legs, and I laid back against his chest.

He used soap and a soft washcloth to clean us both as we kissed languidly. The water helped loosen my sore muscles and I knew I could sleep for two days now. When we were done, he dried us both off and took me back to bed, wrapping himself around me.

I threaded my fingers through his. "Jack?" I whispered. He kissed the back of my neck in response. "I love you."

I felt his smile and it made my heart flutter. "Love you too."

I turned over to face him. "What are we going to do?"

His hand cupped my cheek, his thumb brushing over my lips. His eyes met mine, searching them in the hint of moonlight coming through the curtains. "We'll figure it out. One day at a time. I've waited eleven years to find you again. I can wait a few more."

We kissed each other until we fell asleep, our foreheads touching.

CHAPTER TWENTY-THREE

TODAY'S PICTURE-A-DAY PHOTO: JACK, SHIRTLESS AND LAUGHING

JACK LEFT to get ready for work after a late breakfast. We kissed at the back door until he was nearly late for his shift, unwilling to let the other one go. I watched him pull out of the driveway like a crazy person.

I loved him.

Dammit.

I took a long soak in the tub again to relieve my sore muscles—even veteran porn stars got sore after incredible, marathon sex—and then checked my email to find the new web design drafts I had received for both Happy Endings and Edie's Auto. I bookmarked the Happy Endings site to show Grandma later, then forwarded Edie's Auto to Tamicka for her to get approval.

After firing off a few emails, I did the dishes, changed my sheets, and started a load of laundry, then cleaned the bathroom and the tub.

Nothing made me more productive than avoiding a problem.

Grandma walked in as I finished mopping the floor, a red cowboy hat on her head and an obvious stiffness in her back. I ran over to help her, but she waved me off. "I'm fine. Just too much dancing. I'm going to go take a bath and read a book. We can catch up over dinner."

As the morning dragged on, I grew restless. Yesterday had been one of the best days of my life. Now, I was jittery and agitated. I needed to make decisions and I wasn't sure where to begin. I thought about going to the bakery, but I didn't want to talk. I also didn't need any more sugar or caffeine.

What I needed was a run.

I stretched for double the amount of time I usually did. It had been several weeks since I'd run a few miles, and yesterday had been pretty taxing, but I was going to give it a try. Nothing else had worked so far. When I was ready to go, I stuffed my phone into an armband, put on my wireless headphones, and cranked the eighties music. With "Never" by Moving Picture blasting, I imagined I was Kevin Bacon in Footloose and took off...but without the dance moves.

I pushed myself hard.

Sweat pooled on the back of my knees and down my neck, but I just ran faster. My hips were screaming, but I didn't pay attention to them. I needed to run until I cleared my head.

I thought I knew my heart. It was building a feminist, sex-positive porn company. It was launching my #SayYesToConsent clothing line and working with my best friends. It was creating movies that would stand up to the quality of what was coming out of Hollywood, just with more sex. It was working with foundations that made a difference in the world. It was living the life I wanted in a way my mother couldn't. It was being unapologetically me.

But now my dreams were morphing into something new I didn't understand. Going back to live in my condo alone where I didn't know my neighbors seemed foreign. I was exhausted at the thought of waking up at dawn to prep for a twelve-hour shoot. I wanted to sit in foundation meetings, but I also wanted to screw up baking cookies with Grandma. I loved having sex on camera, but I also wanted to come home to Jack every night and make love until we fell deeper into each other.

Why did it have to be one or the other?

I stopped running, bending at the waist and breathing hard. My midsection was burning. Maybe I had overdone it. I took several deep breaths, trying to get enough oxygen.

I'll figure it out, I promised myself. Either way, I had to go back to SoCal. Some space would help me get my head on straight. Maybe I wouldn't even miss this place when I left.

I didn't believe that for a second.

I had just started walking back to the house when a fire engine turned the corner and zoomed by me, lights and sirens blaring. I stood there in shock. When was the last time there had been a fire in Grenadine? Surely they were just testing out the engine. I watched as it approached the intersection ahead and waited for it to turn right, heading back to the station.

"Please don't turn left, please don't turn left, please don't turn left..."

It turned left.

I took off at a dead run.

I dodged a woman walking a dog and a man pushing a twin stroller. I knew I could be overreacting, but something in my gut told me that I needed to get home. My cell started vibrating and I clicked the headset button to pick up the call, but nothing happened. Stupid headset.

I wasn't about to stop and check my phone.

I rounded the corner to Grandma's street and yelled at a group of women who were standing and chatting to "move their damn asses." I ignored their comments about rudeness as I shoved through them.

The fire engine was in front of Grandma's house, but I couldn't see smoke rising into the sky. I pushed my way through the organized chaos, dead set on walking through the front door and finding Grandma when Michael came out of the house and picked me up like I weighed nothing.

"She's right here, sweetheart. She's okay," he promised, dropping me off at the ambulance where Grandma sat getting examined by Sharon. "Jack's okay, too. Taco and Waffles were on the back porch. They're safe and sound at Jack's house."

I sank down in front of Grandma and grabbed her hands. "You're really alright?"

She pulled the oxygen mask off her face and waved me away. "I'm completely fine. I lit one of those fancy ass candles we got at the store and the damn thing caught the shower curtain on fire."

I looked up at Sharon. "If she's okay, why is she on oxygen?"

Sharon smiled. "It's a breathing treatment. She was running around trying to look for you and her asthma flared up."

I put my head in my hands. "I didn't tell you I was leaving. I'm sorry."

Grandma patted my head. "I saw your car and thought you were still inside. I didn't even call the fire department. But Virginia heard my smoke alarms and made the call. Everything is fine."

There was a screech of brakes and Gertie started yelling, running up the driveway like she was about to win a marathon. Franky jumped from his car and raced up behind her. "We're fine!" I yelled. "Everyone is okay!"

Gertie started fussing over Grandma as Franky bent over and scooped me up off the ground. "Don't you fucking *ever* scare me like that again, you loser," he scolded me in a broken voice. "Gertie called the bakery and I thought my hair was going to go gray. How could you do that to your best friend?! I'm too young for gray hair."

I hugged him tight and we swayed back and forth. "I'm sorry, loser. I'll pay for you to get your roots touched up."

He sniffed. "You better." He took a step back and gave me a once-over. "You're super sweaty. It's really disgusting. But I love you anyway."

I play punched him in the shoulder. He laughed and took a step back, nodding behind him. I turned around to watch Jack walk out of the house. He had his turnout pants and helmet on but was just wearing a Grenadine Fire Department T-shirt. That meant the fire couldn't have been too bad if he wasn't in full gear.

The moment he spotted me, time stopped. It was just him and me, staring at each other through the chaos of firefighters, EMTs, and the police. Without a word, he walked straight toward me and lifted me off the ground, kissing me fiercely.

This kiss was past desperate, full of fear and anxiety. His grip grew tighter just before he set me down and hugged me. "We got the call and..." He trailed off.

"I saw the truck and..." I couldn't finish it.

We stood there for a long moment, just holding each other until our adrenaline eased. "You're both staying at my house," Jack said. "We'll need to get the insurance company out here and a contractor. There's damage to the tub and ceiling."

I nodded.

"I'm staying with Gertie!" Grandma called. "I'm not going to cramp your style."

I groaned and pushed my face against Jack's chest. He just stood there and laughed at me.

"When we clear out, grab whatever you need and head over to my house. I'll be home as soon as I can, okay? I'll unlock the back door and text you the garage code."

I beamed up at him. "Uninterrupted Jack time? Yeah, I'll take it."

Jack lifted his head and frowned, looking at something over my shoulder. I turned around to see a silver sedan driving away. Neither of us mentioned that it was my dad's car.

CHAPTER TWENTY-FOUR

GRENADINE ORDINANCE NO. 13-7-18: THERE SHALL BE NO ARGUING WITHIN ONE HUNDRED FEET OF THE CHURCH DOORS BETWEEN THE HOURS OF 9:00 AM AND 7:00 PM.

THREE NIGHTS in Jack's bed and it was my new favorite place to be. We were wrapped around each other on Sunday morning and I was perfectly content to never leave this room again. "Seriously, how is your bed so comfortable?"

He kissed me softly. "Because you're in it." I hit him with a pillow. "Okay, okay." He laughed. "Because I splurged on it. It's probably the most expensive thing in this house, outside of the furnace. It has a good amount of give while still being firm. It's also really good for some other things besides sleeping." He pulled the sheet down and his mouth followed. We didn't do much talking after that.

After a shower and much-needed breakfast, Jack walked out of the bedroom wearing gray slacks and a white, collared shirt and I nearly dropped my coffee mug. "Why is that so sexy?" I breathed. "Seriously, how are you not married yet?"

He shrugged. "Because apparently, I'm extraordinarily picky. There's only one woman for me." He kissed me softly before trailing his fingers along the bottom hem of my sundress. I closed my eyes, savoring his touch.

Thanks to the power of the internet, I had purchased a few

church appropriate dresses and cardigans to make Grandma happy. I knew the rules. If you wanted the small town to accept you—and I was trying—you went to church on Sunday.

"I've had relationships," he explained. "A few were serious. But when it came down to it, I couldn't imagine making love to them all night then going to church with them on Sunday for the rest of my life."

I bit my bottom lip and shivered. He kissed the tip of my nose. "You think if I ever moved here, you'd get me to church *every* Sunday? Because that's probably not gonna happen."

He smirked and pulled me tight against him. "I was more concerned about the first part of that sentence." He kissed me again and I pushed away, laughing. We were going to be late if he kept this up.

"You know walking into church with me is a declaration to the town. More so than anything else we've done."

His response was to step back and lace my fingers through his. "I've got nothing to hide. You're my girl. End of story." He pulled us toward the back door.

I gripped his forearm to stop his momentum. "Jack, *your girl* makes a living fucking other men—and women—on camera and then releasing those videos to the world. Her job is in SoCal."

He released my hand and put both of his on either side of my neck, his thumbs going under my jaw and lifting it so we were eye to eye. "Vera, I know what you do. Is there a part of me that I need to talk down from being jealous? Sometimes. But all I need to remember is that you give me something different than you give your scene partners."

"Yeah?" I asked, quietly.

"You give me all of you. I haven't seen all your videos, but I've seen enough to know that the way you are with them and the way you are with me are completely different." He pulled our hips together. "You don't shake and cry and scream out their names." He kissed my forehead. "You don't whisper you love them while you fall asleep together." He kissed my eyelids. "You don't share your dreams and hopes and worries with them." He kissed each corner of my mouth.

I smiled and kissed his lips. "That's true."

"We are a team." He gestured between us. "It's you and me against the world, remember?"

I laughed. "You're a nut. But I love you anyway."

He backed up and grabbed my hand again, kissing the back of it. "Me too. Now let's go. The town is already going to gossip like crazy. If we're late, we'll never live it down."

THERE WAS nothing like running through the doors of church at 9:59 am, but we made it. Jack kept my hand tight in his as we walked down the main aisle, and I focused on my shoes instead of the way everyone's heads turned to look at the two of us. The organ started playing which thankfully covered up the whispers. I breathed a small sigh of relief as we slipped into the pew next to Grandma and Gertie. She mouthed, "You owe me twenty," to Gertie, and I bit the inside of my cheeks so I didn't laugh.

Jack held onto my hand most of the service and at the end of Mass, he wrapped his arm around my shoulders. His meaning was crystal clear; he had chosen me, and the town needed to get on board or lose favor with a Grenadine favorite. I had my girls back in SoCal, and I had my grandma. But being part of the "Jack and Vera Team" was the most amazing gift in the world.

After Mass, we stopped to talk with Franky and Franklin. Franky lifted his eyebrows in a silent exclamation, and I mirrored his expression. There was going to be so much texting later.

Jack pulled me closer as the congregation split into its socializing groups, both of us ignoring the whispers and pointed looks. At least, we did until Jack's mother walked up to our group and grabbed my arm, yanking me away from her son. Normally I would've been able to hold my own, but the unexpected confrontation left me in shock. I blinked, staring at her and looking at my arm then at her face.

She was pale except for her eyes, which were a light shade of red as if she had been crying. "Jack Reeves, how could you?" Her words were sharp, meant to cut. "How could you choose her after what she did to us?!"

I stepped in front of Jack, not wanting her to hurt him with her accusations. It was clear she was hurting, but that didn't mean she got to take it out on others. "Mrs. Reeves, please do not talk to your son like that. He is an amazing, brave, loving man."

She narrowed her eyes, turning her vile toward me. Good. "You don't deserve to lick the bottom of his shoes." The conversations around us quieted. We were the after-Mass special, live and in-person.

I held my hands up in a placating gesture. "Mrs. Reeves, with all due respect, we need to find a way to get through whatever it is that you're so angry about. I've apologized to your son about the choices I made when I was eighteen that hurt him. Please forgive me for not coming to talk to you and expressing my sincere apologies as well, as well as my condolences for Danny. It was poorly done of me." I took a deep breath and then reached out to take her hands. "Can we start over?"

I didn't know what I was expecting. Maybe to defuse the situation? Maybe for her anger to lessen even a little?

I certainly wasn't expecting her to slap me across the face.

The crowd gave a collective gasp, and everyone stilled. Out of the corner of my eye, I saw my dad step forward, but he didn't come over. I held my cheek while Jack jumped in front of me and tucked me behind him. Grandma ran over and touched the hand on my cheek. Morris tried to step between Pam and Jack, but Jack shook his head.

"Mom." He used his deadly serious, calm voice. "That was absolutely out of line. If Vera decides to press charges for assault, I will support her. With or without your blessing, Vera is my choice. But you will never put your hands on her without her express permission ever again."

"She destroyed our family and you're just standing next to her like nothing happened!" Pam shouted.

I took a step back at her vehemence and into a hard body. Franky steadied me and wrapped his arms around me. "You okay?" he whispered. I shrugged because I didn't know. I didn't understand why she was so angry about something that happened so long ago or how I had destroyed her family.

"Mom, I'm with Vera now. We're a package deal. You'll have to come to terms with this."

She shook her head violently. "Over my dead body."

"Honey," Morris said. "This isn't the time or place. Let's talk about this at—"

"It's her fault Danny's dead!" she screamed.

Her words were like a gunshot. My body tensed as I tried to process her meaning. My eyes moved to Jack, but he just stood frozen, hand to his chest as if she had actually shot him.

Pam was openly weeping now, pointing her shaking finger at me. "If you hadn't run away, Jack wouldn't have followed you. He would have driven Danny to that party, and I would still have both my sons!" Her words were shrieking, desperate, so full of pain my own heart broke alongside hers.

I couldn't move. *Jack followed me?* Was that true? If so, was I really responsible for Danny's death?

I knew, logically, these were the words of a very damaged mother who hadn't learned to process her grief. But her words were poisonous darts and each one had hit their target.

This time, my dad walked over to Pam. He never looked at me but leaned close to her. "Pam, Lord knows Vera's made a lot of mistakes, but she doesn't deserve the blame for Danny's death."

"Yes, she does!" she cried. My father's shoulders sagged as he sank back into the crowd. What happened to the strong man who taught me not to fear life? I was still in shock over the fact he'd stepped up to defend me. It wasn't much, but it was a start. I hiccupped, too many emotions coming to the surface at once.

Franky gripped my arms hard. "Don't you dare cry, Ra-Ra," he whispered harshly. "This isn't about you. Don't show this town it can hurt you." I started to shake with emotion, but he pinched me under my arm. "Don't fucking cry. Do something positive." He pinched me hard again and it worked. The urge to cry subsided.

I counted backward from five and then nodded. I looked at this poor, broken woman, trying to figure out what to say. So I did the only thing I could think of. I walked around Jack and right up to Pam and wrapped my arms around her. She all but collapsed in my arms, repeating that it was all my fault even as she gripped my shoulders and started sobbing.

"You've been blaming me for eleven years?" Jack asked, his voice absolutely devastated. I turned my head to him, but his eyes were locked on his mom.

"That's not true!" she pleaded. "You're my baby boy—"

"You said you blamed Vera for leaving because I went after her." He inhaled a watery breath and shoved both his hands into his hair. I wanted to run to him, but Pam was leaning her weight on me.

It was killing me to watch the strongest man I had ever known completely fall apart. Thankfully, Franky came up and gripped his shoulder, not pulling away even when Jack tried to take a step forward.

"If she hadn't left, you wouldn't have canceled on going to the party with Danny," Pam explained. "He wouldn't have been driving home alone. He wouldn't have fallen asleep at the wheel!" Her words were a desperate explanation, a way to assign grief. Morris rubbed his hands over his face and shook his head, his eyes wet.

Jack blew out a breath as his face went red from emotion. "If I was in the car with Danny, he would still be alive. If I was there. Not if Vera was there. Me." He hit his chest with his fist. "It's my fault in your eyes. I'm the only variable that could've kept him alive, then? Not if he had pulled over, or left the party earlier, or stayed home, or gotten a hotel room. Only if I was with him?" Shaking his head, he turned around and walked away toward the side of the church.

"Jacky!" his mom wailed, collapsing.

Morris and I caught her as Franky chased after Jack. Grandma called for someone to get Father Wright, but Cynthia was already running down the steps with him following behind. My dad came to relieve me, his eyes meeting mine for a long moment before he turned to help Father Wright and Morris get Pam into the church. Cynthia ordered someone to get Pam a bottle of water and a peppermint candy, in hopes it would help calm her.

She patted my arm in a silent thank you before running after the group in five-inch heels. She might be a dragon, but she definitely knew how to take charge when needed. Will met her on the stairs with a bottle of water and foil wrapped candies in his hand. She kissed him quickly before going through the front doors and closing them.

Grandma started to say something to me, but Gertie told her to hush. "That way," Gertie said, pointing to the side of the church.

I took off running, forever thankful I had worn flats. Jack was sitting against the building with his head resting on his raised knees. Franky had his arm around his shoulders, hugging him tightly. Franky was speaking softly, reassuring Jack that it was the grief talking, that his mother didn't truly blame him, that no matter what, Jack had the two of us.

When Franky saw me approach, he gave Jack one last squeeze and a kiss on the side of the head before standing. My eyes held his, silently thanking him. Franky shrugged out of his suit jacket and set it down on the ground, then nodded his head for me to sit.

I wrapped myself around Jack and he lifted his face to search mine. I nearly broke down right there, seeing his red, watery eyes and disheveled hair. I pushed my hand through his hair and handed him a tissue I pulled from my purse. "We're going to get your mom some help, okay?" I promised.

"She blamed me," he whispered. "All this time."

"It's not your fault." He buried his face against my shoulder, and I rubbed his back in circles. "Not his accident. Not her blaming you. Not her reaction to me." He nodded but didn't move. I sucked in a deep breath, trying to get my courage up for the next question. "You followed me?"

He nodded again. "I went to your house to try to talk to you, but you were already gone." Each word forced out. "I told your dad you had something of mine I needed, and he let me upstairs. You had left your cell phone and computer behind. I looked at your internet and call history."

I kissed the top of his head. "Smart man." Despite Dad kicking me out with only a few hours' notice, I'd had enough time to look up my route and a few cheap motels. I even printed out job postings to look into when I got to Vegas. "But you didn't catch up with me."

He shook his head. "I was probably five hours behind. Figured I'd nap here and there and eventually catch up with you. I was about four hours in when my dad called."

I sucked in my lips and held him tighter. "I'm sorry I wasn't here for you. I'm sorry for a lot of things."

"I know. Me too." We held each other for a long time, understanding the unspoken words between us.

Franky came back over and sat on the other side of Jack, wrapping him in a hug. I loved these men, loved that they weren't ashamed of their friendship with me or each other. They weren't ashamed to give and receive affection. Franky cleared his throat. "Father Wright is with your parents. I think you should be with your mom."

Jack nodded and rubbed his hand over his face. "Okay, okay." He looked between us. "You'll both be at my house later for dinner or something?"

"Just try to get rid of us," Franky said, getting up.

I kissed Jack's cheek. "You're stuck with me." I stood and reached out my hands.

Jack gave a weak smile and let out a long breath before rolling his eyes. "Gosh, just sit here all day. Whatever, losers, I have things to do."

We laughed as Franky and I helped him up. I scooped up Franky's coat and brushed it off, then handed it to him. He laid it over his arm and tipped his head toward the mostly empty parking lot. "I'll meet you at the car."

I walked Jack to the chapel doors and gave him a sweet kiss. "I'll see you soon, okay? Call me if you need anything."

He kissed me and then took a deep breath. He opened the doors and stepped inside. My heart followed after him. I didn't want him to have to go in alone, but I knew I wasn't welcome in there.

I trudged to the parking lot. "This fucking sucks," I huffed as I climbed into Franky's car. "I should've tied him to the bed this morning, instead."

He nodded. "I find it's generally sucky for one to find out their boyfriend's mom blames them for her other son's death."

"That's some solid nutshelling. Thanks for that."

He started the car and headed out of the parking lot. Very slowly.

"There are literally three other cars in this parking lot. Why are you driving like my grandma's grandma?" I moaned.

Franky leveled me with a stare. "*I've* never been in an accident."

Dammit. I rolled my eyes. "I'm never going to live that down."

"Not until the end of time, Ra-Ra."

CHAPTER TWENTY-FIVE

@GRENADINEUNOFFICIAL: GOODBYE VERA EASTMAN! HAVE A SAFE TRIP BACK TO CALIFORNIA #WEMISSYOUALREADY

IN THE BLINK OF AN EYE, Sunday turned into Monday turned into Tuesday. Everything had changed after church, and the feeling of dread in my stomach kept me up late into the night. Jack and I still slept in the same bed and ate breakfast together at the same table, but he was more distant and reserved. I knew his mind was dealing with his mother's breakdown and the resurfacing of his own grief, but I couldn't stop watching the space between us double and then triple. Soon, it would be an entire country.

The only time we found each other again was in the middle of the night. Jack would wake me and make love to me, desperate and earth-shattering. It was like he needed the safety of night and grogginess to handle our connection.

I went to see Grandma every day at the store or at Gertie's. She was still shaken up about what happened but was living it up at Gertie's place. They had already baked so many cookies and so much fudge for the firehouse that they could open their own bakery.

After hunting down Dad's new place, I had taken over a container of cookies, determined to talk to him. He didn't answer the door, even though his car was in the driveway and the curtains had moved as if someone was peering through them. After the third doorbell ring, I left the cookies on the porch. The empty container was placed on Grandma's front porch overnight. Well, that was another small step forward.

My free time had been spent on the phone with insurance companies and repair guys. I had missed two work calls that resulted in a few passive aggressive emails from agents, but I didn't care. Family came first.

I really needed more assistants. I had one in-house who fielded phone calls and urgent emails, but I needed someone who could deal with pissy-ass agents and my travel schedule while I spent time with people I loved. I emailed Payton and she promised to have a list of candidates by the time I got back.

Without fanfare or remorse, Wednesday morning arrived. Every movement I made seemed wrong, backward. Putting the suitcase in the car was like the too-soon end of a story that hadn't yet reached the middle.

Franky had picked up Grandma and Gertie and brought them over to Jack's before I was even out of the shower. We all ate breakfast together in near silence, each of us lost in our own thoughts. Jack and I hadn't even discussed our plans yet. I didn't want to be selfish when I knew he was working through so much, but his silence was suffocating me.

But goodbyes happen whether you're ready or not. How different they were this time. We all stood in the driveway, looking at my car. "You have a full tank of gas?" Grandma asked.

"Filled her up yesterday."

"And paper maps? You know that GPS is a kook."

I smiled. "Yes, two of them in case another traveler needs one."

She cupped the side of my cheek. "Good girl. Remember to call and check in when you stop for the night."

"Promise."

Gertie handed me a container full of baked goods and gave me a kiss on the cheek. "I'll take care of Bea, don't you worry."

"You'd better," I whispered, struggling to keep an even tone.

Franky hugged me tight and kissed my cheek. "You know you can't get rid of me, loser."

I squeezed him harder. "Right back at you, loser."

Then Jack kissed me sweetly and set his forehead against mine. "I love you. Call me later, okay?" I nodded. He took a step back and searched my face. "We'll figure it out."

I smiled but couldn't find the words I needed to say. My gut knew the moment I left Grenadine was the moment our relationship would fail. I couldn't do this; I couldn't leave him. But somehow, I gave him one more kiss and then turned toward my car, each step harder than the last. Left, right, left, right. I wanted to throw up everything I had ever eaten.

"Vera!" Grandma called. "Make sure you always lock your doors while getting gas! And keep your cell phone charged! And park under street lights!"

Don't cry, don't cry, don't cry. I ran back to her and wrapped her in another hug. "I promise I'll be back soon." When I pulled back, her eyes were wet.

She play-slapped me on the shoulder. "Get out of here before you embarrass both of us."

I climbed in the car and pulled out of the driveway. When I looked back, the people I loved were standing there, waving vigorously. They were still in the driveway until I could no longer see them in the rearview mirror. I made it exactly ten minutes before I burst into tears.

THAT SAYING, "You can't go home again?" It seemed to apply much more to my California life than my Grenadine life. I felt like a tourist in my empty, sugarless condo. The bed was uncomfortable, the kitchen was too modern and too big—really, who needed a dining room table and a breakfast bar when they lived alone?—and the entire building too noisy to sleep. I bought a sound machine and noise-canceling headphones my second night back.

Then it was Saturday night. The big night.

I stood in front of my full-length mirror applying a second coat of deep red lipstick. It felt like slipping into battle armor. I was wrapped up in a designer top and short-shorts, which were just a bit snug, channeling Zoe Hart from Hart of Dixie. Chunky jewelry and lots of concealer distracted from the dark circles under my eyes.

I opened my impeccably organized walk-in closet and slipped my feet into four-inch heels. Everything in here was calculated. There weren't piles of shoes or rainy-day clothing. Everything had its place and use.

When I had bought the condo, I turned everything to white and mahogany and stainless steel. Clean lines and clutter free. It was the result of moving past all the years we'd lived in filthy, falling down places. But maybe now I needed something in-between.

I checked the time and jumped. I was going to be late. Shaking out my shoulders, I grabbed my purse and a bottle of champagne. I could do this. I could walk in and see my best girlfriends and celebrate our success. This was everything we had been dreaming about and working toward.

My phone lit up with Jack's picture and for a moment I couldn't move. I missed him so much I found it hard to breathe. I couldn't talk to him right now and then face the party.

A text came through after I ignored the call.

Jack: Have fun tonight! Call me tomorrow and tell me all about it.

I shut off the ringer and shoved it into my bag.

When I stepped off the elevator, my doorman, Wilson, smiled at me. "You look ready to take over the world, Ms. Eastman."

I gave him a half smile. "Every day. All I need is a good pair of shoes and champagne."

He chuckled as he buzzed me into the garage. "Have a safe night."

When I got to my car, I climbed in and set my bag down on top of the paper map sitting on my passenger seat. Carefully, I picked up the map and ran my hand over it. I had called Grandma twice a day since I'd left, but it wasn't the same. How did you even begin to catch up on eleven years?

I flipped the map over and saw a little hand-written note in the white space. *Just in case you ever needed to find your way home. Love, Grandma.* I breathed out a string of obscenities to keep from crying before shoving the map into the glove compartment. I turned up my eighties rock and went a good twenty, or thirty, miles over the speed limit on the way to Jasmine's.

When I walked in, she screamed at the top of her lungs then launched herself at me. She was all copper arms and legs. Her familiar candy scent made me realize just how much I missed her, and I held her tighter. "I missed you, baby girl," she purred. She kissed me and then wrapped me back in another hug.

Darrin, all curly dark hair, fair skin, and green eyes, came up and gave me a quick hug and kiss. He was so easy on the eyes. "Missed you, Vera. Welcome back." He took the champagne out of my hands, inspecting it. "We're celebrating something? I didn't think you drank alcohol."

"I mean, I am a National Treasure. I should be celebrated wherever I go." I smiled, or tried to. "And I'm drinking tonight."

Payton walked into the room, statuesque and drop dead gorgeous. She was nearly six feet tall, perfectly toned and sculpted. Her complexion rested somewhere between fawn and gold, as if it could change with her clothing and hair color. She was a chameleon, adapting her entire body to fit her mood, while simultaneously creating a perfect mask.

Today, she had long blue extensions, a huge change from the black bob she had when I left. She gave me a big hug, squeezing so tight my ribs ached. She gave me a lingering kiss with her full red lips.

"I'll be honest, I wasn't sure you were going to come home," she admitted.

"Well, here I am." I went for excited-to-be-home voice, but it came out a bit more passive-aggressive than I'd intended. I pressed my forehead against her shoulder, her love filling a Payton-sized hole I had been carrying since I left.

She smiled, but it didn't reach her charcoal eyes. I knew she could see right through me. "We want to hear all about your adventures...but first, I have some news."

As expected, Jas did a lot of screaming and crying. She graciously accepted the promotion, just like I knew she would. All the commotion woke up her six-month-old daughter—my goddaughter—and I volunteered to put her back to sleep. I had missed her new baby smell and cute little noises more than I realized.

I rocked her, singing her a song my mom used to sing to me every night. She quieted, her eyes closing and her breathing evening out. She looked so much like her parents. She had Jasmine's complexion, dark hair, and temper. She was already a diva and she had just started eating solid foods. But she was a happy baby, always smiling and laughing like her dad. She even had his big, green eyes. My heart practically burst with love as I took in how much she'd changed since I last saw her.

How could I leave her behind if I moved back to Grenadine?

With a soft kiss to the top of her head, I placed her back into her crib. If Jack and I had kids, who would they look like? Would they have his reddish-brown hair or my brown? His brown eyes or my blue? His easy-going personality or my crazy, passionate temper?

I shook my head and left the room. Jack and I would need to actually figure our shit out if we were going to start a family. Right now, that seemed as likely as time travel.

When I rejoined the group, I quickly downed a glass of champagne. Payton kept looking over at me, sizing me up. I hadn't had alcohol since Payton helped me get sober, too afraid to go back to that mess of a girl I used to be. But tonight, I just wanted the bubbles to go to my head. When I reached for a second glass, Payton pulled me into a hug and whispered, "It's not going to fix whatever you're running from."

My cheeks heated and I set the glass down. She was right; I didn't need any more.

Jas demanded that I share the highlights of my trip. I stuck to the academic version, skipping how deeply I'd fallen for Jack and how devastated I was to leave my grandma again. I couldn't tell them more. I couldn't take the questions tonight.

"But you finished a lot of your mom's list?" Jas asked.

I nodded. "Half. Everything that could be done locally."

Payton put her hand on my forearm. "I'm so glad." She leaned back and finished off her glass of orange juice. "I'll be honest, this job sucks without you. I'm so glad you're back to work on Monday."

Come on, face. Form a smile. Make a smile. I must have made it happen. "Yeah, it'll be nice to get back."

Jas cheered. "Want to do a shoot together? I have a few ideas."

"Um..." I tucked my hair behind my ear. "Let me get back into the swing of things. I have a lot to catch up on, you know?"

She watched me for a long moment. "Sure. We'll talk about it next week."

I glanced at my phone, looking for an escape. It had been a while since I'd drunk the champagne and I knew I was sober. It was only 9:30, but I was done. "You know, I'm exhausted. The time difference and all." I made a show of stretching. "I'm feeling it."

Jas gave a dramatic sigh, and Payton studied me for a long moment. "Alright, babe," Payton said. "We'll see you Monday, okay?"

"Yep. See you Monday."

With hugs and kisses, I headed back to my place, to my empty condo. There were no animals underfoot, no cute firefighters next door, no Grandma testing out different recipes in the kitchen.

Just me.

CHAPTER TWENTY-SIX

"YOU CAN'T LIVE YOUR LIFE FOR OTHER PEOPLE. MOST OF THEM HAVE TERRIBLE TASTE IN MUSIC, AND YOU DON'T NEED THAT KIND OF NEGATIVITY. HERE, HAVE ANOTHER COOKIE." – GRANDMA BEA

THE NEXT THREE weeks went by in the blink of an eye, yet tragically slow. I knew logically that crossing post-vacation blues with major life events was always going to suck. Jack and I barely had time to talk between my newly crazy schedule and the time difference. By the time I got off work, he was asleep or hanging out with friends.

I used to love working seven days a week. We'd built this company with our entire selves—physically and emotionally—and it used to be my whole life. But now my long hours were punctuated by resentment and a low, burning anger in my stomach.

I was taking an omeprazole every day, trying to ward off the acid reflux that was burning a hole through my chest at night. Last week, I'd managed to get through two shoots before I decided I didn't want to be booked for any more, at least for the foreseeable future. My heart wasn't in it. My life felt like it had been pulled apart and pieced back together wrong.

The turning point came when Payton stopped by my office, her hair now blonde and curly, to find me crying over a chocolate chip cookie. I was crying. Over a cookie.

"What is happening here?" she asked, gesturing everywhere.

I grabbed a tissue and dabbed at my face. "You just gestured to everything."

"And the cookie. You don't eat cookies. Jesus, Vera, I can't remember the last time you ate a dessert. Do you need me to throw the cookie away?"

She reached for it and I slapped her hand. "No touchy." She held her hands up and sat in a chair across from my desk. "Grandma sent these."

I reached into my desk and pulled out the container, opening it for her. She took one and inspected it as if it were the first cookie she'd ever seen. She took a bite and closed her eyes for a long moment, then continued chewing. She ate the rest of the cookie in two bites. "Okay, I can see why these would make you homesick."

I shoved the rest of my cookie in my mouth and for a split second, it was like Grandma was there. But when I blinked, I was back in my office. The tears started all over again. "Payton…" I whispered.

Her head hung for just one moment and she looked completely defeated. Then, like she always did, she sighed and straightened, ready to attack head-on. "I know, baby girl," she said, reaching over to grab my hand. "I could tell the moment you got back."

I sniffed and searched her face. "What are we going to do?" I whispered.

She blinked rapidly and then sat back in her chair. "I dunno." Her voice wavered, a vulnerability I had only seen a handful of times. "This company was always you and me. You and me against the industry. You and me against the haters."

"I know." I grabbed another cookie and I pulled out a pad of paper. "Well, what do we know?" I asked, trying to imitate her.

She smiled and snagged another cookie. "We know that I can't imagine this place without you."

"Ditto," I whispered.

"Our options are dissolving the partnership…"

We both took in a deep breath, unable to put into words how much we didn't want to do that.

A knock at the door made us both jump. Jas stuck her head in. "Hey, ladies, I was just..." She looked between us, spotted the cookies, and slipped into the office, closing and locking the door. "Why is there refined sugar on your desk?!" she whisper-yelled. "How many people did you kill? Darrin can dig really fast; he grew up on a farm."

Payton and I burst into laughter as she pulled out the second chair at the desk. I shoved the container of cookies toward her and she inspected them even more than Payton had. "What are they?"

I smiled. "They're Grandma-Made Cookies. Full fat and full sugar."

She gingerly picked up one and took a cautious bite. She sucked in a breath and put her hand over her mouth, looking between us. "No wonder you want to move back home."

"Wait, what?" I asked.

"You knew?" Payton gasped, offended.

I put my hands up. "I didn't tell anyone."

Jas rolled her eyes. "Oh my God, Vera, I could tell as soon as your constant texts stopped. You reconnected with your family and the love of your life. Of course you weren't going to stay in SoCal."

"Uh..." I motioned around us with my finger. "The multi-million-dollar business of my dreams is in SoCal. I don't have a choice."

She took another bite of the cookie and moaned. "This may be better than sex." Her eyes went wide. "Don't tell Darrin I said that."

Payton crossed over her heart with her finger.

Jas finished the cookie, licked the crumbs off her fingers, and then crossed her arms, leaning back in the chair. "You two are my best girls besides my daughter, but you can't see the forest for the trees." She pointed at me. "Anyone who saw your disaster of a last video knows that you don't want to have partner scenes on camera anymore."

I scoffed. "It wasn't that bad."

She raised an eyebrow. "They had to dub your incredibly fake orgasm with audio from an old video. It *was* that bad." She held up two fingers. "Secondly, your product videos were hilarious. I think I watched the lube-tasting video a hundred times. The first time, I literally had to change my underwear because I was laughing so hard I peed."

Payton covered her ears. "Gross!"

Jas rolled her eyes. "The joys of childbirth. Loss of bladder control." She grabbed another cookie and talked around it. "Three, the solo videos are cool. Get your groove on when you want to. Upload them to the server. Done. Four, your clothing line is handled by mail. They can ship anywhere. None of this stuff needs to be done from California."

I looked between her and Payton. "That was...a lot of things."

"What about meetings and foundation work?" Payton asked. "She can't attend fundraisers and award shows from Michigan. We are as much a philanthropic company as an adult film company."

Jas shrugged. "They have these things called planes—perhaps you've heard of them—she would climb on board and BAM. Five hours later she could be here, or we could be there. We could expand our charity work to Michigan, maybe even hire a few people out there. Those events are scheduled months in advance."

"Meetings?" Payton prompted.

Jas turned to look at her. "Your meeting schedule is terrible and unproductive."

"Hey! You've been VP for like three weeks!"

"Yes, and you should've made me VP years ago. Listen, I get that you both want to be involved in every aspect of this company because it's your baby, but at your projected growth rate it can't keep happening. You both work seven days a week as it is. Fuck that."

Payton stood up. "Excuse you!"

Jas grabbed Payton's arm and pulled her back down. "We're going to hire more people, the kind of people you trust to do the lower-level meetings and give you notes." She pointed to me. "Your assistants will be your eyes and ears. Make sure one can handle the projects here, and a virtual one for everything you do in Michigan. You have the budget. Fucking use it."

Jas wiped her hands on her pants and stood. "Vera, you're going to have to fly back for the important shit, including my daughter's first birthday, or I will kill you, and Darrin will hide your body. Payton, you're going to take up tennis or quilting or stamp collecting or whatever else isn't work. You're going to spend at least an hour not working every night."

She put her hands on her hips. "Now. I'm going to lunch and I don't want to see the two of you for the rest of the day. I'm too irritated at your complete disregard for logic." She stormed out of the room and we both stared after her.

"So…" I finally said. "Looks like we're going to need to figure out some paperwork. And you need to learn how to quilt."

Payton gave me the middle finger.

CHAPTER TWENTY-SEVEN

TODAY'S PICTURE-A-DAY PHOTO: A CRUMBLED BALL OF PACKING TAPE STUCK IN BRIGHT RED HAIR

THE LAST TWO weeks had been spent obsessively going over every detail with Payton and Jas. I hired my assistants and Payton hired a slew of management to take over the low-level day-to-day operations. Trying to learn everyone's name was proving more difficult than I thought, but Jas promised she'd send me a cheat sheet.

I hadn't told anyone back in Michigan my plan. I was too afraid to jinx it. Until the day I started packing up my essentials in my condo, it was a secret. Unfortunately, it was a secret that was so hard to keep I was avoiding my phone like it was the plague. I lied about having a cold and laryngitis, which bought me a few days.

Before I moved home for good, I had to do something I really didn't want to do. Or maybe I did but was really afraid to do. I picked up my phone and dialed. I still had his cell phone memorized after eleven years.

"Hello?" The formalness of his voice caught me off guard. Of course he wouldn't have this number, but I still somehow wanted him to instinctively know it was me. "Hello?" he asked again.

"Hi, Dad." There was no response. I pulled the phone away from my ear to check if he had hung up. Surprisingly, the call was still connected. "I'm moving home. I'll be running my business from Grenadine. I just...wanted to let you know."

More silence.

"I know that things between us haven't been good for...a long time," I continued. Talk about the understatement of the decade. "But I'm hoping you can learn to talk to me when we see each other out in public. Maybe one day even in private. Because Grenadine is a small town and life is hard enough without your father hating you."

"I don't hate you." His voice was anxious and quiet, as if he were afraid to talk too loud. "I just wished..." He sighed. "Parents always have wishes for their kids."

Neither of us spoke for a long moment. Then I cleared my throat and asked the question I needed to ask. "Why did you tell me Grandma was dead?"

He let out a long breath and fumbled with the phone. "It was...an ill attempt to get you to come home."

Bitter words filled my mouth, but I swallowed them down. "You're the one who told me to leave," I whispered.

"I was grieving and angry. I was so afraid of losing you like I lost your mother and I didn't handle any of it well. I'm sorry."

I didn't respond. I didn't know what to say to that.

"You didn't come home," he added.

I looked at the window, clutching my phone so tight it was likely to crack in my hands. "I didn't get the email until a few weeks after you sent it. I didn't have a cell phone or a computer for awhile. I had to get a job and save up."

"Oh."

"You could have just asked me to come home instead of making me think Grandma had died! You could have told me Danny died. That would've been true, and I would've come home for the funeral. You could have apologized or told me you missed me! You could have welcomed me back home."

He didn't say anything.

"I know you don't like my profession, but I won't apologize for it.

Dad, I'm an incredibly successful businesswoman. We have a foundation that helps save lives and educates about abuse. I'm always trying to find ways to give back like you and Mom taught me."

I started pacing and pushed my fist against my forehead, trying to calm my racing thoughts. "I'm not a bad person. I'm simply a person who earns her living with both her body and mind."

He still didn't respond.

"Okay...well...I guess I'll talk to you later. Bye." I hung up, not waiting for him to speak. I didn't know if we would ever fully reconcile, but I had done what I needed to do to feel like a good daughter. I did it for me, and I did it for my mom. It's what she would've wanted. His reactions were all on him.

I texted Jas and Payton. **We having this girls' night packing party shit or not?**

Payton: How'd it go with your dad?

Jas: U called UR dad?!

Me: It went about how I expected. Lots of awkward pauses

Payton: Proud of you.

Jas: *heart emoji*

Jas: Be there in 1 hour

Payton: You made seven figures last year and you can't hire packers?

I laughed. **This is just an excuse to have a girls' night. Read between the lines.**

Payton: Thank god. I'm wearing yoga pants. Fuck heels

Jas: Whatever. My wedges R cute

Jas: *sends picture of cute wedges*

Jas: Also I luv packing

Payton: You're a special kind of weird. Also yes, killer shoes

Me: I love your weird. Someone bring pizza. I have cookies

Jas: I'll carb or sugar, not both

Jas: I'll bring salad

Payton: Wait...

Payton: You're not baking, right?

Me: Everyone thinks they're Paul Hollywood

Payton: ...

Payton: But no, really...

Me: No you bitch. They're from the bakery down the street

Payton: Whew.

FIRE TRUCKS, GARTER BELTS, & MY PERFECT EX

Jas: *kissing emoji*

Me: I hate both of you.

DESPITE BEING able to order cheese in four languages and having three degrees, I was struggling with a damn tape gun. It had seemed so simple to assemble boxes, but no. There was most definitely tape in my hair and a cardboard box cut on my arm. Seriously, packing was a dangerous job.

I sighed, looking at the disaster of cardboard and adhesive around me. Maybe I did need professional help. I thought it'd be fine to do it on my own. I was only taking what I couldn't live without to Michigan and was planning on keeping the condo for my trips back.

I got a text on my cell from the front desk. **Guest here to see you.**

Okay to send up. Payton and Jas were on my approved list. My guess was the computer was down again. As good as technology was, it only worked when it wanted to.

When the knock sounded, I had just taped my hair to another box. I was amazing. "Thank God!" I yelled, unlocking the door and opening it. "I don't think this new hairstyle is a good lo—" All my words left my head. It wasn't Payton or Jas.

It was Jack.

He just stood there, trying not to laugh by the way he bit his lower lip. I opened my mouth to say something, but nothing came out. He looked so damn sexy in a gray, fitted T-shirt, worn jeans, and a backpack over his shoulder. He had dark circles under his eyes, but his smile was huge and genuine.

He took a step toward me. "I don't know," he said as if he were seriously considering me. "I'm told the box look is in. Besides, you look good in everything." He winked. "And nothing."

"I-I-I..." Nope, brain would not engage. "What?"

He shrugged. "Phone calls, or lack of them, weren't working for me anymore. Glad to hear you've got your voice back."

I opened the door wider to let him in, my heart hammering so hard I could see the veins in my eyes. He set down his bag as I closed the door. Without mocking me, out loud anyway, he took the tape gun out of my hand and disentangled me.

"Maybe you should let me help." He chuckled. His brow creased as he looked around. "Why are you packing?"

Why were we standing here talking? Why was he here? Why were his lips not on mine? I had so many questions. "I'm moving," I admitted. Jack's face morphed from amused to focused, intense. "Back to Michigan." His eyes never left mine and I felt them burn straight to my bones. "I'll have to come back for a few weeks every other month and for major events. It won't be easy, but I—"

I couldn't finish the sentence because he placed his hands on either side of my face and kissed me. He kissed me like I was oxygen and he couldn't get enough air. He kissed me like I was an oasis in the desert. He kissed me like he couldn't live without me.

"Vera," he whispered over and over, kissing every part of my face. "You're giving up so much."

I stilled his face and searched his eyes. "But I'm gaining so much more." I gave him a quick kiss on the lips. "Besides, I'm not giving up my dream. I'm adapting it to fit around my new dreams."

Then I kissed him deep, that familiar rush of *home* engulfing me. We grabbed each other, desperate to be closer. He pushed me against the front door, his mouth dragging down my neck, his hands gripping my butt and pulling me so close I could feel how hard he was everywhere. I needed more, more, *more*.

I shoved my hands between us and unbuttoned his jeans while he helped me kick off my shorts. In one smooth move, he gripped my thighs and put them around his hips as I guided him into me. We both cried out so loud I swear the building shook. "Jack," I pleaded when he didn't move.

He smiled. "There's my girl." Then he started moving and I was lost to the world.

It was rough and the doorknob dug into the side of my leg, but it was perfect. The desperation and anxiety that had been fueling the last five weeks melted away with each press of his lips on mine, each roll of his hips.

"You. Are. Mine." He growled against my mouth, making my legs quiver.

"You're mine," I whispered just before I came apart. He followed with a groan so loud it filled my own chest with unspoken emotion. I knew, without a doubt, that my heart was irreparably bound with his.

"I love you," I told him, running my fingers over his jawline.

"I love you." Jack kissed me softly. "Move in with me."

I nipped his bottom lip. "Actually, I think I'm going to stay with Grandma for a while, if that's okay? I want to make up for some lost time, and it'll give us both a chance to get settled."

He growled and kissed me again. "Fine. You know I'll wait for you however long you need."

A pounding on the door made us both gasp, then look at each other with shocked expressions. "Are you still getting banged against the door or can we come in?" Jas shouted. Loudly. For all my neighbors to hear.

"Oh my God, it's girls' night." I gasped, just remembering there was a world outside of Jack. "Give us like thirty seconds!" I called, disengaging from Jack and quickly pulling up my pants, then helping him with his. "Get to my bedroom!" I ordered, pushing him toward the last door in the hall. I had just closed my door when I heard the front one open. Jas and Payton both had keys. Thank God they had knocked first.

Jack and I were a laughing mess as we cleaned up and I changed. We stole kisses and touches the entire time. When we were both fully dressed, I grabbed his hand. "Are you ready to face Payton and Jas? They're both crazy."

He kissed my cheek. "Princess. They're your best girlfriends. Of course they're crazy."

I started to protest, but he opened the bedroom door and walked into the living room. Both Payton and Jas were staring at us. "This is Jack," I explained. "He came by for a surprise visit."

Payton smiled and shook her head. "I'll be honest, I was secretly pretty mad at you for leaving."

My eyes went wide. "Payton!"

She waved me off. "But if I had a man that smokin' who looked at me like that, I'd leave

too." She nodded. "Nice to meet you, Jack."

Jack laughed and pulled me into him, kissing the side of my head.

Jas pursed her lips and then nodded. "He seems like the kind of guy who'd take splinters out of your ass if you fucked against a picnic table."

Jack laughed and lowered his head to my shoulder. "I would definitely pull splinters out of your butt."

Jas gestured toward him. "See? That's how I knew Darrin was the one. We had only shot together twice, but that picnic table scene." She let out a low whistle and shook her head. "Splinters for *days*, if you know what I mean." She gestured between her legs.

"We get it, Jas. You got wood in your vag," I said.

Jas beamed. "Girl, you know how much I like wood in my—"

I held up my hand to cut her off. "Yeah. We know."

Payton tapped her chin. "Technically, it was her labia."

I put my hand to my forehead. "Jesus Christ..."

Jack wrapped his arms around my waist and kissed the side of my neck. "I like these two."

"You're in a room with three successful, incredibly hot porn stars," Payton countered. "What's not to like?"

Jack was laughing so hard he had to sit down on a bar stool as he tried to catch his breath.

"Thanks for breaking my boyfriend," I told her.

She winked at me and blew me a kiss, then stood. "Now then. Let's get this shit packed."

THE NEXT MORNING, I called Grandma on speaker phone to let her know I was moving back to Grenadine. She immediately ordered me to take her guest room, now that the renovations on her bathroom were done. "Don't you be moving in with Jack yet. Not until there's a ring on your finger."

Jack had to leave the room because he was laughing so hard.

The "you do know what I do for a living" response was taken as well as I expected it to be. I got a five-minute lecture about how matters of the body and matters of the heart were two different things.

When Jack had calmed down enough to talk, he pulled me into him and gave me a slow, breath-stealing kiss. "How much did you bribe the contractors to get your grandma's house done so soon?"

I winked at him. "I'll never tell." It was amazing how far a few phone calls and a check could go.

It took a lot of late nights, and a few crying sessions between me and my best girls—even Darrin's eyes teared up—but I was on a plane with a moving truck following two days before my thirtieth birthday. When I landed at the Detroit airport, Jack was waiting for me in baggage claim with a sign that read "Grenadine Cherry Queen."

I screamed like I had won another AVN award.

When we got to the truck, Jack handed me the Grenadine Herald with a smile. On the front page was *Grenadine's own 'Roni Vegas' nominated Cherry Queen in honor of late mother.*

"How is this a thing?" I asked, sniffling.

He reached into his center console and pulled out a tissue, handing it to me. "You know that Gertie is the town social media manager, right? She does all the social media posts and gives scoops to the paper. The story about you wanting to be Cherry Queen in honor of your mom circulated just in time for voting."

My hand went over my mouth. "I can't believe people voted for me."

"You helped my mom, you know. And your grandma. That didn't go unnoticed."

I couldn't speak for a long moment. That was true, but that wasn't it. "Jack, this is one of the most coveted awards. It's nearly impossible to win as someone who hasn't lived in Grenadine for eleven years."

Red tinged his beautiful cheekbones. "It's possible that a few of us went door-to-door to make sure people voted for you."

"A few of you went door-to-door?" I repeated in disbelief.

He smiled sheepishly. "Well, I wasn't going to tell Paul and Michael that they couldn't come with Franky and me. Although Jami being there got a little sticky."

I narrowed my eyes. "Sticky, how?"

His grin grew wide. "Cynthia's crew was also out campaigning."

I covered my mouth with my hand. "I beat out *Cynthia* for Cherry Queen?" I leaned back in the seat and shook my head.

"Yeah...talk about a win out of left field!"

"Church is going to be so awkward on Sunday."

He kissed my hand. "Naw, I got you. You and me against the world, remember?"

Grandma and Gertie were waiting outside when we pulled up in the driveway an hour later, and I was greeted by a flurry of hugs and kisses and demands to know what took so long. The doorbell didn't stop ringing until after nine when the neighbors finally stopped coming around to congratulate me and welcome me back.

Jack took me back to his house for the night, where we made love until we were too tired to move. I fell into a deep, dreamless sleep, finally at peace.

EPILOGUE

@GRENADINEUNOFFICIAL: HAPPY 30TH BIRTHDAY, VERA! WILL JACK BE JUMPING OUT OF A CAKE AT YOUR PARTY? INQUIRING MINDS NEED TO KNOW. #SENDPICS

I WAS BLINDFOLDED and in high heels. Not in a sexy way, although I was pretty sure I could get Jack to agree to that later, but in the being-led-across-the-parking-lot-to-a-surprise-location kind of way. He pulled me into a building then took off my blindfold.

"SURPRISE!"

It took me a few moments to take in the scene. We were at Edie's Auto, which was filled with pink balloons, tables of food, and pretty much every person in Grenadine who liked me. I laughed and shook my head.

Franky ran up and hugged me, spinning me around once. He kissed my cheek. "Happy birthday, Ra-Ra."

Chieka and Edie came at me from both sides, sandwiching me in a hug. "The shop is doing awesome because of your help," Edie said. "Thank you."

Tamicka gave me a wave and then pointed between Jack and me. "It's about damn time."

Rosa bounced up and wrapped me in a tight squeeze before we excitedly talked about how the shop's social media had been getting a lot of positive attention. I promised her I'd be by the shop next week to grab some lunch with her.

Then the shop door opened, and Payton and Jas walked in. I screamed and ran to them, nearly taking them both to the ground. I started crying and Jas swatted at me. "Stop it, your makeup is perfect. Don't waste it on us."

Payton cupped my cheeks. "I told you I was going to be where you were for major events. Don't ever think you can get rid of me that easily."

"Never," I promised.

She gave me a kiss and then grabbed Jasmine's arm as they went to greet Jack and Edie's crew. But it was the person who walked in after my best girlfriends who silenced the entire room.

"Dad," I breathed.

He nodded, his face betraying how truly uncomfortable he was to be here. "I'm not staying. But I wanted to give you this." He handed me a thin, square box, then took a step back. "It's not wrapped."

I nodded, even though I was in a stupor. I blinked down at the box for a long moment. My dad had brought me a gift on my birthday.

Carefully, as if it could disappear at any moment, I opened the box. Inside was the round, sterling-silver locket Mom had worn my entire childhood. The front was intricately engraved with different kinds of flowers while the back was worn smooth. I popped it open and found a picture of her and Dad on their wedding day on the left and a picture of Grandma and Mom holding me as a baby on the right.

I covered my mouth with my hand, trying to keep any embarrassing sounds from escaping. So of course, I hiccuped instead. I lowered my hand and looked him in the eyes. "Thank you," I mouthed.

He nodded. "Happy birthday." He turned around and left and I stared after him, wanting to invite him to stay and have cake.

Grandma came up next to me, a crumpled tissue in her hand. "You'll get there. Give it time." She helped me put the locket on and then patted it once. "I gave that to your mom when you were born. I'm glad it's where it should be."

Jack rubbed my back and cleared his throat. "If anyone else is going to make my girlfriend cry, can we get it out of the way? We have cake to eat."

Everyone laughed, including me.

Edie came up with a clothing box that was decorated with ribbon to within an inch of its life. "Rosa," she explained. "That girl loves ribbon."

Jack pulled out a pocket knife and cut the ribbon off after I struggled with it to the point it was almost embarrassing. Inside the box was a set of cherry red Edie's Auto coveralls. "Yes! Thank you!" I cheered and hugged Edie.

"You're officially part of the team. Even though I'm not actually paying you," she teased.

The handsome man she'd been with at the fundraiser came up beside her and reached out his hand. "It's good to see you again, Vera," he said, shaking mine. "I'm Luke. I don't think we were formally introduced."

"Well, it's really nice to see you again, Luke."

"Hey." Luke took a step forward and lowered his voice. "You didn't happen to make a thirty-five-thousand-dollar donation recently on Fund Me Now, did you?"

I shook my head. "No, I'm sorry."

He shrugged. "One day I'll find them and thank them."

Music played, delicious food catered by Ray's and Barwell Bakery was consumed, and a two-tier ice cream cake was demolished. Jack had even thought ahead and gotten Edie her own gluten-free cupcake. I loved his thoughtfulness.

Chieka bumped my shoulder. "When's your car getting here? I miss that baby."

I closed one eye, trying to do the math. "Should arrive Wednesday. Wanna take a ride?"

She nodded. "Abso-fucking-lutely." She took a step closer and lowered her voice. "I need a favor."

"Name it."

"Edie had to sell her 1967 Camaro Rally Sport Coupe to save the shop."

I let out a low whistle. "That's a damn fine car."

She nodded. "It was her late grandpa's. I've been looking for it but can't find who bought it. Think with your contacts you could locate it?"

Jami leaned in. "We talking about Ella-Jean?" Chieka nodded. "Edie's lips have been sealed, but I've got a few leads."

I nodded. "I'm in. We'll start looking next week."

Chieka gave me a salute and went to mingle more.

"What'd Jack get you?" Jami asked as he stuffed a forkful of cake into Caden's mouth.

I snorted at Caden's surprised look. "He is taking me to Italy to check off some more things on my mom's list."

Jami lifted a fork full of cake in a toast. "Good man, that Jack."

I nodded. "The best."

"Excuse me!" Edie shouted over the din of the party. The music stopped and we all looked toward the door. She was holding it open for two police officers.

Caden frowned and straightened, wiping the cake off his face. "Why are they here?" he asked quietly. He pulled his wallet out and flashed his badge as he walked over to the door. Whatever they were discussing had Caden shaking his head in disbelief. "Chieka," he called. "Can you come over here please?"

Chieka wiped her hands on a napkin and muttered, "Not again."

Tamicka walked up next to me and held out a bowl of popcorn. "Here we go!"

FIRE TRUCKS, GARTER BELTS, & MY PERFECT EX

In case you missed it, stay tuned for an excerpt from:

Headlights, Dipsticks, and My Ex's Brother
Edie's Automotive Guide: Volume 1

CHAPTER ONE

EDIE'S TIP #42: BLINKER FLUID IS NOT A REAL THING, REGARDLESS OF WHAT THOSE AUTO SHOP GUYS TELL YOU.

There was only one ballroom in Grenadine, Michigan and it wasn't big enough for the both of us. I had no choice but to take a third—or was it a fourth?—champagne glass to keep my fist from finding its home square in my ex-fiancé's throat. The fizzy bubbles tickled my tongue as I silently congratulated myself on my self-restraint. His perfectly tailored gray suit was new, but the purple striped tie had been a birthday gift from me two years ago. Asshole.

His dark brown eyes snapped to mine before quickly blinking away. He wouldn't come over; confrontation wasn't his way. He would just spend the evening passive-aggressively glancing at me and then telling my family he hoped I'd found "some stability" after our "devastating breakup." The comment would spiral, as small-town gossip always does, and make everyone believe I'd gone off the deep end. And business would continue to plummet.

New life motto: never ever, ever (again) get romantically involved with someone you share a business with.

An arm slipped around my shoulders and I looked up from my seat to find the bride, my younger cousin, Kristy, smirking at me.

CHAPTER ONE

"Edie, what's with your 'I'm going to punch someone' look? Make sure to use your elbow so you don't break your thumb. Again."

"Yeah, yeah, love you too."

She kissed the top of my head and I smiled, leaning against her awesome cleavage. "Your boobs look phenomenal," I said, garnering a raised eyebrow from a nearby table.

"Don't they?" her new husband Sam said reverently. "Thanks for picking this dress." The ivory dress complemented the pink undertone of her light skin, and it fit like a glove. He was right; she did look absolutely smashing. He smiled at her, love and adoration filling his eyes. I bit my lip, looking away from their intimate expressions. I was so happy they'd found each other.

I gestured between the two of them. "Congratulations, by the way! Sam, you should've run while you had the chance. You're a hostage now."

He kissed Kristy's hand, the movement making her beautiful ring sparkle under the thousands of twinkle lights. She thumbed the gold band adorning his dark brown skin, her lips curving into a smile. "Hostage, huh?" he asked. "Good thing I have great company." Kristy rolled her eyes but smiled so large my cheeks hurt for her.

I leaned over. "How many 'Oh! I didn't know he was black' comments have you gotten so far from the extended family?" I whispered loud enough to get a few more side-eyes from the neighboring table.

Kristy and Sam looked pointedly at each other, then back at me. She tilted her head to the side. "Now, are we counting the rehearsal dinner when Great-Grandma Mildred told him he was a terrible waiter?"

Sam rolled his eyes. "Or that weird second cousin of yours who thought I was LeBron James?"

I winced. "Dude. You really shouldn't play anything sportsball related."

He pointed at me. "Accurate."

Kristy was the athletic one—basketball, soccer, golf, she could do

CHAPTER ONE

it all. Sam, however, couldn't catch a ball to save his life. But he looked damn good in a pair of glasses, holding a book.

My mother's laugh cut through the ballroom and a chill ran down my spine, successfully chasing away the warm, fuzzy fog of alcohol. That was my mother's patented I'm-about-to-make-a-scene laugh. I threw back the rest of my champagne, preparing for the apocalypse. "By the pricking of my thumbs, something wicked this way comes," I muttered, grabbing Kristy's drink from her hand and finishing it too. It had far too much rum—any rum was too much rum, let's be honest—but I soldiered through. I was a trooper like that.

"Holy crap," Kristy whispered, leaning over my shoulder. "Is that? No way..."

"Is that my mother with her hand on Will's chest?" I narrowed my eyes, the seven layers of mascara protesting the movement. "Why, yes. Yes, it is."

The man I'd thought I'd spend the rest of my life with was leaning just a little *too* close to my mother and smiling as she whispered something in his ear. My stomach tightened in the same way it had when I'd found that three-week-old banana in my duffel bag after a road trip. To be fair, it could also have been all that alcohol combined with a lack of food...

"Why? How?" Kristy whisper-shouted. "He definitely wasn't invited! Is she trying to hook you guys back up?"

"I mean, her older sister's daughter is getting married at twenty-four, a whole year younger than *her* daughter. I wouldn't put *anything* past her." I shrugged, trying to be nonchalant. By Kristy's well-practiced side-eye, I could tell she wasn't fooled for a second. "What? Don't look at me like that. I want nothing to do with him. I thought throwing all his stuff out the window was a pretty clear message."

She frowned, then turned to study Sam, who had suddenly become very interested in his cufflink. "Samuel, what do you know?"

He sighed, resignation pulling his shoulders forward. He clasped

CHAPTER ONE

her hands in his and kissed the top of each one. "My dearest wife, please forgive me."

She raised an eyebrow. "You're so weird. What am I forgiving you for?"

He flashed her a sheepish grin. "Your mom told me Aunt Cynthia demanded a plus one. You were stressed out, so we didn't tell you and just added an extra chair to the family table."

She cocked her head and studied him before nodding. "Good man. I would've committed homicide if I had to do that seating chart one more time, and then I wouldn't have gotten to wear this pretty dress." They kissed, eliciting some hoots and a chorus of silverware clanging against long-abused glasses. Kristy smiled but growled low. "Remember to use plastic glasses when you get married," she advised me before kissing her husband again.

My mother's laugh rang out again. Jami, my older brother, weaved through the crowd in his impeccable navy blue tux. He jumped onto the small platform that housed the head table. "Mayday, mayday," he said. "We better start the speeches before Mom laughs again. Twice is a warning. Three times is detonation."

As best man and self-appointed disaster-avoidance coordinator—a full-time job, really—Jami's advice was heeded immediately. Kristy and Sam signaled their DJ to begin the speeches as I stood to snag another glass of champagne from a passing waiter. My brother snatched it out of my hand and put it back on the tray. "Nuh-uh. Your cheeks and ears are turning pink and you have the maid of honor speech to give. How drunk are you?"

I snatched it back. "Whatever. I'm as pale as a ghost. I turn pink with a four-degree temperature change."

He grabbed it back from me and drank it down. I pouted.

Then my mother laughed for the third time. Into a microphone.

We both froze.

"Ground control to Major Tom," I whispered, spinning to face the woman—nay, *dragon*—who had somehow given birth to both of

CHAPTER ONE

us. All of the delicious alcohol in my bloodstream disappeared and I was suddenly stone cold sober.

Mom's ice-blonde curly hair was perfectly straightened and coiffed, magically hiding the devil horns beneath her impressive mane. Her floor-length ivory ball gown—because really, what else would she wear to her niece's wedding?—glittered as she lifted the microphone to her mouth with one hand and grabbed Will's hand with the other.

"Oh, this can't be good," Jami said.

"The last time she had a microphone, she told my senior class about getting knocked up with me!" My face heated from the memory. Grenadine High School Class of 2010's prom had gone from fairytale-themed to an abstinence lecture the moment my mother found the microphone.

Jami shook me, breaking me out of my trance. "I'm going to go stop her before this turns into her telling the entire summer camp at the closing ceremony that you started your period."

I let out an exaggerated sobbing sound. "Oh my God, I forgot about that." Guiding me by the shoulders, he pushed me down into my chair and then speed-walked toward my mother. I slumped, defeated. Why was I always the one she made look bad in these microphone exchanges?

I glanced around, trying to see where our plan for speeches had failed. Kristy and Sam hovered on the edge of the dance floor with a shocked Aunt Mary blustering about the order of speakers. Really, Aunt Mary should've known better than to leave any audio-visual equipment unattended. My mother could sniff out a microphone hidden on Ford Field during a blizzard in mid-February.

"Now, I know it's Kristy and Sam's day," my mother said, and I pressed my palm to my mouth to keep from laughing out loud. No, she most certainly did *not* know that. "But I believe they would be as happy for me as I am for them!"

"Timber!" I whispered, making a falling sound, followed by an explosion. Kristy's other two bridesmaids, both cosmetology school

CHAPTER ONE

friends who clearly hadn't known what they were getting into with this wedding, looked at me with identical expressions of horror. I slid lower in my chair, hoping to slip under the tablecloth and stay there until tomorrow morning.

"This afternoon, William asked me to marry him, and I said yes! Third time's a charm, ladies. So from one happy couple to another, congratulations, Kristy and Sam!"

The sound of screeching brakes filled my ears and the room tilted sideways.

No.

Nope.

God, I was drunker than I thought.

I needed an ambulance. I was obviously dying. At least hallucinating.

I couldn't have heard that right.

But then why was my mother—MY MOTHER—locking lips with my ex-fiancé in the front of a ballroom? Lips that until eight months ago had belonged to me? Oh God, he was dipping her backward like a scene in a movie. He'd never kissed me like that.

I was losing my mind.

This didn't mean what I thought it meant.

Like, she wasn't *engaged* engaged, right?

Glancing around the room, I spotted the table of my mother's best friends—the pack she'd brainwashed into adoring her—swooning. Why had Kristy even invited them? Stupid small-town inclusiveness. One of the Barbie bombshells was dabbing at her eyes with a monogrammed handkerchief. Another was clapping above her head as if she were in church and the pastor had just said something enlightening.

My gaze snapped to Jami, who was wrestling the microphone from the dragon's claws. "Congratulations to my mother and William and cheers to Kristy and Sam," he said quickly before turning off the device and handing it back to the DJ. My mother raised her right

CHAPTER ONE

hand and gave her queen wave, making sure to blow a few kisses to the audience.

I needed to move. I needed to get out of here. I couldn't feel my legs.

Kristy let out a sob, then slapped her hand over her mouth, turning away from me. Sam had his arms around her, probably trying in vain to convince her that the reception wasn't ruined. I wanted to tell her not to cry because it would destroy her amazing makeup. But if I'd been in her shoes, I'd probably cry too.

Oh God, I'm not crying, am I?

Somehow, I unclenched my fists and pressed my palms to my scalding cheeks. No wetness. Good. I wasn't crying. I could *not* show weakness in front of these hyenas. I could already hear the gossip from the nearby tables.

"Did she know?"

"Obviously not, look at her face."

"Poor thing. I can't even imagine losing a guy like William to *my mom*."

"There must be something really wrong with Edith if he prefers Cynthia over her."

The DJ, clearly struggling for what to do next, mumbled something about the rest of the speeches happening soon before playing an upbeat swing track. I wrapped my arms around my middle, trying to convince myself I didn't want to throw up.

I closed my eyes and concentrated on tuning out everything around me. *Deep breath in, deep breath out.* When I was 90 percent sure I could stand without fainting, I opened my eyes and searched each corner of the room, looking for a quiet and easy exit. I didn't want to make Kristy's wedding even more of a spectacle, but I couldn't stay here another moment. I knew she'd understand.

The closest door to me was the kitchen, which probably had a back door. I plastered a giant smile on my face and stood, gripping my clutch as if it were a life preserver. *Good. You didn't fall flat on your face. Now, put one foot in front of the other. Smile, SMILE!*

CHAPTER ONE

I had to make it past three tables and fifteen feet of open floor before I walked through the swinging double doors. I could do this. Each step was carefully calibrated to be fast, but not look like a run, and not cause me to fall on my ass. I hated heels.

I waved and smiled to those calling my name, even uttering an "I'll be right back!" and "So good to see you!" in a clear and calm voice. *Move aside, Frances McDormand. The Oscar goes to me.*

I slipped into the kitchen and inhaled a deep breath of relief, leaning against a nearby wall. I tucked my hand just below my collarbone and concentrated on slowing my heart rate before I passed out. All this wedding needed was an ambulance. Especially an ambulance after my ex had announced his engagement.

José, my employee Rosa's older brother, walked by with a tray of full champagne flutes. Without saying a word, he handed me one and gestured to the kitchen's back door. I made a mental note to give Rosa a raise. I lifted my glass to him in a silent toast and all but sprinted into the humid July evening.

New life motto: never ever, ever (again) go to another wedding.

AUTHOR'S NOTE

As with many of my books, I've pulled ideas from real life. Here are a few highlights:

Chocolate Chip Cookies:

This is one of my favorite—and last—memories with my grandma. They weren't the best tasting cookies I've ever had, but they were by far the best I've ever made.

The Kaitlin Elizabeth Foundation

While this foundation is entirely fictional, the sentiment behind it is not. I lost a dear friend to domestic violence. If you are abused or need guidance, here is a link to a variety of hotlines that can help: http://victimsofcrime.org/help-for-crime-victims/national-hotlines-and-helpful-links

Sharon, the EMT

Named in loving memory of my baby cousin, who loved being an EMT. Miss you "lil' coz."

All-Female Auto Shop

These exist in real life! One of my favorites is Girls Auto Clinic. Check them out at www.girlsautoclinic.com.

AUTHOR'S NOTE

The Cover

Did you catch that the cover is based on an automotive manual? It's one of my favorite Easter eggs.

ACKNOWLEDGMENTS

To my readers: Thank you, from the bottom of my heart. Time is the most important gift you can give someone, and I'm so grateful that you spent some time with me.

When I picked the concept for book two, I didn't realize quite what I was in for. I couldn't have done this without my right-hand woman, Janna Bonikowski. Thank you for not jumping off this runaway train.

A huge, enormous thank you goes to Tristan Taormino (author, educator, activist) for helping me make this book—and Vera—as realistic as possible while still working within my fictional world. Your guidance was crucial, and I'm honored to have worked with you (and I hope even with artistic license, I followed your advice as intended). To learn more about Tristan's work, visit www.tristantaormino.com.

Another giant thank you to firefighter Zahi Kassab who answered so many, *many* questions. I truly appreciate your kindness and wisdom!

To Tori Renaud, who is my go-to for all sex positive and alternative lifestyle questions! Thank you for going along with all my fictional (and crazy IRL) ideas.

Thanks to Lindee Robinson Photography and Najla Qamber Designs for my amazing cover, and to Danielle for all my logos.

Thanks to my editors: Erika Cooper, Janna, Ellie from My Brother's Editor, and Rosa Sharon at IScream ProofReading Services.

A shout out to the women behind the scenes who helped keep this book on track: Elyssa Mann, Michelle Lux, Shelly Bell, Sage Spelling, Aliza Mann, MK Schiller, Elizabeth Heiter (and all of GDRWA), and T-Money. Special thanks to Tamara Lush for talking with me about Vera's journey in the early stages of this manuscript.

My assistant, Nicole, you are the reason anything gets done. To Chris and Alex for picking out Vera's car and making sure I knew what I was (mostly) talking about. To Lucie and her crew for always saving the day.

To my Tacos: You're the best reader group I could ask for. Thank you for your honesty, your discussions, and for sharing my love of sex-positive romance! I adore you.

Beta readers and review team, what can I say? My life would suck without you. Thanks for your forever support.

To the band Marianas Trench, whose music kept me sane and helped me write through the IRL hard stuff. I know it's trite to thank your favorite band, but seriously, your words helped me find my words.

And finally, to Mr. Heather, my family, and my friends: You could have had a nice normal life if it wasn't for me. Thanks for sticking around .

XOXO,
Heather

ABOUT THE AUTHOR

When she's not pretending to be a rock star with purple hair, Heather Novak is crafting sex positive romance novels to make you swoon! After her rare disease tried to kill her, Heather mutated into a superhero whose greatest power is writing romance that you can't put down.

Heather tries to save the world (like her late mama taught her) from her home in the coolest city in the world, Detroit, Michigan, where she lives with Mr. Heather and their hypoallergenic pets.

You can find her online at:

HeatherNovak.net
Heather's Tacotastic Facebook Fan Club
Visit the Heather Novak Zazzle Store for merchandise from your favorite books!

Made in the USA
Lexington, KY
18 May 2019